RAM
c/o
ANANDHI

RAM c/o ANANDHI

AKHIL P. DHARMAJAN

Translated from
the Malayalam by
HARITHA C.K.

This English edition published in India by Harper Fiction 2025
An imprint of HarperCollins *Publishers*
4th Floor, Tower A, Building No. 10, DLF Cyber City,
DLF Phase II, Gurugram, Haryana—122002
www.harpercollins.co.in

2 4 6 8 10 9 7 5 3 1

Published by DC Books in Malayalam
This edition is published by HarperCollins *Publishers* India
By arrangement with DC Books

Malayalam copyright © Akhil P. Dharmajan 2020

English translation copyright ©Haritha C.K. 2025

P-ISBN: 978-93-5489-995-9
E-ISBN: 978-93-5489-936-2

This is a work of fiction and all characters and incidents described in this book are the product of the author's imagination. Any resemblance to actual persons, living or dead, is entirely coincidental.

Akhil P. Dharmajan asserts the moral right
to be identified as the author of this work.

For sale in India only

All rights reserved. No part of this publication may be reproduced, stored in a retrieval system, or transmitted, in any form or by any means, electronic, mechanical, photocopying, recording or otherwise, without the prior permission of the publishers.

Typeset in 11.5/15 Adobe Garamond Pro at
HarperCollins *Publishers* India

Printed and bound at
Replika Press Pvt. Ltd.

This book is produced from independently certified FSC® paper to ensure responsible forest management.

Author's Note
Chennai Ungale Anpudan Varaverkkiradhu!
(Chennai welcomes you warmly!)

Dear friend,

Thank you for choosing this book from the many available. To start, let me clarify a few things. If you are expecting a perfectly crafted novel, please forgive me. I am more of a storyteller than a writer. Imagine we are sitting next to each other as I tell you this story. If you are an avid reader of literature, my storytelling style might disappoint you.

Now, let me tell you about *Ram C/O Anandhi*. I consider this to be a cinematic novel. Imagine you are entering a cinema hall with a ticket. The story is set in various places in Tamil Nadu, including Chennai. I completed this novel after living in Chennai for almost two years. To add some spice to the story, which was moving slowly, I took some unconventional routes that landed me in some embarrassing situations. My Tamil friends and I suffered the repercussions of those impulsive acts for a long time. However, everything has settled now, and it's time for this novel to come to life.

One last thing, some characters and locations in this novel are connected to current events. It's your responsibility to keep those surprise elements intact. So, I humbly request you not to share any spoilers with those who haven't read the story yet. I have conducted a lot of research to write this novel. I hope you will forgive any human errors that may have occurred. Well, I warmly welcome everyone to Chennai city.

Chennai Ungale Anpudan Varaverkkiradhu!

One

23 JANUARY 2018

5.45 A.M.

Avadi is a quaint little station, a few kilometres shy of Chennai Central railway station. It was that hour of the day when the great Indian Railway tracks became the great Indian latrine lines in many parts of the country. Those accustomed to the tracks as their morning loo swiftly relocated as the Alleppey–Chennai Express approached, its horn blaring a warning. As the train pulled into platform 4, passengers waiting to get off crowded around the doors. Before it could stop completely, they were spilling out, eager to get on with their day.

Avadi station, a busy spot for people living and working outside Chennai, was bustling with activity. The crowd ebbed and flowed like the tides of the ocean. Among the throng of people was Sriram, navigating through the masses with his bags in tow.

Once on the platform, Sriram breathed a sigh of relief, unscathed by the chaos around him.

As passengers scattered in all directions, the train rumbled back to life, its whistle signalling its departure. In no time at all, the entire station had emptied out, leaving behind nothing but silence. Dropping his bags to the ground, Sriram scanned the platform.

Bineesh, who was supposed to pick him up, was nowhere in sight. Sriram walked over to the cement bench nearby with his bags. Placing them on the bench, he headed to the drinking water tap on the platform to wash his face. He turned the handle expectantly, but all he heard was a feeble hiss. He tried again and again, but despite his efforts, the tap remained dry, denying him any respite from the heat. Disappointed, he abandoned his plans and returned to his seat.

As he glanced around, Sriram spotted a man across the tracks, puffing on a beedi while clutching a bottle of water. Taking in the scene, he noticed some people sitting between the tracks, while others were squatting on the rails for relief. His gaze shifted to the public toilet nearby, but its door was shut tight.

'Well, this is quite the welcome to Tamil Nadu,' Sriram muttered to himself.

With a sigh, he reached for his phone and dialled Bineesh's number.

'Hey Ram, have you reached?' came Bineesh's voice from the other end.

'Of course! Where are you, bro? I'm surrounded by a pooping squad here,' Sriram replied, a mix of frustration and humour in his voice.

'Ha ha ha! That's pretty typical around here. Here's what you should do. Head over to the road across from where you're standing on the platform.'

'Is it near the SBI ATM?'

'Yep, that's the one. Come over there. I'm waiting,' Bineesh replied before ending the call. Sriram looked around once more, grabbed his bags and made his way towards Bineesh.

Bineesh had been working for a software company at the DHL IT Park in Chennai for almost nine years. Sriram felt a brotherly affection and respect for him, as he was the elder brother of his best friend, Manish. Despite being thirty years old, Bineesh was content with his life as a bachelor, resisting his family's pressure to get married.

Sriram had visited temples in Palani and Rameswaram many times with his family, but he confidently chose to pursue his passion for cinema in Tamil Nadu only because Bineesh was in Chennai.

As Sriram reached the opposite road, he spotted the SBI ATM. There, leaning against a Royal Enfield Classic Black Bullet, stood Bineesh.

'Hey, Bineesh Etta!' Sriram said and rushed to hug him.

'You've got so many bags! Did you bring your entire village or what?' Bineesh remarked, surprised at the sight of three large bags.

'Yeah, had to bring everything with me. My whole life has been packed into these bags.'

'Alright, alright. Let's not waste time. We should head to the apartment before the roads get too crowded,' Bineesh urged and picked up one of Sriram's bags, slinging it over his shoulder.

With one swift movement of his leg, Bineesh kick-started the Bullet. Sriram hopped on, holding on to the remaining two bags. Bineesh revved up the engine and moved the bike forward in first gear, the thunderous rumble of its engine filling the air. Sriram took in the bustling city of Chennai as they rode along.

Two

The roads buzzed with vehicles zooming away, stirring up clouds of dust. Most people zipped around on trusty two-wheelers, affectionately known as Lunas. Tea stalls, lining the roads, were teeming with people sipping tea and munching on samosas and cakes while chatting away. Elderly folk and women lounged in front of the stalls.

Next to them lay baskets brimming with flowers, vegetables and construction tools, offering a glimpse into the daily lives of the locals.

'That's their breakfast,' Bineesh remarked, catching Ram's curious gaze in the rearview mirror.

Ram continued to enjoy the lively scene.

After about half an hour, they arrived at Iyyappanthangal, where Bineesh lived. The apartment was situated on a busy street, housed in a two-storeyed building with a staircase at the centre. Four apartments faced each other on the two floors. Bineesh's apartment was located on the second floor, on the right side.

As Ram stepped into the apartment, a wave of anxiety washed over him, similar to the one he had felt when he had boarded the train at Alleppey. He had never stayed so far from home before. He retrieved a bottle from his bag's side pocket and took a swig from it, draining the last of the pale red liquid in it.

'If you're thirsty, there's cold water in the fridge,' Bineesh offered, noticing Ram's frantic gulps.

'It's an old habit, Etta,' Ram explained. 'Whenever I'm away from home, my mom boils water with karingali and gives it to me in bottles. When I miss home, I drink some of that water. It kinda eases my homesickness a bit.'

Bineesh looked suspicious. He dropped Ram's bag from his shoulder and opened it. His eyes widened as he saw about ten one-litre bottles filled with pale red karingali water.

'Ten bottles? Why would you bring so much karingali water to Chennai?' Bineesh exclaimed.

Ram chuckled at the question.

The apartment had two bedrooms, a kitchen, a small hall and a shared bathroom. In the hall, there was a sofa, a small table and photos of Hindu gods on a shelf. One of the bedrooms had a long balcony that offered a view of the street.

'Check out your room,' Bineesh said, pointing to the room with the balcony.

'Nice, a balcony!' Ram exclaimed, pleased.

With a grin, he entered the room. Suddenly, he noticed colourful sticky notes with some English words plastered on the walls. The room also had a shelf that was filled with clothes.

'Who else lives here?' Ram enquired, turning back to Bineesh.

'My friend's younger brother, Kiran. He studies B.Com. here,' Bineesh replied. 'He's out right now, but will be back soon. He is also a little crazy fellow; you both will get along well.'

Ram nodded and then asked, 'Even though there are plenty of colleges in Kerala that offer B.Com., why did he choose Chennai? He doesn't seem only "a little crazy"! "Totally crazy" would be more like it!'

Bineesh shrugged. 'Why did you choose Chennai even though there are many film schools in Kerala?'

Ram grinned. 'Well, my intention isn't limited to the academic part alone. I'm here to learn about people's lives and to turn them into stories.'

Bineesh nodded, looking serious. 'That's cool. But Chennai's not all sunshine. There are some dark corners, too. If you're good and behave yourself, I'll treat you right. But if you step out of line, whether you're my brother's buddy or a storyteller, I won't hesitate to give you a whack with the rolling pin lying in the kitchen. Got it? Now, go freshen up. Then, we'll go downstairs and grab some breakfast,' he said and headed to his room.

Ram mulled over Bineesh's words. 'Hmm, he's probably joking. But wait, could Manish's scar above one of his eyebrows be from a similar whack?'

As Bineesh returned to the hall, he caught Ram's gaze fixed on the ceiling. 'Hey, haven't you freshened up yet?'

'Yeah, yeah, I'm on it,' Ram hurried into the bathroom.

The apartment was near Oil Mill Road, surrounded by a mini-supermarket, several vegetable stalls, electronics shops and food carts.

Elderly Tamil women with ornate nose studs sold flowers, adding a touch of tradition.

Ram and Bineesh went to a small eatery for dosas. Ram savoured the flavours of the coconut chutney, mint chutney and sambar with each bite. The mint chutney seemed like an exotic choice to be paired with the dosas. But, one thing puzzled him: *why did a dosa cost fifteen rupees here when nearby shops advertised dosa batter for just thirty rupees per litre?*

'Isn't this a bit unfair, Etta?' he asked Bineesh on their way back.

'Ha ha ha! Who has time to buy dosa batter, make dosas one after the other, grate coconut and make all those chutneys? Very few bachelors in Chennai manage to do that. Time is a luxury here. They know people will buy dosas even if they charge twenty rupees for one.'

'Bineesh Etta, let's start making dosas at home from tomorrow. I will do all the cooking. Eating out isn't that healthy anyway,' Ram suggested.

Bineesh laughed out loud. 'Ah, the initial enthusiasm! Don't worry, it will all fizzle down once your classes start tomorrow. You'll be too busy and exhausted from chasing buses and trains.'

Ram remained quiet, pondering over Bineesh's words.

Three

When they reached home, Bineesh announced that he had some work to do and headed to his room. Ram decided to open the balcony door from his own room. Planning to get a chair for the balcony, he was surprised to find one there already. He figured Kiran, who shared the room, liked spending time there.

Ever since Ram had noticed the English words and strange clothes of Kiran, he had been wondering if he would get along with him. If it became too difficult, Ram decided he would move his bed to the living room.

Later, while lounging on the balcony, Ram tried calling home but got an automated message saying that the landline wasn't working. He called the neighbour's house to let his mom know that he had arrived in Chennai. His dad, Aravindan, a big ambassador of natural living and good health, didn't allow mobile phones at home. He had reluctantly given Ram a mobile phone before he left for Chennai, but only after he promised to use it sparingly. Ram had to really beg for a good phone with a camera, saying it was needed for his course.

His family was all about nature and farming. They grew rice, vegetables and fruits on a big plot of land, selling the surplus to folks who loved organic food. Ram resented his dad when he was younger, but he began understanding him better as he grew up. His dad became his hero once Ram realized how peaceful their lives were compared to others. Growing up with such a dad, Ram had big dreams, like studying films and writing books. His dad supported his writing but wasn't thrilled about the film part. It took a lot of convincing from Ram, his mom and his sister, till his dad agreed to let him pursue a one-year film course.

For Ram, Tamil Nadu and its people had always been fascinating. He wanted his first book to capture the essence of the state, but just visiting temples occasionally wasn't enough for a complete story. That's when he seriously considered studying cinema there. He quickly found out about the best film schools from Manish's brother and decided to pursue cinema. Although Ram's dad didn't expect him to choose Tamil Nadu, he supported his son's decision. When the time came for Ram to set off on his new adventure, he felt a twinge of sadness at leaving his family behind, especially his mom, for the first time.

So, on the day Ram arrived in Tamil Nadu, his dreamland, he spent his time lost in thoughts, repeatedly sipping karingali water when he felt homesick.

2

One

Early next morning, Ram woke up to the balcony door creaking open slowly. He remembered that the door didn't have a lock. In the dim light streaming in from the streetlight outside, he saw a figure entering the room. At first, he felt scared, but after a moment he plucked up some courage. He quickly covered himself with the bedsheet and crept towards the door. As the intruder took a few steps inside, Ram sprang into action, slamming the door shut and tackling him to the ground, wrapping him up in the sheet.

'Thief! Thief! Bineesh Etta, come quickly!'

Ram was about to shout, but to his surprise, he heard the same words coming from under the sheet in a much louder voice. He paused for a moment, wondering if he had made a mistake. Nevertheless, he too called out for Bineesh, who rushed in and turned on the lights. He found Ram pinning down the intruder who was sprawled on the floor. Bineesh pulled Ram away.

'How come you are here now?' Bineesh asked the 'intruder', astonished.

The 'intruder' turned out to be Kiran.

'I sent you a message on WhatsApp last night, saying I'd come today,' Kiran replied, sitting up and rubbing his back. 'Ow! Hey, who's that?' he winced, glaring at Ram.

'Remember I mentioned someone coming from my hometown? That's him. Sriram,' Bineesh explained.

'Oh, got it. Ow, my back!' Kiran groaned as he got up from the floor and stretched. Then he gulped down half of the karingali water from Ram's bottle that sat on a table nearby.

'Sorry about that. The way you entered the room, I thought you were a thief,' Ram apologized, frowning slightly.

'No worries. I sneak in like that at night so I don't wake him up,' Kiran said looking at Ram and tossing the bedsheet back on to the bed. 'Nice to meet you. I'm Kiran,' he said and extended his hand.

'I'm Sriram,' Ram replied, shaking his hand.

'Perfect timing!' Bineesh chimed in, sarcasm lacing his sleep-induced voice, before heading back to his room, muttering to himself.

Ram and Kiran chuckled behind his back. They continued to chat and got to know each other. Kiran's family, including his parents and elder brother, had been running a hotel in Salalah, Oman, for about ten years. Two years ago, Kiran, who was living with his uncle's family in Kollam, Kerala, expressed a desire for a change. So, he was sent to study in Chennai and live with Bineesh, his brother's best friend. His family supported him financially, sending a monthly allowance to take care of his expenses. After talking for a while, Ram and Kiran called it a night.

Two

The morning of Ram's first day at college dawned. Bineesh took a half-day leave to accompany him.

'What time will you pick me up this evening?' Ram enquired as he got off the bike, tucking his shirt into his jeans.

'Let's see how you handle life's lessons,' Bineesh teased before firing up his motorcycle and riding off. As Ram watched Bineesh roar off into the busy streets of Chennai, he felt like a lost puppy for a moment before turning his attention to the college.

The entrance had a quaint green gate covered with vines, which gave it a rustic charm. A pathway between two tall buildings guided Ram ahead, covered in gravel and with grass peeking through the gaps. At the end of the pathway, two flights of stairs led to the buildings on either side. The one on the right stood four storeys tall, while the one on the left had three storeys. Both were painted a vibrant red. Flowers and vines adorned the walkway, adding a splash of colour. Moss clung to the walls, with the college's name—The Chennai Academy—standing out in white letters. The lush greenery created a serene atmosphere. The breeze carried a hint of chill.

Ram entered through the gate and spotted two girls dressed in Bharatanatyam dance attire, their ghungroos tinkling against their ankles as they walked.

He knew from the college's website that it offered courses in dance and music, in addition to film studies.

'Excuse me, college reception enke?' Ram asked for directions, mixing Tamil and English.

The girls smiled and pointed towards the building on the right.

Ram climbed the stairs and found a young woman, probably in her early twenties, sitting in front of a computer. She didn't look like a typical receptionist to him. Instead, she wore an old-fashioned kurta with a dupatta, her hair tied back and an ID card hanging down her neck. He wasn't sure if she was the receptionist.

She noticed his suspicious glance. 'Can I help you?' she asked in Tamil.

Ram managed to reply in broken Tamil, mixing it up with English. 'I'm looking for the new DFM (Diploma in Film Making) class.'

'Are you Mr Sriram Aravind?'

Ram felt relieved hearing his name. 'Yes, that's me.'

'Why are you so late?' she asked sternly.

Ram's feeling of relief quickly turned to shock. 'Late? I was told classes start at ten.'

'No, classes start precisely at nine-thirty here and end at three. This is your first and last warning. Don't be late again, or I won't allow you upstairs,' she said with a glare. 'Okay, follow me. I'll show you to your class.'

With that, she stood up and led Ram upstairs. With his excitement dwindling, Ram felt like he was back in school.

Quietly, he followed her until they reached an air-conditioned room on the third floor. She called the young man, who was taking a class inside and introduced Ram as the latecomer of the day.

Ram apologized, and the teacher waved it off. 'No problem, come in,' he said, ushering Ram inside while the receptionist returned downstairs.

'Everyone, this is the only Malayali in your class. Let him introduce himself,' the teacher announced as Ram entered. Despite feeling hesitant, Ram took off his bag and began to speak.

'Hello everyone! I'm Sriram and I'm from Alappuzha in Kerala. I studied mechanical engineering.'

As he spoke, he heard people mentioning 'Kuttanad' and 'houseboat'—iconic words associated with Alappuzha.

'I don't know much Tamil, so I'll share more about myself later. Thank you,' Ram said.

The class welcomed him with applause. Ram smiled warmly at his batchmates.

He thought it was essential to thank them in their own language. 'Thanks for the kayyadi,' he said gratefully.

Ram's words made everyone, including the teacher, stop clapping and start laughing.

'Ram, some Malayalam words have different meanings in Tamil. Be careful, okay?' the teacher advised.

Ram nodded, not quite understanding, and looked for a seat.

There were fifteen students in the DFM batch, including Ram They had all been selected after clearing three rounds of tests, including a video interview. Only one of them was a girl. Ram found an empty spot at the back. A young man named Vetri sat beside Ram, waving more than shaking his hand.

'Hi, I'm Vetri,' he greeted enthusiastically.

Ram smiled back.

The teacher, Mr Shiva, resumed his lecture about world cinema.

'Machaa, just so you know, "kayyadi" means "clap" in Malayalam, but it means "masturbation" in Tamil,' Vetri whispered.

Ram was shocked for a moment. 'Oh my God!'

Vetri stifled a laugh as Ram grinned.

'Hi, I'm Reshma,' the girl sitting next to Vetri introduced herself, reaching out to shake Ram's hand.

'No, no, that's not her name. Meet Ms Greedy Guts. She loves free food at weddings.'

'Get lost, you kummanamoonji,' she swore, playfully slapping Vetri on the head.

At this, Mr Shiva intervened, 'Are you and your sister also planning to bring that boy down to your level?'

'No, sir,' both of them replied in unison.

Ram was surprised to find out that Vetri and Reshma were siblings, taking a course together. During the break, everyone in the class approached Ram. Most of them were curious about Kuttanad and the houseboats. Ram didn't engage in much conversation, wary of potential expenses caused by wannabe tourist friends. At lunchtime, he went to a nearby restaurant and had biryani. He realized that Tamil Nadu biryani was spicier than what he was used to in Kerala.

Three

After classes ended at 3 p.m., Ram's next challenge was to find his way back to Iyyappanthangal, which was over fifteen kilometres away as per Google Maps. He walked from his college to the main road. When he saw a sign that said 'Nungambakkam Railway Station, 200 meters,' he headed in that direction.

The road in front of Nungambakkam station resembled the chaotic street markets from Tamil movies. Half of the road was crowded with vendors selling fruits, vegetables, flowers and even electronics. An auto stand, too, had made its place amidst the clamour.

As Ram pondered over how to ask for directions to Iyyappanthangal, someone tapped him on the shoulder. It was Vetri. Ram smiled, relieved to see a familiar face in the crowd.

'Why are you standing here?' Vetri asked in Tamil.

'I need to get to Iyyappanthangal. That's where I live. But I don't know how to get there,' Ram explained in a mix of Malayalam and Tamil.

'Machaa, I can understand Malayalam, but slow down … speak slowly,' Vetri requested, struggling to follow.

'I want to go to Iyyappanthangal, but I don't know how,' Ram repeated slowly.

'Oh, Iyyappanthangal! It's far from here, machaa. First, you need to take the local train to Guindy station and then catch a bus from there.'

'That sounds like a long journey,' Ram said and remembered Bineesh's warning about his situation after class when he had volunteered to cook at home.

'What's wrong?' Vetri asked, noticing Ram's distant look.

Ram gazed at the flyover leading to the railway station, swarming with people.

'Machaa, I will be going via Guindy railway station on my bike. I can drop you near the bus stop there,' Vetri offered.

Ram gratefully accepted, hoping Vetri wouldn't ask for houseboats rides and Kuttanad visits in return.

On the way, Vetri pointed out different places and shops, explaining their specialties.

'Is your house in Guindy?' Ram asked during the ride.

'No, I'm from Madurai,' Vetri replied.

'So, where do you live here?'

'I'm staying as a paying guest in a house.'

'How about Reshma?'

'She is a native of Chennai.'

'But you said she is your sister.'

'Machaa, we have one dad but two moms. Dad is with them now. My mom remarried and lives in Madurai,' Vetri shared matter-of-factly.

Ram was shocked by Vetri's casual attitude towards his complicated family dynamics.

'So, machaa, what's your dream role in the movies?' Vetri asked, steering the conversation away from personal matters.

'I want to be a great scriptwriter and director. What about you, Vetri?'

'I want to do it all: direct, act, shoot ... everything,' Vetri replied eagerly.

'Adipoli!' Ram exclaimed.

'What's "adipoli"?'

'It means "super",' Ram said with a grin.

Ram felt confident that he could learn to speak Tamil well. He had, after all, managed that entire conversation in Tamil except for the word 'adipoli'.

Vetri dropped Ram off at the bus stop near Guindy station. He nodded in a unique manner and Ram, too, nodded in response before they parted ways.

Ram asked a policeman which bus to take to Iyyappanthangal. He was told four bus route numbers: 54, 49, 149, 154.

How am I supposed to remember all these numbers for one place? Ram was confused. As he stood wondering, bus number 54 arrived, but it was too crowded. Seeing more people waiting to board it than the number inside, Ram decided to wait for the next one.

By four o'clock, schools had closed and the traffic had increased. After about twenty minutes, another bus came, but it was also overcrowded. Eventually, Ram squeezed into it with other passengers. Despite the conductor's warnings not to stand near the door, Ram and three others still ended up hanging on to the door.

Suddenly, the door with the air compressor locking system started closing. The four of them, squeezed together, screamed. The bus screeched to a halt.

'How many times do I have to tell you to move inside?' the conductor yelled, sticking his head out of the door. 'Those standing at the door, get off. Get off!' he shouted angrily.

In the ensuing chaos, Ram managed to sneak inside the bus. The other three people got off, cursing. Then, the bus resumed its journey.

The bus was packed to the brim, with not an inch of space to spare. Traffic congestion was at its peak. Passengers swayed back and forth as the driver manoeuvred the bus through the traffic. Ram held on to the railings tightly, feeling like he was on an adventure park ride. With each brake, his shirt came untucked from his jeans, changing his look from executive to casual.

He glanced at the seated passengers. Majority were women, mostly engrossed in their phones, either watching soap operas or listening to music with headphones on.

As the bus passed a small lake at Porur, Ram felt something brush against the front of his jeans. When he looked, he noticed an old man with a sling bag, struggling to keep it on his shoulder.

At first, Ram thought it was accidental, but then he felt it again. He realized that the old man was deliberately touching his zipper.

He couldn't understand how the old man found pleasure in such behaviour, especially in a crowded bus. He decided to act and firmly stamped on the elderly man's toes.

Ram chuckled as he watched the man wince in pain. He then shifted his sling bag to the other shoulder and moved away to escape Ram's ire. By that time, the bus had reached Iyyappanthangal bus depot.

3

One

Bineesh looked surprised to see Ram back, looking like a lost puppy that had finally found its way home.

'Wow, so you managed it!' he said in amazement.

'Oh, that was easy-peasy,' Ram replied disdainfully.

'Well done, my boy. So you've decided to learn about life, huh? By the way, how was your first day?'

'Everyone's cool. I'm the only Malayali in the class though.'

'Isn't that great? Your Tamil will improve, you'll understand a new culture and you'll make good friends. It's the perfect situation to learn about the Tamil way of living and write a story. Why go abroad just to be among other Malayalis? This is the real experience. In other news, Kiran and I felt like cooking. We made rice and amazing fish curry. Freshen up and let's eat together.'

'Oh, you cooked, huh? That's great. Where's Kiran?'

'He's in the balcony. His main hobby is watching what goes on in the neighbouring apartments at night.'

Kiran was relaxing on a chair on the balcony, enjoying the breeze, when Ram entered the room from the hall.

'Hello, Mr CCTV.'

Hearing Ram, Kiran smiled and looked back.

The wind was strong, making the washed clothes clipped to the clothesline flutter.

'What's so interesting to see here?' Ram asked as he approached him.

'Ram Annaa, just ask what you can't see when you sit here. Look, there are so many apartments around, each with different lives and emotions. There's anger, love, lust, poverty and so much more. If you stay here, you'll get to see so many different emotions.'

Ram, surprised to hear such profound thoughts from someone so young, asked in a mock-serious tone, 'Are you high on weed?'

'This is the problem with us Malayalis. If a young person brings in seriousness and depth to what they say, they're immediately assumed to be a pothead.'

'Ha ha ha, I was just pulling your leg,' Ram chuckled, running two fingers through Kiran's hair.

He looked at the surrounding buildings. Kiran was right. Many lives could be seen from a distance, through the windows and balconies of each apartment. In a way, it was like an invasion of privacy, but to Ram it seemed like scenes from different movies playing out. Some people sat on the balconies with their babies, watching the vehicles go by on the street. Others stayed indoors watching TV. In some places, people were fighting. Love lingered in the shadows on some unlit balconies. Then Ram noticed many beds lined up side by side, covered with mosquito nets, on the open terrace of a two-storeyed building on the right. In some of the beds, he could see the glow of mobile screens.

'What's all that?' Ram asked, pointing at the terrace.

'That's a kind of lodging here. People can rent one bed on that terrace for one thousand rupees per month. Along with the bed, they get a phone charging station and a storage area under the bed. There's also a common bath on that terrace.'

'Oh. And when it rains?'

'During the rainy season, you can see them putting up tarpaulin sheets overhead. Unlike our Kerala, there are rarely any occurrences of unexpected rain here, or rains that last for three months straight. People here are happy if it rains at least once a year, I guess. I can't imagine what they'd do during sudden rains. Maybe they'd simply get wet.'

Ram looked at the beds on the terrace once more. It seemed like a small world of people, weaving dreams under the mosquito nets.

After dinner, the three young men fell asleep before the clock struck ten.

Two

The next day at 6.30 a.m., Bineesh left for work in the company cab. Around 8 a.m., Kiran left as well. Shortly after, Ram headed off to college.

When he reached the Iyyappanthangal bus depot, bus number 47 was ready to depart. Ram took it, got off at the Guindy bus stop and then walked through the subway, which was full of vendors. The subway was right in the middle of two routes: one leading to the starting point of the railway overbridge and the other to the starting point of the Guindy Metro overbridge.

There was a ticket counter next to the overbridge. Ram asked someone about the route and was told to board a train bound for Chennai beach to get to Nungambakkam.

He learned that every fifteen minutes, a train that went through that area stopped at platform no. 2.

He bought a ticket for five rupees, crossed the bridge and reached platform 2 just as a train arrived. After confirming with someone again, he boarded the train. It was quite crowded, given that it was the morning rush hour. Most people stood or sat with serious faces, paying no attention to anyone else. Many were wearing headphones or earphones.

Realizing that he wouldn't get a chance to have a conversation, Ram put on his earphones and began listening to a Tamil song. The train kept moving forward, passing stations along the way.

While hanging on to the handrail and listening to music, Ram felt a tap on his shoulder.

Turning around, he found himself face-to-face with a woman who had a jasmine garland in her hair and wore dark red lipstick. Ram suspiciously pulled one earphone out.

'Aruvani,' she said.

Ram had heard that word many times during his youth, often used derogatorily by the women in his village during fights. Thinking she was insulting him for no reason, he turned away.

'Hey! Aruvani,' she repeated, patting him on the shoulder again, determined to not let him go.

Shaking his head to indicate that he wasn't an aruvani, he moved away again.

'I'm an aruvani. Give me money, my dear,' she insisted.

Ram was bewildered. *What nonsense is this? Is she calling herself an expletive to get money?*

'Dear, you look so handsome. I love your beard,' she teased, placing a finger on his chin and pressing hard on his arm, as the others watched.

Feeling humiliated, Ram reached into his shirt pocket and found a twenty-rupee note, leftover change from the bus and train tickets. He showed it to her.

'This is all I have,' he said.

She quickly took the money, tucked it into her blouse, blessed him with both hands and moved on to the next person.

'Are you a Malayali?' a fellow passenger hanging on to a handrail nearby asked him.

'Yes.'

'"Aruvani" means eunuchs. They say all sorts of things. Don't fall for it. We shouldn't give them any money. They're all frauds. Are you new here?'

'Yes, bro. This is the first time I've seen and spoken to such people up-close. And the woman who just came up to me didn't seem like an aruvani at all.'

'Some people don't look like they are aruvanis,' the fellow passenger said. 'Chennai railway stations have so many beggars and people like this. Look over there.'

As the train stopped at T. Nagar station, he pointed to a bench. There were a few men dressed as women, chitchatting and laughing loudly.

'See? There's a group like this at every station. When people like them approach you, don't give them any money. Got it? I'm getting off here.' Giving his two bits of advice, he left.

After stopping at the station for a minute, the train started moving again. Ram cast a brief look at the aruvanis once again. Despite their plight, they seemed to be living in a world of their own, where only their laughter and happy moments echoed.

Three

Finally, by the time he got off the train at Nungambakkam and walked quickly to the college, it was almost 9.30 a.m. As he ran up the stairs, the girl at the reception looked at him with a frown, her brows furrowed.

'Why can't she at least smile when she sees someone in the morning?' he muttered to himself, hurrying towards his class on the third floor.

Just as he reached the classroom and took a seat at the back, Mr Shiva walked in.

'What timing, machaa. You are impossible!' Vetri whispered.

'Good morning, everyone. A good film-maker needs, above all, punctuality. You all are perfect at that,' Mr Shiva said as he entered, while Ram tried to catch his breath.

During the lunch break, as Ram was heading to the same eatery as the day before, Vetri and Reshma stopped him and took him to a different place.

'Which restaurant is this?' Ram asked, standing in front of a building just across the street from the college, adorned with J. Jayalalithaa's picture.

'This is Amma Unavagam,' Reshma explained like a tour guide. 'From seven to ten in the morning, you can get idlis for one rupee and pongal, sambar rice, lemon rice, curry leaves rice and curd rice for just five rupees. From six to nine in the evening, you can get two chapatis and dal for three rupees.'

Ram remembered reading about this initiative by former Tamil Nadu chief minister J. Jayalalithaa in a newspaper long ago.

As they walked into the cafeteria, which looked like a big hall, it seemed that everyone from the college was there. People were standing around round steel tables, eating together, while others sat on the slabs attached to the walls.

Ram saw the girl from the reception there, too. She pushed someone aside to buy curd rice.

'Moodevi,' Reshma cursed under her breath upon seeing her.

'Machaa, here you go,' Vetri said, handing steel plates to both Ram and Reshma. The three of them joined a queue of about twenty people.

'What should I eat?' Ram said out loud.

'Machaa, you should eat thevidiyaa,' Vetri suggested.

'Thevidiyaa? What's that?'

'It's a super thing, machaa. It's like biryani. Only five rupees. Just ask the lady over there to serve it. You'll get it hot.'

'Ram, don't ask. You'll get a good beating,' Reshma whispered, pinching Vetri's hand. She then explained to Ram that the word meant 'prostitute'.

'You dog,' Ram exclaimed, playfully hitting Vetri on the head with a steel bowl. The impact created a loud sound, like a cymbal.

'If you break the plate, you'll be charged fifty rupees. Got it?' the lady serving the food yelled.

The three of them fell silent and waited for their turn. They ate quietly and soon left the place.

This was Ram's first time exploring the street near the college, so he carefully observed his surroundings. It seemed like if you had even three feet of land, you could open a shop. Nungambakkam Street was bustling with a variety of stores and numerous shrines dedicated to Hindu gods.

The roadside was lined with flex banners for weddings and birthdays, each featuring photos of the bride or groom alongside headshots of family and friends. The banners were well-used, with not even an inch of space left blank.

After wandering around for a while, the three of them returned to the college.

Four

After classes ended that afternoon, Ram waited outside the college for Vetri to arrive on his bike. He watched as the receptionist sped away on an old Luna adorned with a garland in the front. The urgency with which she left made it seem like she was riding an ambulance.

'Dude, come to my place for a bit. I want to introduce you to someone cool,' Vetri said once he arrived.

'Boys, I'm joining you. Let's go,' Reshma announced, arriving on her blue Fascino scooter.

'I really can't spare much time. If I start roaming around on my second day in the city, my flatmate will kill me,' Ram said.

'Ram, don't you stay in Iyyappanthangal? I have to go to Poonamallee later. I can drop you on my way there. Is that fine?' Reshma offered.

Hearing that, Ram jumped on Vetri's bike.

About a kilometre after Guindy, Vetri took a turn on to a road leading inland from the beginning of Kathipara bridge. They travelled a bit further along a cemented road lined with crowded houses. Children were playing cricket on the streets and women stood around chatting, hands on their chins. After navigating through a series of zigzag paths, they finally stopped in front of a gate.

Ram got off the bike. The first thing he noticed was a beautifully designed kolam outside the gate. The house was an old two-storeyed building with a small courtyard enclosed within a wall. The courtyard had an overgrown neem tree and several ornamental plants.

Though the house was two-storeyed, it had only two rooms on each floor. A black water tank was mounted on the terrace above the second floor. Ram's eyes lingered on the tank for a moment. To his surprise, he saw the college receptionist standing there, cleaning it. She was wearing a worn-out check shirt, her hair was tied up and her face covered with dirt. Noticing Ram looking at her, she glared at him for a moment before resuming her work without any change in expression.

4

One

'What is she doing here?' Ram exclaimed in shock at the sight of the receptionist perched atop the house.

'Don't you dare ask me about that Moodevi,' Reshma retorted, nudging the gate open with the front of her scooter and riding inside.

Vetri followed Reshma, parking his bike in the long car shed in front of the house. An old green Premier Padmini stood inside, next to the receptionist's garlanded Luna.

Though both Vetri and Reshma rode over the kolam, Ram managed to enter without stepping on it. His gaze drifted back to the receptionist standing on the terrace.

'Paatti, start that motor!' she shouted from above.

'Yeah, I am turning on the switch,' a woman's voice responded from inside the house.

'That's enough. Now turn off the motor and turn on the tap.'

'Okay, done.' With that, an elderly woman pulled back the curtain of the door, stepped outside and turned on the tap in the washbasin in the sit-out area.

Brownish water flowed through the tap.

'Oh, my little sweetie pie,' Vetri called out teasingly when he saw the old lady.

Ram observed her closely. Her hair was cut short to her shoulders, resembling a little schoolgirl's hairstyle. It was entirely white; whiter than any hair he had seen before. Black kajal accentuated her large eyes and square and black-framed spectacles enhanced her beauty. Small jhumkas dangled from her ears. Her high eyebrows, also white, looked like perfect bows. She wore an orangish-yellow saree. Ram estimated that she was at least seventy years old.

Though there was only a subtle divergence in appearance, Ram assumed that the receptionist was the old lady's granddaughter.

'Turn on the motor, Paatti,' her voice echoed from above once more.

'Anandhi, keep it down. You'll disturb the bees,' Paatti shouted back.

Ram looked around and noticed a sizable beehive hanging from the highest branch of the sprawling neem tree in the courtyard. The bees seemed to be rather big. He had only encountered such hefty ones near government water tanks and similar places.

'I'm exhausted. Reshma, go and start that motor,' Paatti instructed Reshma upon seeing the three of them.

'I am not lifting a finger for her,' Reshma snapped.

'Is she the sole user of water from that tank, you idiot? Isn't your brother using it too?' Paatti shot back.

'Oh! She's pocketing five hundred rupees every month from you for cleaning the tank. Tell her to come down to the ground floor herself if she wants to operate the motor,' Vetri interjected, siding with Reshma.

'Paatti, could you please start the motor? I've got plenty of other work too,' Anandhi's voice rose again, tinged with frustration.

Paatti shot Reshma a stern look, muttered something under her breath and then swiftly retreated indoors to switch on the motor.

'Now shut it off and open that tap,' came the command from above. This happened a couple of times, after which Paatti returned to the group standing on the ground floor.

'By the way, who's this?' Paatti enquired, eyeing Ram.

'Paatti, this is the Kerala guy from our class, the one I mentioned earlier.'

'Oh. Sriram. Your film school classmate.'

'Let me ask you something. Who are you all?' a completely confused Ram demanded, eyeing the three of them.

Paatti, Reshma and Vetri exchanged amused glances before bursting into laughter, which ceased abruptly when they noticed Anandhi descending to wash her feet at the front yard tap. Ignoring everyone, she cleaned up, took her maroon towel from the clothesline and disappeared into the outdoor bathroom, closing the door behind her.

'Moodevi,' Reshma muttered once more.

'Enough of that nonsense. Ram, sit down and I'll get you some coffee,' Paatti commanded, giving Reshma a sharp look before heading inside.

'Alright, spill it. What's going on here? Why is that receptionist here? Who's the old lady?' Ram demanded impatiently as soon as Paatti disappeared indoors.

'First, have a seat,' Reshma insisted, guiding him to a chair in the sit-out area.

'Ram, Paatti's name is Kolanjiammal. This house belongs to her. Vetri is a paying guest here. She started renting out rooms recently. Vetri and that girl are her first tenants. That Moodevi stays in one of the rooms upstairs; this idiot is in another. As for Paatti—'

'Wait! So, that girl is also a paying guest here?' Ram interrupted, anxiety writ all over his face.

'Let me tell you the full story, Ram. Paatti doesn't have any children. Thaathaa passed away four years ago. After his death, Paatti and this house seemed to have lost their purpose. Many people advised her to move back to her hometown in Thanjavur, but she refused. Young Paatti came to Madras with Thaathaa in the 1970s, when he got a government job here. Together, they built this house with savings from Thaathaa's salary. Paatti is determined to spend her remaining days here, in the house where she shared so many beautiful memories with Thaathaa. She insists that when she passes away, her body should be taken to the cemetery only in Thaathaa's old Padmini, which is why the car is still kept in good condition. Both of us have tried to convince her to let us drive it, but she refuses. Paatti has vowed to sit in the car only after her death. She doesn't have any financial worries as she receives Thaathaa's pension. Plus, she prefers to take care of all the cooking herself and not hire any household help. In addition, she spends her days making a variety of sweets. Initially, she used to share them with the kids in this neighbourhood, but soon local bakeries began asking her to supply to them. Many of the sweets you find in the bakeries nearby are Paatti's original recipes. Eventually, someone suggested that she should have people around to help in case of emergencies, which is why she decided to rent out the rooms on the upper floor.

'Anandhi came here through a broker. Solely driven by the desire to make money, she grabbed the receptionist's job at our college within a week of her arrival in the city. Knowing that Paatti had more rooms available, Anandhi went ahead and posted an ad online to rent out the room next to hers on the upper floor; her intention was to make some extra cash. Vetri, upon seeing the ad, contacted her and came here. However, she demanded a commission from each month's rent from both Vetri and Paatti. Poor Paatti complied, but Vetri refused to pay, knowing that Paatti was already giving her a commission. Since then, she has held a grudge against him and has been trying to get rid of him. Once he's gone, she can bring in another tenant and pocket commission from them as well, right? It's been a year and a half since that Moodevi came here. Vetri came to Chennai from Madurai soon after, to pursue his passion for movies. Anandhi manipulates Paatti by taking her to the park, mall and beach, while subtly causing trouble for Vetri whenever she gets a chance. Thankfully, Paatti doesn't pay much heed to her accusations against Vetri. Paatti truly loves both him and me, but Anandhi's a fraud who will do anything for money.'

'I'll try to fill in the gaps,' Vetri interjected. 'When I first arrived here, there was a woman who used to sweep the yard and make the kolam. Moodevi drove her away. Similarly, a man used to come to clean the water tank once a month, but she got him dismissed, too. Eventually, she took over both these tasks herself and deducted the money from the rent she was supposed to pay.'

'Truth be told, she's living here rent-free,' Reshma added.

'Ram, don't believe a word they say. They're both incredibly jealous of her,' Paatti said, as she approached with three cups of coffee, distributing them as she continued to speak. 'She's a hardworking girl, you know. Came here about a year ago through a broker. She is from a village called Vaniyambadi. Let me be honest, life's been a lot brighter since she arrived. She's nothing like these two. She takes me out whenever she can. What really ticks these two off is that they tried to get admission to the film school you're attending now, through her. They were so dramatic in their efforts that, one fine morning, they even went as far as to show her a lot of affection, but she just flat out refused to help. That's why they're so angry with her.'

'It wasn't just a simple "no". You should have seen the way she talked! "Do you have any shame, trying to get everything the easy way? No matter how hard you try, you'll never get admission there. You and your sister always resort to drama to get what you want." It was a long, scathing "No!"' Vetri recalled the incident.

'So what? Didn't both of you eventually get admission there? It's all thanks to her,' Paatti exclaimed excitedly.

'It seems like Moodevi's been doing some serious brainwashing. Your praise for her is proof of that. We got admission there because our uncle is a member of the ADMK party,' Vetri confessed, causing Ram to look at them both in surprise.

'Ah, so you're both there under the recommendation quota!' Ram teased.

Just then, Anandhi emerged from the bathroom, freshly bathed. She hung her towel on the clothesline and hurried upstairs.

'Why's she always in such a rush? She zoomed out of college, too, like a rocket,' Ram commented, watching her disappear.

'She never sits still for a moment, Ram. Money, money, money. That's all she thinks about. She's constantly selling apartments and land, buying vegetables and flowers at wholesale rates to resell them to small shops, and dealing in all sorts of second-hand goods, including vehicles. Whatever jobs there are in Chennai to make money, she does them. And she's incredibly stingy, too. Have you seen the phone she uses? It's an old keypad model with a rubber band holding it together, also second-hand. Would any of us young people use something like that? You can get a touchscreen phone for just twenty-five hundred rupees now. And that dumb Luna she rides? Can anyone really say its safe enough to be driven about? Plus, the garland on it!' Reshma said, rolling her eyes at Anandhi's two-wheeler that stood in the car shed.

'She's not stingy. She knows how to run a business by playing on people's sympathy. She can grab anyone's attention because she's beautiful. She must have studied MBA,' Vetri mused.

Ram listened to Vetri and Reshma talk about Anandhi, while Paatti seemed absolutely unfazed by their words.

'Look, oldie. One day she'll beat you up, ransack this house and leave,' Reshma warned, noting Paatti's indifferent expression.

Just then, Anandhi came downstairs, talking on her phone. She was wearing a yellow kurta and churidar. 'Exactly at 9 p.m., Paatti,' she announced the time by when she would be back and sped off on her Luna.

Ram checked his watch; it was 5 p.m. 'Oh, it's getting late. Let's go,' he said hurriedly.

'Come back on Saturday. Reshma will be here, too. We'll have some good food,' Paatti invited Ram before he and Reshma left.

'Of course, Paatti,' he smiled, bidding farewell to Vetri and Paatti before they drove off.

Two

This time, Ram was the one driving the scooty. He navigated slowly because the road was busy and he wasn't familiar with Chennai. At every junction, Reshma, who was seated behind him, gave directions.

After Guindy, Ram had stopped at a traffic signal, waiting for it to turn green, when he saw a curious sight. Anandhi's Luna was moving slowly down another road. A goddess's crown adorned her head and a large garland hung around her neck. In front of her, on the Luna, was a tall oil lamp leaning over her shoulder. Medium-sized banana plants were strung along the back of the Luna, their leaves peeping out of the newspaper wrapped around them. On the back seat were two bunches of bananas tied with a rope, with a basket placed on top of them. If all that was not enough, there were also two bundles of tender coconuts that were tied to the back of the vehicle. The traffic policeman, bystanders and other drivers stared in astonishment as she passed by.

'Reshma, look! Anandhi! There!' Ram called out, pointing in her direction.

Reshma was shocked to see Anandhi riding with all that paraphernalia, while people gaped in surprise.

'She is quite thick-skinned,' Ram commented, amazed at the scene unfolding before his eyes.

One

When Ram returned to the apartment, Kiran was on the balcony as usual, keeping an eye on the neighbourhood, while Bineesh was in the room working on his laptop.

Ram called home to chat with his mother for a while and then freshened up.

Later that night, as the three of them sat on the floor in the hall to have dinner, Ram shared stories with them about Paatti and Anandhi.

'Why was that chechi going around with a crown, banana plants and an oil lamp?' Kiran asked, puzzled.

'She seems to dabble in all sorts of businesses. She was probably providing supplies for some rituals that are performed when girls here reach puberty, or something similar,' Bineesh speculated.

'But what about those banana plants? Why would someone pull them out of the ground just to place them in an auditorium or house?' Kiran mused.

'Wish your father had planted a banana tree instead of making you that night,' Bineesh remarked dryly.

'Your knack for finding a different angle on everything is impressive, Kiran,' Ram taunted.

'I despise a civilized society that confuses parental lust with banana cultivation. Befriending the heartless is the folly of the ignorant. The bull that gored the father will gore the calf,' Kiran retorted, taking his plate to the kitchen.

Ram and Bineesh looked at each other, bewildered.

By 10 p.m., the three of them had gone to bed.

The next morning, during the train ride to college from Guindy, Ram saw the same aruvani he had encountered the day before. She was moving through the same compartment, asking for money. As soon as Ram spotted her, he tried to hide behind another passenger clinging to the handrail.

She noticed him immediately. 'Oh, you there, my darling! Give me money!' she said, stroking Ram's hair as he stared at the ground.

He continued to avoid eye contact, his gaze fixed on the floor. She kept touching him, caressing his hair incessantly.

Laughter erupted from the other passengers. Finally, Ram finally looked at her angrily.

'I can't give you money. Go away,' he said firmly.

'Then I'll somehow get it from you.' She began clapping her palms obnoxiously close to his ears. The other passengers chose to be mute spectators, never making any attempts to intervene.

'Give money, darling.' She caressed Ram's body again, prompting him to grab her hand and twist it. Her smiling face turned serious.

'Give money, you bastard!' She moved closer.

Ram's heart rate spiked. The scent of turmeric and jasmine flowers from her body filled his nostrils. The stares from the onlookers made him feel as if he were losing his grip on reality.

'I'm a student. I don't have money to give you every day,' he tried to explain.

'People are watching. Today, you have to give me money,' she insisted, clapping near his ears to make her point.

'Don't you understand? I can't give you money. Go away!'

Ignoring him, she reached into his shirt pocket. Ram tried to push her away, but she was stronger than he had anticipated. He only had one hundred rupees left, a significant amount for him, and he wasn't willing to let it go. As they struggled, the train stopped at Kodambakkam station. A sudden thud came from behind the woman.

To his utter shock, Ram saw a policeman kick her. In the scuffle that ensued, Ram's shirt pocket tore and the hundred-rupee note fell into her hands. She bolted from the train, but the policeman chased her and struck her with a baton, causing her to tumble on to the platform.

As the train started moving again, the policeman turned and ordered Ram to get off, but Ram quickly pulled his head back inside. Everyone on the train was staring at him. Ram lowered his head in embarrassment and tried to act invisible until he reached the next station, Nungambakkam.

Though it was already 9.30 a.m., Ram went to a shop, drank some water and sat down for a moment to calm down before trudging to the college.

Two

Anandhi was sitting at the reception. Ram quietly strode down the cobbled corridor towards the film-making class.

'Well, where are you going?' she enquired, her tone resembling that of an authoritative parent questioning their child who had come home late.

'It's a bit late. It won't happen again,' Ram assured.

'I don't care. You can't go to class.'

'I'm really sorry. I'll ensure it doesn't happen again,' he apologized without looking up at her and began to head up the stairs.

'I already told you that you can't go,' she insisted.

Ram shot her an angry glance over his shoulder. 'It's not your father who is paying for my studies here, alright? And this isn't a rocket science class where being ten minutes late matters!'

Hearing this, she leapt up from her chair and marched up the steps, blocking his way.

'The principal has instructed me not to allow anyone upstairs after nine-thirty. There is no way you will attend class today.'

Infuriated, and at his wits end already, Ram grabbed her and gave her a shove before continuing upstairs. Anandhi stumbled and fell to the ground.

Mr Shiva had already commenced the lecture. Ram knocked and was summoned in. Instead of entering, he gestured for Mr Shiva to step outside. Once they were in the corridor, Ram explained the situation to him. Hearing his account, Mr Shiva comforted him and escorted him into the class. Despite Vetri and Reshma's persistent inquiries, Ram remained silent.

A while later, Anandhi entered the classroom and announced: 'The principal is calling Sriram.'

'What's the matter?' Mr Shiva enquired.

'I don't know.'

'Then I'll come too,' Mr Shiva said.

Ram glared at Anandhi with hatred before rising from his seat.

Standing in Principal Srinivas's office, Ram remained silent while Mr Shiva spoke on his behalf. Despite him explaining that Ram's actions were due to some unfortunate circumstances, the principal remained unmoved.

'This institution prioritizes respect towards women. If a student misbehaves with a staff member, it's my duty to address it publicly. Therefore, Sriram must apologize to Anandhi in front of his classmates. That's my decision,' the principal declared.

'I'll do that, sir. If you want me to fall at this girl's feet and apologize, I can do that too,' Sriram blurted, revealing his inner turmoil.

'Very good,' the principal replied cheerfully.

When the principal, Anandhi, Mr Shiva and Ram entered the third-floor classroom, no one understood what was happening.

'I apologize to Anandhi, a staff member of this institution, in front of all of you for my rude behaviour towards her. Sorry!' Ram said, addressing the class.

Vetri and Reshma exchanged confused looks. After the principal and Anandhi left, everyone in the class started bombarding Ram with questions.

'Leave Ram alone for now. It's a minor issue. Nothing serious,' Mr Shiva said, switching off the lights and starting the projector to show the movie *Colour of Paradise*. He clearly wasn't in the mood to continue the lesson.

Three

In the afternoon, while standing in line at Amma Unavagam, Reshma and Vetri noticed Anandhi sitting on a cement bench nearby, eating curd rice.

Ram stood quietly with them in the queue. The three of them ate in silence, with Vetri and Reshma occasionally throwing a glance at Ram.

'She deserved a tight slap, not just a push,' Reshma said as they walked back through the streets of Nungambakkam.

'Please, let it go,' Ram replied calmly.

'Do you know what's wrong with you? You don't stand up for yourself. You're too naive. Otherwise, would an aruvani on the train have torn your shirt? And with Anandhi, you just need to stand strong with us. We'll handle it,' Vetri said decisively.

Reshma nodded in agreement.

'My dear friends, please spare me. I don't want to get involved in any more problems. This issue is resolved. Don't drag me into your conflicts,' Ram snapped and started walking ahead.

Vetri and Reshma exchanged looks of despair.

The trio had almost reached the college gate when they saw Anandhi standing under the shade of a tree in front of the building.

'Mr Sriram, can you please come here?' she called out.

Ram glanced at Vetri and Reshma, who signalled with their eyes for him to go.

Ram slowly approached her. 'What do you want?'

'Can you come with me?'

'Why?'

'Please hurry. Break time is almost over,' she said and began walking.

'Hey, Ram!' Vetri called from behind.

Gesturing with his hand that he would be back soon, Ram followed Anandhi.

Anandhi stopped abruptly as they entered a side street, out of sight from Vetri and Reshma. Ram, unsure of her intentions, found himself standing uncomfortably close to her.

'Sriram, do you know our college has cameras everywhere?'

'Yes, I know.'

'The principal made you apologize in front of the class because he saw everything on a camera. I had no part to play in that decision.'

With that, Anandhi looked around and delivered a stinging slap to Ram's face.

'That's for hurting me and for insulting my father!'

Ram was stunned.

At that moment, Mr Shiva, having had his lunch at a nearby hotel, chanced upon them.

'Why are you two here?' he asked, noticing the tense atmosphere.

'Nothing, sir. I was just resolving my issues with Ram,' Anandhi replied coolly.

'Very good. Very good. Come on, break time is over,' Mr Shiva said and headed into the college.

Anandhi glared at Ram and then walked with Mr Shiva. Ram stood stock-still, frowning and trying to process what had just happened.

6

One

'What did she say?' Vetri asked Ram as they left college and headed to Guindy. Ram had been silent in class all evening.
'Nothing.'
'Oh, so you're on her side now, huh?'
'I am not on anybody's "side",' Ram replied angrily.
They rode in silence for a few minutes as Vetri carefully navigated through the traffic.
'Can you promise me you won't tell Reshma if I share something with you?'
Vetri abruptly stopped the bike by the roadside. 'What's going on?'
Ram didn't answer; he kept staring at the road instead.
'Come on, I won't tell anyone. What's the matter?'
'It will be humiliating if anyone finds out, but I can't keep it from you. Anandhi slapped me.'
'What? Slapped you?' Vetri was shocked.
Ram continued looking at the road. Vetri noticed his eyes were tearing up.
'Aren't you embarrassed at being slapped by some random girl?'
When Ram didn't respond, Vetri put the bike on its stand and pulled Ram to a nearby tea shop. He bought Ram a glass of Horlicks milk to help soothe his nerves.
'Let it go. It doesn't matter. It's actually good that you didn't hit back. If you had, you'd probably be sitting in a police station right

now. Ever since Jayalalithaa became the chief minister, women have special privileges in Tamil Nadu. People always believe the woman's side of the story. And Anandhi is really bold. She might even accuse you of trying to assault her. Don't worry, bro. We'll give her a taste of her own medicine. At least no one else saw you get hit.'

For a moment, Ram felt that Vetri was justifying his helplessness to ease his own distress.

'I feel terribly ashamed, even if no one else saw it. It's like I've lost my self-respect. I feel so small in front of her. I've never experienced anything like this before.'

'Come on, Ram, you're too naive. That's why you get stuck in situations like this. In a place like this, if you stand dumbstruck, people will take advantage of you. If you don't have the courage to speak up firmly, people will walk all over you. No one will respect us or our words. This is how people in Tamil Nadu are. Dude, you need to get rid of your Kerala style and switch to the Tamil Nadu-mode.'

To show that he practised what he preached, Vetri promptly called out to a schoolboy walking in front of them. 'Hey, dickhead!'

'What do you want, you asshole?' the boy retorted, turning around.

'Nothing, bro. Just showing a sample. Take care.'

The boy walked away, cursing Vetri under his breath.

'See? Even that kid knows how to handle himself. This isn't Kerala, Ram. This is Tamil Nadu. This is how things work here. You need to adapt.'

Just then, a large man returning from the tea shop accidentally bumped into Ram.

'Hey, are you blind?' Ram roared, letting out all the rage that had been building up inside him.

'Sorry, bro. My bad.' With that, the man scurried away.

'That's my boy,' Vetri chuckled.

'Remember when you said you and Reshma could come up with a plan to get back at her? Count me in. Anandhi isn't just any girl, she's an arrogant Moodevi. We can't take her down in one blow. We've got to chip away at her, piece by piece,' Ram suggested, making Vetri smile menacingly.

Before parting, he informed Vetri that he'd be visiting Paatti's house the next day, which was a Saturday.

Ram couldn't sleep that night. He kept replaying every moment from the day—Anandhi slapping him, the aruvani touching him and demanding money—the embarrassment of it all. He could still smell that aruvani's turmeric and jasmine scent. Unable to calm down, Ram wandered out on to the balcony and started reading some of the books he had brought from home. Soon, he drifted off.

Since Kiran and Ram did not have to go to college the next day, they hadn't set an alarm. Ram, however, woke up at 8 a.m. sharp.

From his bed, he sent Bineesh a WhatsApp message, informing him about his plan to visit Paatti's house to meet friends. Then he woke up Kiran who was fast asleep.

'Hey, wake up, wake up! It's time for college!'

Kiran got up, alarmed. After a moment, he realized what was happening and gave Ram a death stare.

'What's wrong with you, bro? No college today. Let me sleep,' Kiran groaned.

'Oh, really? My bad, bro. Go ahead, get some sleep,' Ram said, secretly pleased with himself for screwing up Kiran's morning.

'Kerala-mode off. Tamil Nadu-mode on,' he muttered to himself wickedly, appreciating his reflection in the mirror.

Later, on the bus to Guindy, he dialled Vetri's number.

'Has Reshma arrived?' he asked.

'Yeah, she just got here. She's pumped up for this,' Vetri was all charged up.

'Great. I'll be there soon,' Ram said before ending the call.

After reaching Guindy, Ram called Vetri again, who promptly arrived to pick him up.

Two

Outside Paatti's house, Ram quickly dismounted Vetri's bike and opened the gate, stepping on the kolam meticulously made by Anandhi without any hesitation. Not finding her Luna in the car shed, he glanced up at her room on the second floor, but it was locked.

'Ram dear, you're here? Come in, I've made some delicious kesari,' Paatti called out, setting down the watering can and wiping her hands on her pallu before heading inside.

'Quick, eat up and join us upstairs,' Vetri urged, already making his way up the stairs.

Reshma stood on the balcony, giving Ram a thumbs-up.

After devouring the kesari, Ram went upstairs. The room was spacious and had a double cot, a wooden table and a large wardrobe.

Not seeing an attached bathroom, Ram deduced that the one downstairs must be the shared facility.

'So, what's the plan?' he asked, joining Vetri and Reshma on the bed.

'She left in the morning, saying she would be back by noon. She's very punctual,' Vetri remarked.

'We're not here to praise her,' the displeasure was a little too evident in Reshma's voice.

'Okay, okay. If she's back at twelve, she'll go straight for a bath. She'll use that towel hanging on the clothesline. Let's start there.'

'What can you do with a towel?' Ram was curious.

'Look at this. This is the dried powder of the senthatti plant,' Reshma said, holding up a small metal box.

'Senthatti? What's it used for?'

'Just wait and watch.'

Reshma tiptoed down the stairs and, without Paatti noticing, sprinkled the powder on the maroon towel on the clothesline, rubbing it in well. Then she calmly walked back upstairs, humming an old song, as if nothing had happened.

By then, it was past 11 a.m. Ram, Vetri and Reshma waited on the second-floor balcony for Anandhi to return.

In between cooking lunch, Paatti made lemonade for the three of them. Reshma didn't even peek into the kitchen, as she was so focused on successfully executing their plan.

Time passed. When Anandhi's scooter approached the gate, the three mischief-makers rushed into Vetri's room and stood by the door, intently listening to the sound of Anandhi wheeling in her scooter, parking it at the usual spot, walking up the stairs, opening her room and going back down to take a shower.

After about two minutes, Reshma stepped out of the room, casually walked up to the balcony and then hurried back into the room.

'She's in! She's gone in for a shower! Yay!' Reshma exclaimed with great joy, jumping up and down and doing a little dance to a hit Tamil song playing on Vetri's 5.1 home theatre system.

Paatti, in the final stages of cooking, heard the music from upstairs and tapped her feet in time with the beat. After checking the salt in the coconut milk chicken curry, she turned off the stove, covered the dish and climbed up the stairs, enjoying the song.

When she reached Vetri's room, she saw Vetri and Reshma were dancing, while Ram sat nearby, laughing and enjoying the scene. Paatti joined in, her enthusiasm infectious even at her age. Ram joined in, too. Vetri and Paatti danced together, while Reshma cranked up the volume. The four of them danced to upbeat Tamil tunes, adding some comic moves here and there.

'Stop! Stop it, I say!' A voice louder than the home theatre system interrupted them from outside.

'Oh, Anandhi. What happened, dear?' Paatti rushed to the door of the room upon seeing Anandhi's body covered in reddish rashes. The songs continued to blare in the background.

Vetri, Ram and Reshma exchanged amused glances at Anandhi's ruffled appearance.

'Who did this?' Anandhi asked, trying to keep her anger in check.

Suddenly, Reshma caught her brother pointing at her with his eyes.

'You traitor!' Reshma exclaimed.

Before she knew it, Anandhi dashed inside the room and pressed her towel against Reshma's face.

Paatti, bewildered, didn't understand what was happening.

Realizing that Anandhi was getting back at her, Reshma started crying.

'It wasn't me. They did it. Put it on their faces too, you Moodevi!' Reshma cried out.

Vetri and Ram, aware that things had spiralled out of control, retreated to the corners of the room to evade Anandhi.

'No, Anandhi, no,' Vetri pleaded as Anandhi turned her attention to them. Despite the itching on her body, Anandhi advanced towards them with the towel. At the same time, Reshma's face also began to itch.

Vetri and Ram managed to restrain Anandhi, pushed her on to the bed and then bolted out of the room.

'Do you have any more of that stuff?' Anandhi panted, lying on the bed and looking at Reshma.

Reshma picked the tin of senthatti powder from the table and tossed it to Anandhi.

With a sudden spurt of energy, Anandhi grabbed the box of powder and rushed after Vetri and Ram. Not one to miss the drama, and despite her itchy face, Reshma dashed to the balcony to watch the chaos unfold.

Poor Paatti was yet to figure out whether the commotion was a joke or a serious matter.

'Have you all lost your minds?' she asked, baffled.

'Anandhi, let's please sort this out,' Vetri half-pleaded and half-shouted as he ran into the car shed, while Ram darted into the outside bathroom and locked the door.

'If my Padmini gets a scratch, I'll kill both of you!' Paatti yelled from the balcony, watching Anandhi chase Vetri around her beloved car.

'Don't waste time running around. Act quickly. Rub it on his face!' Reshma screamed from above.

What no one had noticed was that the ruckus was beginning to stir the beehive hanging from the neem tree close to the second floor.

'Hey, kummanamoonji! Throw that tin at his face!' Reshma's scream set off a chain reaction. The next moment, the air was filled with the buzzing sound of very angry bees.

Paatti clutched her chest in shock and ran into Vetri's room, slamming the door shut behind her.

'Let me in, too, you old lady!' Reshma ran after her, banging on the door in desperation.

Paatti quickly opened the door and yanked Reshma inside, but several giant bees swarmed into the room.

Both Anandhi and Vetri were alarmed, when they understood what had happened. Panicking, they tried to run inside, only to realize with horror that Paatti had locked all the doors before going upstairs.

Vetri ran towards the bathroom and shouted, 'Ram, we're doomed! Open the door!'

Anandhi was close behind.

'No matter what you say, I won't open it,' Ram yelled, pushing against the door from inside.

Upstairs, the bees started attacking Paatti and Reshma. Paatti got stung on the nose and Reshma on the forehead. Both of them flung the door open and ran outside, only to be stung repeatedly by the bees waiting outside.

Meanwhile, Ram still refused to open the bathroom door. Anandhi and Vetri raced towards the gate and out on to the road, chased by a swarm of bees.

Hearing the screams of Paatti and the others, Ram sensed something was wrong. He opened the door slightly and peeked out. In the distance, he saw Vetri and Anandhi running frantically down the road.

'What's going on?' he muttered to himself, flustered.

He cautiously opened the door a little more and stepped out, only to see Paatti and Reshma running towards him, screaming in pain and trying to escape the bee attack. They dashed into the bathroom, but the bees followed them, forcing them out again.

Realizing that the bees had spotted their new prey, Ram also bolted down the road, screaming. Reshma and Paatti ran out after him, desperate to get away.

7

One

'Whoosh!' Vetri winced as a doctor extracted the bee's stinger from his head.

Around nine people were sitting in the emergency room, all thanks to bee stings.

Five of them were Paatti and her companions, while the remaining four were residents from their neighbourhood. Apart from Paatti and her group, the bees had also targeted four women who had been gossiping near a roadside community tap. Eventually, someone had gathered all nine individuals into a car and rushed them to the nearby hospital.

Ram burst into laughter when he saw Reshma's swollen nose, a result of the rashes caused by Anandhi's vicious attack with the towel. Ram had been stung below both his eyes, giving him a comical appearance. Anandhi had stings on both her cheeks, forehead and neck. Vetri endured stings on his head, forehead and buttocks, while Paatti suffered stings on her lips, nose and hands. The four of them looked at each other and couldn't stop laughing.

Meanwhile, the four women who had also been stung were lying on nearby beds. They watched the five of them laugh, their expressions conveying no amusement.

'A rascal bee stung me on the breast. I didn't tell the doctor,' Mallika, one of the women, confided to the others. 'I'll have to go home and have my husband take a look at it.'

It was five in the evening when they finally left the hospital.

'When we get home, we should burn the bees down, Paatti,' Vetri remarked as they walked along the street. Thanks to their swollen faces, all the passersby couldn't help but stare and try to hide their chuckles.

'The bees have been there since Thaathaa's time. Let's not disturb them,' Paatti replied calmly, continuing her stride.

'You're crazy, old lady. So, memories of grandpa came and started stabbing at you? Had a good time, huh?' Vetri retorted, his tone edged with frustration.

He didn't say anything more after that.

When they reached Paatti's home, Anandhi's towel and the tin of senthatti powder lay in the courtyard. Ram looked at Anandhi, feeling relieved to see both her cheeks swollen, as if she had been slapped. Anandhi returned his gaze with a glare. She doubted whether he could see straight as both his eyelids were swollen.

Reshma remained quiet throughout, convinced that she was to be blamed for agitating the bees. Loud music was still playing in Vetri's room upstairs.

All four of them looked up at the neem tree's top branch. The bees had regrouped as if nothing had happened!

After a quick meal, Ram borrowed Vetri's sunglasses and headed to Guindy with Reshma.

'Ram, we need to avenge this,' Reshma insisted as he got off the scooter.

Ram took off his sunglasses, looked at her with as much anger as he could show through his unbelievably swollen eyes. 'How dare you look at my face with your swollen nose and say this, you idiot? Go home, or I'll kill you! You and that senthatti powder. Get lost.'

Reshma lowered the visor of her helmet and rode away. Ram boarded a bus and eventually reached his apartment. Kiran opened the door and smiled at the sight of Ram with sunglasses on.

'Is this a new look?'

'Oh yeah, yeah.'

'Oh yeah, come on, baby,' Kiran teased Ram playfully. Bineesh, who had just returned from work, came out from his room.

Seeing him, Ram took off the sunglasses. After the initial few minutes of being shocked and horrified, Kiran and Bineesh burst into laughter when Ram recounted everything that had happened. Resigning himself to his unbelievably unlucky fate, Ram gulped down the medicine given by the hospital and went to bed early that night.

Two

The next day, the first thing Ram did after waking up was to look in the mirror. Relieved to note that the swelling had reduced a bit, he went to the bathroom to freshen up. Since it was Sunday, Bineesh didn't have to go to work. Kiran got up around 8 a.m.

'I've ordered food online. Don't bother entering the kitchen with those eyes,' Bineesh said, coming out of his room.

'How about cooking some biryani for lunch?' Kiran suggested.

'If you chop everything, I'll handle making the biryani,' Bineesh said, rolling up his sleeves.

Later, when Bineesh and Kiran stepped out to buy the ingredients for chicken biryani, Ram made a video call to Vetri and Reshma. He felt a little more at peace when he noticed that both their faces were the same as his. The fact that he wouldn't be the odd one out in class the next day provided much-needed relief. Then he called home and shared all that had happened the previous day with his mother. His mother, too, couldn't stop laughing.

Half of Sunday was spent making the biryani. During the other half, the three of them took turns to go to the toilet, as the extra spices they'd enthusiastically and generously added to make the biryani tastier had ended up having a 'strong' effect on them.

Three

The next day, the swelling on Ram's face had come down significantly.

'Thank God! Tamil Nadu-mode is off from now on. Back to-Kerala mode. Best to stick with that for my health, too,' he mumbled at his reflection in the mirror.

As usual, Ram and Kiran exited the house after Bineesh. Ram boarded bus number 52, got off at Guindy and walked to the railway station by the subway. When he saw the aruvani and her allies by the side of the road, he stopped for a moment. Consumed by the fear of her confronting him, Ram, in an attempt to hide, quickly joined a group of Bengali labourers who passed by him and walked towards the overbridge.

Ram looked at his watch as he scurried towards platform 2.

It was 9.05 a.m. The train was still ten minutes away. Someone tapped him on the shoulder while he was trying to find a corner to stand in. He turned around with a start and was relieved to see an old woman selling small samosas.

'Mone, hot samosas. Take five pieces, only ten rupees,' the old woman tried convincing him.

'No, Ammachi, no. I usually don't eat them,' Ram replied, moving away. Just then, there was another tap on his shoulder, causing him to turn around in agitation. It was the aruvani. Ram involuntarily recoiled at the sight of her, clutching his shirt pocket and the money in it tightly.

She extended a small tin box towards him. 'Here, take this.'

'What is it?' Ram asked, wary.

'It's my spit from betel leaves. Take it,' her voice was stern.

Ram was taken aback. He recalled Vetri's advice about standing up to people who bothered him. 'If someone bothers us, we should have the courage to give it back. That's how you survive in Tamil Nadu. Kerala mode should be turned off, and Tamil Nadu mode should be on,' he had said.

With these thoughts in mind, Ram hesitated to accept the tin box. 'Just leave. If you don't, I'll call the police,' he said, avoiding eye contact but feeling the gaze of others on the platform.

The aruvani moved closer. The familiar scent of turmeric and jasmine, which had haunted him in his dreams, flooded his nose and made him feel uneasy.

'I said, take it!' she insisted through gritted teeth.

Ram realized he was being watched by everyone around, and that his resolve to adopt the Tamil Nadu-mode had dissolved.

Reluctantly, he took the box from her hand. He felt like a coward. As soon as he took the box, the aruvani moved away.

In the distance, the train's horn echoed. People rose from their seats and moved to the edge of the platform. When the train came to a halt, Ram looked at the aruvani once more before entering the compartment. As he climbed aboard, she followed him. When the train started moving, she didn't ask anyone in that carriage for money. Instead, she clung to the handrail next to where Ram was sitting, staring at him. Ram, holding the tin box, occasionally peeped at her, only to find her still staring. He quickly looked away each time.

After ten minutes, he reached Nungambakkam station. When he got off, she did the same. Ram quickly walked towards his college. Every few seconds, he looked back to see her still following him. His plan to discard the box after getting off the train had been thwarted.

'Oh my God, what kind of destiny is this? I'm carrying a box full of an aruvani's spit and walking around,' he muttered, cursing himself.

He glanced down at the box. *I am a coward. If I weren't, why would I be running away, fearing an aruvani who is marginalized in society? As Vetri said, Chennai is not the place for someone like me. What satisfaction do they get from harassing me like this?*

Lost in these thoughts, he reached the trees in front of the college. Memories of the slap he got from Anandhi resurfaced, making him feel even more unsettled. He looked back once more as he entered the college. He saw the aruvani standing under one of the trees, still watching him.

Anandhi, noticing Ram climb the stairs with a tin box in his hand, eyed him suspiciously. She wondered if it was more senthatti powder. To Ram's satisfaction, Anandhi's cheeks were still slightly swollen.

'What?' he snapped at her in response to her scrutinizing look.

'What?' Anandhi replied scornfully.

'Podi!' Ram sneered, asking her to get lost.

'Poda!' Anandhi shot back.

'Your punishments aren't over yet. There's more to come,' he warned as he continued to climb the stairs.

On his way up, he kicked open the lid of a dustbin and threw the tin box into it. Then he marched his way into the classroom.

8

One

That day, Mr Thayalan's cinematography class extended well into the afternoon.

During the lunch break, Ram told Vetri and Reshma about the tin box the aruvani had given him. They scolded Ram for hastily discarding it, without even examining its contents. When they checked the dustbin, it had already been emptied.

As they walked towards Amma Unavagam, Vetri and Reshma continued to reprimand him. They found Anandhi seated on a cement bench there with her usual curd rice. While waiting in line, the lady serving the food noticed Vetri, Reshma and Ram, and their swollen faces. A cheeky smile flickered across her face.

'I knew someone would get back at you soon,' she remarked casually, looking very pleased with herself.

Reshma snapped at her. 'You wretched woman, I'll hit you with my sandal!'

Vetri intervened quickly, restraining Reshma. 'Please, let's not create a scene here. The next eatery is two kilometres away.'

Reshma quietened down. Vetri proceeded to order his food, followed by Ram and then Reshma.

'Chee!' the lady serving food exclaimed in anger.

'Chee!' sneered back Reshma.

After the trio washed their hands and returned their plates, Reshma and the lady exchanged hostile looks one last time.

'Reshma, you're crossing the line with your impulsive behaviour and talking back too much,' Vetri said as they exited the restaurant.

'I was just about to say the same thing,' Ram chimed in, backing Vetri up.

Reshma sullenly walked alongside them.

The hot sun beat down, yet the street refused to slow down. Most of the benches and chairs outside the tea shop were occupied.

'Hey! Hello!'

The three of them turned around upon hearing Anandhi's voice from behind. They stopped in surprise.

'Sriram, can you please come here?'

Ram glanced at Vetri.

'Dude, she's calling him the same way as she did yesterday,' Vetri observed.

'Well, if she dares to lay a hand on Ram today, she'll see my true colours. I'll give this Moodevi what I have reserved for the other Moodevi in the unavagam,' Reshma declared before striding towards Anandhi.

'Wait, what? You told Reshma that I got slapped? You cheater,' Ram stamped on Vetri's leg.

'Are you Sriram?' Anandhi asked Reshma.

'Yes, for now, I am Sriram. Just tell me what it's about.'

After a moment's thought, Anandhi retrieved a tin box from her side bag and placed it in Reshma's hand.

'There was money in it. The lady who came to collect the trash gave it to me,' she explained.

With that, Anandhi gave Reshma a once-over before walking away.

Ram and Vetri hurried over to Reshma; Anandhi had already turned and walked away by then. Reshma opened the box and found a hundred-rupee note along with some rolled-up ten- and twenty-rupee notes inside. There was also a neatly written note in Tamil on a piece of paper. It read: 'I don't usually harm anyone. But I couldn't help myself when I saw you. I apologize. Enclosed is the same note taken from your pocket and money to buy a new one to replace the torn shirt.'

Ram was shocked. 'Do people feel an urge to hurt me when they see me?'

'Don't think so,' Vetri and Reshma replied in unison.

Even after returning to class, Ram couldn't shake off his feelings about the message from the aruvani. She had actually admitted to hurting him intentionally.

'Ram, what's wrong?' Mr Shiva, who was conducting the class, enquired.

'Nothing, sir. Sorry.'

'Alright, let's continue then, class. Today, I'm assigning you your first task. You need to shoot a two-minute short film in which a guy proposes to a girl in a unique way. You can borrow cameras and equipment after signing at the reception. After shooting, those enrolled in the video editing course will assist with the editing. Similarly, if dubbing is required, it can be done with the help of the sound engineering department. You have the whole of tomorrow to complete this task. We'll screen everyone's work the following morning,' Mr Shiva explained.

'Sir, who will be the hero and the heroine?' asked Deva, one of the students.

'You can choose anyone you like. You can act, too, if you wish. It's just a test to gauge your creativity. Best of luck, guys.'

Two

After class that day, Vetri and Reshma invited Ram to watch a Hindi movie, but he declined and returned to the apartment since he hadn't informed Bineesh that he could be late.

It was his first time travelling back to Guindy by train.

The train was packed to the rafters, with four times the morning crowd. Ram managed to squeeze in somehow. At the door, schoolboys happily hung half-out, showing off by banging their hands on nearby posts whenever the train slowed down at stations.

After arriving at Guindy station, he ascended the steps of the overbridge that led to the bus stand. Ram scanned the area carefully. Except for the lady selling samosas, he didn't recognize anyone.

By the time he reached his apartment, it was 5.30 p.m.

He took out the tin box given by the aruvani from his bag and showed it to Bineesh and Kiran, recounting the events of the day.

'They usually don't give money to anyone. If they voluntarily do so, it means you're going to be prosperous,' Bineesh remarked wisely.

'You and your wild theories! While I'm wondering why they tried to harm me, you're talking about prosperity.'

'Well, now your life will be prosperous.'

'Of course,' Ram said sarcastically.

'It's quite surprising that so much has happened to you in just a week here. It took me until my second year in the city to have any crazy stories to share,' Kiran mused.

'He's different from you. He came here to study life, create stories and become a director. I suspect he dives into every problem he sees to gain new experiences,' Bineesh added.

'Now you're blaming me for everything. Just so you know, Vetri and Reshma invited me to watch a movie, but I came home instead,' Ram replied, looking at Bineesh, as if complaining.

'You're missing out on good times with your friends. I only advised you to avoid trouble, not to miss out on having fun. You're not a little boy. Don't hold back from doing things you enjoy because of what I say. Just send a message next time,' Bineesh said.

'Okay, thanks,' Ram smiled.

'But if you have any intentions of going astray, I'll give you a whack on the head. Understand?' Bineesh added with all the seriousness he could muster, looking at Kiran who was smiling and shaking his head.

'Men who are partial to laws are devils. We'll grow wings on the day fire rains down upon you,' Kiran said.

'You two better resolve this issue by talking it out. I'm going to freshen up,' Ram said, laughing.

That night, Ram spent time on the balcony with Kiran, brainstorming ideas for the short film that Mr Shiva had assigned.

Three

The next morning, Ram looked in the mirror and saw that the swelling on his face had disappeared. He boarded the bus from Iyyappanthangal at 8 a.m. and reached Guindy before 9 a.m., thanks to the light traffic.

While descending the steps to the platform, he saw that a train was just about to depart. Since he was early, he decided to sit on a bench, opting not to rush. Instead, he watched others hurry down the steps to catch it. Platform 2 was more or less empty as most people had boarded the departing train. Ram took out a marker pen from his bag and wrote 'Ram' in small letters on the bench. Seeing his name in red letters gave him a sense of ownership over the railway station.

People began to gather on the platform again, but the aruvani was nowhere to be seen. They usually jumped on the moving trains leaving the station. He assumed they would show up when the usual train came. However, as the next train pulled in with its horn blaring, the aruvani still didn't appear. Ram began to think he might never see her again.

When he reached college from Nungambakkam station, he heard his classmates Arun and Karthik shouting at Anandhi in the reception area. Ram ignored the commotion and walked up the stairs.

'It's not a camera donated by your father for you to say you'll lend it only during college hours. We only have one day.'

Upon hearing Karthik refer to Anandhi's father, Ram paused halfway up the steps, covering his mouth to stifle his laughter. After a moment, he began climbing up again and entered the classroom where Reshma was sitting with her legs crossed, pouting and looking like a leading actress.

'That blabbermouth is the heroine in everyone's work. She even demanded one hundred and ninety-nine rupees from me to act,' Vetri informed Ram as he approached.

'One hundred and ninety-nine rupees? What's that for?' Ram asked incredulously, surprised at the specificity of the amount.

'Who knows! If I ask her, she might round it up to five hundred. Those guys just offered her food and movie tickets.'

'And what's your plan?'

'Let's check out the college's dance academy. Maybe we can find someone learning Bharatnatyam or Kuchipudi. We can get it edited while the rest shoot with Reshma,' Vetri suggested.

'Alright, let's do it.'

Ram and Vetri left the classroom.

Poor kids must be off to the ATM, Reshma thought slyly.

As Ram and Vetri came down the stairs, they encountered Karthik and Arun; they held a camera they had retrieved from the reception.

'Hey, got the camera?' Ram asked.

'Yeah, that girl is very adamant. She handed it over to us at exactly nine-thirty,' Arun replied with a huff.

Seeing Ram and Vetri, Anandhi brought out another camera and its bag to the table.

'Maybe we should take a camera, too,' Vetri said as he approached her.

After writing their names in the register, Ram and Vetri went to the dance academy, carrying their camera bags. Despite having been on campus for days, the surroundings of the dance academy building and its vibrant atmosphere felt new to them. Dancers in academy uniforms with ghungroos on their ankles moved gracefully along the corridors. The rhythmic sounds of classical dance lessons emanated from some of the classrooms.

'How should we introduce ourselves?' Ram asked, looking around nervously.

'Wow! There are so many beautiful girls in our college. Why on earth do they have different lunch timings than us?' Vetri sighed.

'Look, that girl seems nice,' Ram said, pointing to one of two girls who were busy drinking water at the end of the corridor.

'The tall one, right? She looks good.'

'Not her.'

'Oh no, no. The tall one is fine. Let's try to talk to her.'

Ram watched as Vetri approached the girl who seemed to be as tall as a ladder. She had curly hair, like noodles, and fair skin. He mumbled to himself, 'What a pathetic sense of beauty he has.'

Even before Ram could finish his sentence, Vetri was beside the two girls.

The girls looked at Vetri suspiciously as he approached them with his camera bag. The second girl's complexion was a bit darker than the tall one. She had a certain grace that Ram thought would be striking on screen.

'My name is Vetri. I'm a DFM student. We need a girl to act in a small project. It will take just half an hour. Just one scene. Can you act?' Vetri asked, looking at the tall girl.

'Me?'

'Yes.'

'Well, what is that one scene?'

'It's a proposal scene.'

'Ha ha ha, alright. No problem. We only have practice in the afternoon. How about we shoot it now?'

Vetri's face lit up. He smiled from ear to ear and looked at Ram. The tall girl's name was Chinkavi, and her friend was Soumya. Quickly, Ram and Vetri made plans to shoot on the road in front of the college. Chinkavi and Soumya observed with curiosity as they set up the camera on the tripod and made the arrangements. Ram handled the camera for Vetri's project.

Vetri patiently explained the scene to Chinkavi several times. Before long, Chinkavi and Vetri became very comfortable together. Ram and Soumya noticed this.

Meanwhile, Ram requested Soumya to act in his project.

'Thank you, chetta. I was wondering how to ask you. If not, Chinkavi would have my head today. She always jokes that she looks like a foreigner. She makes fun of my complexion and calls me "karuppamma" whenever she gets a chance. She lives near my house. If I can get into her good books, I can hitch a free ride to and from college in her car every day. That's why I put up with all this,' Soumya explained.

Ram chuckled at Soumya's candidness.

'Then there's another thing. Her main hobby is seducing men and then dumping them. If she sees carefree men, "branded men", who enjoy life, she'll try to seduce them. Then, when she is tired of them, she'll snatch away their happiness and walk out of their lives.'

'Why is that?' Ram was surprised.

'That's how some girls find happiness, chetta. Chinkavi is also one such girl.'

'By the way, what do you mean by "branded men"?' Ram asked suspiciously.

'She evaluates everything a man wears, from his undergarments to his watch, and calculates. If it comes to over ten thousand rupees, she introduces herself to them,' Soumya said casually.

Ram frowned in disbelief. 'How is that even possible?'

'Wait, let me scan you and tell you your worth now,' Soumya said mischievously.

Ram's eyes widened at the comment. Soumya stared at him for a moment, seemingly contemplating something.

'Your underwear? It's the red and black Jockey combination, isn't it? Briefs or boxers?' she asked, her tone matter-of-fact.

Ram was taken aback by her accuracy. 'How did you know the colour?'

'Tell me which one,' Soumya insisted, impatient to complete her assessment.

'Briefs,' Ram replied, trying to recover from the shock of it all.

'Hmm ... three thousand four hundred. She probably wouldn't even look at you,' Soumya said with a sigh of relief.

'Very insightful,' Ram said, impressed despite himself.

Soumya smiled and winked at him. 'I learned all this after hanging out with Chinkavi. Just don't tell Vetri I spilled the beans. If she finds out, I'll be hanging off the bus tomorrow.'

Ram chuckled.

Soon, Vetri and Ram finished filming with Chinkavi and Soumya. Ram filmed his project near Nungambakkam railway station, incorporating some beggars from the area. Grateful, he treated each of them to a packet of biryani. Before returning to class, Chinkavi shared her phone number with Vetri.

After the girls left, Ram decided to scan Vetri. As soon as he checked out Vetri's jeans, shirt and watch, he realized his friend's worth was well over ten thousand.

'Vetri, which brand of underwear do you wear? What's its price?' Ram asked.

Vetri shot him an annoyed look. 'It's not branded. It's just a loincloth. Happy now?'

'Well, whatever it is, you're still in trouble,' Ram sighed.

As they walked back to the college, they saw Karthik grabbing Anandhi by her hair and planting a tight slap on her face.

9

One

'Super! She deserved that,' Vetri said excitedly as he watched Anandhi get slapped. Ram was stunned.

When Karthik had mentioned Anandhi's father earlier, in a fit of anger over not getting the camera, Ram had expected some sort of confrontation. However, he hadn't thought that Anandhi would dare confront Karthik, who was tall and well-built, in such a deserted place and get slapped herself.

'Vetri, we need to help her. If he hits her any more, she could be in serious trouble,' Ram said, moving forward, only to be stopped by Vetri.

'What's wrong with you? Let her get a couple of more slaps. Maybe it'll knock some of that pride out of her,' Vetri said cheerfully.

Anandhi was leaning against a wall nearby, panting, while Karthik stood gnashing his teeth and glaring at her. Just then, a police jeep slowly came down the road. Karthik panicked at the sight of the police, but Anandhi leaned against the wall with a smile on her face, acting as if she were his girlfriend. Her left cheek was red.

Seeing the police jeep, Vetri and Ram quickly turned on their cameras and pretended to review footage, and discussing its details to avoid drawing attention. After looking at Karthik and Anandhi, the police jeep stopped next to Ram and Vetri.

'What are you doing here?' one of the policemen asked.

'Nothing, sir. We're students from that film school. We're taking photos for an assignment,' Vetri blurted out.

The police did a quick lookover before moving on.

Once the police had left, Ram and Vetri turned their attention back to Anandhi and Karthik. To their surprise, they saw Anandhi step forward and punch Karthik in the groin. He jumped in shock and pain. Before he landed on the ground, Anandhi swiftly struck both sides of his neck with her palms.

As he knelt on the ground, groaning in pain, she gave him a tight slap. She then calmly picked up her hair clip from the ground, which had fallen when he had grabbed her hair, tied it back up and walked away towards the college as if nothing had happened, but not before throwing a smirk Vetri and Ram's way.

Vetri blinked and looked at Ram, whose jaw had dropped to the ground, aghast at what he had just seen.

'It's a good thing you didn't fight back that day, machaa,' Vetri mused.

Once Anandhi was out of sight, Ram and Vetri rushed to Karthik, who was still down. Together, they helped him to a nearby milestone and helped him sit.

Karthik couldn't walk for half an hour, and his neck had such a bad sprain that he couldn't turn his head.

Eventually, Karthik called one of his friends, who helped him on to a bike to take him home. Vetri and Ram returned to the college and walked up the stairs to the class, deliberately avoiding eye contact with Anandhi at the reception.

Most of their classmates had gone to the video editing department to work on their projects. When Ram and Vetri arrived, they saw a long queue that included even those students who had shot their videos after them. Reshma was there, too, waiting to edit her work. She turned away when she saw Vetri and Ram, clearly upset that they had asked girls from the dance academy to feature in their shoots.

'I think I'll just go home and edit the video on my laptop,' Vetri said, eyeing the crowd.

'Do you know how to edit videos?' Ram asked

'This is a good chance to learn, isn't it? Would you like to come along? I can edit yours, too, if you want.'

'Forget it, my friend. I'll stay here, edit carefully and then head home.'

Vetri copied the video files from the camera on to his pen drive and left for home.

Two

It was almost 5 p.m. when Ram finished editing his video. At Nungambakkam railway station, a train was waiting to depart. He, along with a throng of other commuters, rushed into the compartments.

After fifteen minutes, he got down at Guindy. As he started to climb the steps of the flyover, he noticed the aruvani. She was laughing with her friends, sitting on the cement bench where Ram had written his name. After a moment's hesitation, he walked towards her.

'Hey!' he called out.

About thirteen aruvanis were sitting on the handrails and ground. All of them turned when they heard a handsome bearded boy calling out.

All but one of them smiled.

'Tell me, dear,' a plump aruvani asked charmingly.

'I was calling her,' Ram said, pointing to the one he knew.

'Hey, Malli! Looks like he is here for you,' the plump one teased, causing the others to burst into laughter.

'Malli,' Ram repeated to himself.

'He's not here for *that*,' Malli said, getting up and walking towards Ram.

'What do you want?' she asked sternly.

'Oye Malli, he's a good boy. Don't be harsh,' the plump aruvani said, prompting more laughter.

'Come,' Malli said to Ram and moved away a little. 'Why did you come to me?'

'What should I call you?' Ram asked.

'Is that what you came to ask?'

'No. There was more money in the tin you gave me yesterday than what was taken from my pocket. Why?'

'I wrote it on a piece of paper.'

'I can't read or write Tamil. I'm from Kerala,' Ram said, feigning ignorance.

'I figured that from your Senthamil accent.'

Ram laughed at her observation. 'How old are you?' he asked.

'Why do you want to know?'

'Please, just tell me.'

Malli thought for a moment and then replied, 'Twenty-three.'

'Aha, so we're the same age. I thought you were older than me.'

Malli remained silent and avoided eye contact.

'When I first saw you, I thought you were really a girl,' Ram continued.

Again, Malli didn't utter a word.

Ram decided to change his tactics. He took out the money Malli had given him, still wrapped in a rubber band, and handed it back to her. He didn't want to push her further or risk her anger.

'I don't want it,' Ram said.

'I gave it to you to buy a shirt,' Malli insisted, looking at the money.

'Why are you buying me a shirt?'

'I'm the one who tore your shirt, so I'm the one who has to pay for it.'

'Well, then tell me where I can get a Peter England shirt for this money,' Ram quipped, meeting her gaze.

Malli hesitated. 'Oh! So, that's not enough money for a shirt,' she admitted and started to untie the knot at the end of her pallu, which held together the money she had.

'No, no. You must come with me to buy the shirt. Just give the money directly. I heard there are good shops in T. Nagar. If you're free, we can go now.'

Malli looked at Ram in surprise.

'Should I come with you to the store and buy you a shirt?'

'Yes, why not? If you're free, we can go now. If not, we can go another day.'

Without saying a word, Malli turned to see what her friends thought of this. All twelve of them were watching intently. At that moment, a train bound for T. Nagar slowly arrived on platform 2.

'Wait a moment.' With that, Malli quickly walked over to her friends, exchanged a few words and hurried back to Ram, agreeing to go with him to T. Nagar.

'Let's go,' she said, eyeing the departing train.

'Oye, what's your name?' the plump aruvani called out from her seat on the bench as Malli and Ram boarded the train.

'Ram,' he replied, taking a step towards the train and then turning to look back.

They smiled at him.

Even Ram wasn't entirely sure why he had invited Malli along. He knew that walking with an aruvani would draw stares and maybe cause potential misunderstandings, but for some time, he pushed all those thoughts aside. After its one-minute stop at Guindy, the train resumed its journey. For Malli, it felt like travelling with a purpose for the first time in a long while.

The train arrived at Mambalam station. The two walked quietly towards T. Nagar, one of Chennai's busiest streets, located right next to the station.

There were around two hundred shops in T. Nagar. As they navigated through the crowds, Malli occasionally looked back to ensure Ram was still with her.

'It's easy to get lost here,' Malli remarked when she realized he had noticed her frequent glances.

'Have you ever lost someone here?' Ram asked.

Malli paused for a moment and then continued walking.

'Let's try that shop,' Ram suggested, pointing to a decent-looking store.

Malli followed him without a word. The shop was bustling with activity. When Ram and Malli entered, everyone present, from the customers to the staff, whispered to each other and exchanged comments while stealing glances.

Malli, who had felt confident near the railway station, suddenly felt vulnerable. She stayed behind Ram, avoiding eye contact with anyone. Ram noticed her apprehension and, after enquiring about the shirt section, led her there.

A young man showed them various shirts, but they didn't find an exact replica of Ram's torn shirt. Ram then asked Malli to help him choose another shirt that suited him. Malli silently assisted him in selecting one, hoping to resolve the issue quickly. They both liked a black and white checked shirt. After it was packed, Ram took Malli to the saree section.

'Could you please choose a saree for one of my friends?' he asked, making a request gently.

Initially reluctant, Malli eventually selected a beautiful saree at Ram's insistence. Many women and young girls shopping in that section giggled and whispered about them. Malli pretended not to notice, trying to stay hidden behind Ram.

The new shirt was a bit costlier than his old shirt. Ram paid for their purchases with his debit card and then told Malli to pay the difference amount to him later.

As they stepped out of the shop, Malli breathed a sigh of relief, feeling a sense of liberation.

'Let's have something to drink,' Ram suggested cheerfully.

'Aren't you embarrassed enough yet?' she retorted.

'What's there to be embarrassed about? I don't have a problem; you don't have a problem. Who else has a problem here?'

Malli did not reply.

The two of them made their way to a comparatively less-crowded shop run by an elderly man. They ordered two lassis and settled at a table.

'Let me show you a project I did in college,' Ram said.

'What project?' Malli asked.

'I'm studying film-making. This is one of our assignments. Have a look.' Ram then played a video on his phone, the one that featured Soumya.

In the video, Vetri played a boy who always followed a girl who came down from the railway station every evening. Each day, she gave a packet of food to four beggars who sat on the steps of the overpass. One day, she revealed to him, the boy who followed her, that she was an aruvani who begged in trains. The next day, she was surprised to see the boy waiting for her at the same spot, his affection unchanged. When he confessed that he loved her for who she was, and was ready to accept her if she agreed, her eyes filled with tears and she accepted his proposal.

After watching the two-minute video, Malli's eyes welled up.

'What do you think? I have to present this in college tomorrow. I owe this to you. The seed of this idea germinated on that day when you followed me,' Ram exclaimed eagerly.

Malli managed a small smile.

It was already 7.30 p.m. Bineesh called Ram, concerned that he wasn't back yet. Ram assured him that he would reach shortly and hung up.

After finishing their glasses of lassi, Malli and Ram walked back towards Mambalam station.

'This is for you,' Ram said, handing Malli the bag that had the saree.

'But didn't you say this was for your friend?' Malli asked, not accepting the bag immediately.

'You are my friend now. A friend who inspired my short film. I knew you wouldn't agree if I told you this in that shop, so I lied. I'm sorry.'

Though Malli was reluctant, Ram insisted and pleaded till she finally took the bag and walked quietly to the platform with him.

'Why did you say you felt like slapping me when you first saw me?' Ram asked as they waited for the train.

Malli frowned at him. 'And you said you couldn't read Tamil. Was that a lie, too?'

'I may not know Tamil, but others do. Now, answer my question.'

Malli didn't say anything; she just looked into his eyes.

'There was someone in my life, like the person in the video you showed me. A bearded guy. He looked just like you,' she said innocently, studying his face.

'And then?' Ram asked.

'And then ... he left me,' she said, sounding heartbroken.

Ram sensed that she was revisiting painful memories.

'Why did he leave you?' Ram asked gently, looking into her eyes.

She hesitated, unsure whether to share her past with someone she had just met.

'If you're still angry with me, you don't have to tell me,' he added quickly, sensing her hesitation.

'I am not angry with you now, but I doubt you'll understand what I've been through.'

'Don't lump me with the others. If you trust me, you can share,' Ram replied firmly, turning away slightly.

Taking a deep breath, Malli decided to confide in him. 'I trusted him completely and moved in with him. He became my world. I cared for him like a wife—washing his clothes, cooking his favourite meals. I even did things I didn't like in bed, just to please him. Every day, I waited eagerly for him to return from work.

'Over time, his two closest friends started coming over for drinks when he wasn't home. After a few weeks, they started touching me inappropriately. I tolerated it because he had said they had helped him through tough times. I felt I shouldn't stop him from maintaining his relationships.

'Then, one day, he told me he had been promoted and had planned a small celebration at home. I prepared everything and waited for him and his friends. That evening, he arrived with some unfamiliar people. All of them were drunk. There were seven of them, including him. As their party got underway, I served the food and retreated to my room. But later that night, his two friends barged into my room and forcibly took me to the main hall. The lights were off. They were waiting for me like a pack of wolves. All six of them pushed me to my limits. I didn't regret what they did to me, but he was the one who covered my mouth as I screamed his name in pain. In the darkness, you can always recognize the scent of someone you love. He kept kissing my forehead while holding my mouth shut. I still don't know if he was showing me affection or causing me harm. The next day, the twelve people you met a while ago at that station found me lying under the Kathipara bridge and took care of me. I never saw him again. We even searched the house later, but he had already moved out. Years later, I saw you. You resemble him so much, which kept haunting me. The incident in which your shirt got torn was beyond my control. When you hurt me, it brought back memories of the day he had left me exposed before his friends. Only after the police beat me did I come back to my senses. The cops always find it amusing to harass us whenever they get a chance. However, I should be thankful to the one I loved for one particular thing. On some nights, the local cops, when they feel lustful, come looking for the attractive ones amongst us who live under the bridge. I'm often their target. If they take me away, I can't walk for three or four days afterwards. My body is scarred from their belts and cigarette burns. However, the pain inflicted by the police pales in comparison to what I experienced because of the one I truly loved.'

By the time Malli finished speaking, the train to Guindy had arrived at the platform.

10

One

Even while travelling by bus from Guindy to Iyyappanthangal, Malli's screams from that horrific night echoed in Ram's ears.

He arrived at the apartment around 9 p.m. When he rang the doorbell, it was Bineesh who opened the door, with Kiran standing behind him.

'Exhale with your mouth,' Bineesh instructed Ram.

'What?'

'Exhale, I said.'

'Hoooooofff ...' Ram exhaled.

'It wasn't a drinking party then. So, where have you been all this time?' Bineesh asked sternly.

'Didn't you tell me the other day to do what I want and go where I please?'

'Oh, so as soon as I say that, you decide to roam around, huh?'

'Huh? Everyone in this apartment is crazy!' Ram muttered as he walked inside and gulped down half a jug of water in one go.

At bedtime, Kiran and Ram discussed the lives of people like Malli. Neither knew whether to refer to them as 'aruvanis', 'hijras' or 'transgenders'.

Two

The next day, Chennai woke up to light rain.
Ram opened the balcony door and looked out. The entire stretch of Oil Mill Road was rain-soaked. This was the first rainfall since he had arrived in the city. All the rented beds on the nearby building's terrace were covered with plastic sheets.

At the bus depot, while standing with an umbrella, Ram observed everyone—from the street vendors to the beggars—happily moving around in the drizzle.

It was rare to see happiness on the faces of people living in Chennai, but that was the predominant emotion on most faces he saw that day. Ram deduced that Chennai's weather had a direct impact on the emotions of its residents.

While walking through the subway, he spent fifty rupees to buy a box of strawberries from one of the vendors. On reaching platform 2, he saw Malli talking to the old lady who sold samosas. She smiled sweetly when she saw Ram coming down the stairs.

Ram noticed that she was wearing the saree he had bought yesterday, her hair was adorned with jasmine flowers that were just starting to bloom, there was sandalwood paste on her forehead and she wore matching earrings.

Seeing Ram, the old lady glanced at Malli, as if asking if he was the guy. Malli smiled and nodded.

Ram walked towards them.

'Super,' he said, looking at her.

'Thanks.'

By then, the train Ram usually took had arrived. As soon as he boarded, Malli bade farewell to the old lady and got on the train as well.

Unlike the other days, Malli did not ask anyone for money that day. They both stood by the train door, hanging on to the handles on either side. The train was less crowded than most days. Ram opened the box of strawberries and held it out to her. She took one and bit into it.

The rain poured down on the train, occasional drops splashing on Ram and Malli's faces. Malli smiled slightly at him.

'Well, do I sense a bit of romance?' Ram asked teasingly, noticing her smile.

'Oh, no. I won't fall for any bearded man again in this life,' Malli said, folding her hands and laughing. Ram laughed, too.

'Until two days ago, I was afraid of you, Malli. Now we've become friends,' Ram said and handed her another strawberry.

'All this will last for two or three days, Ram. Many people become friends after feeling sympathy for us. When this sympathy runs out, they return to their busy lives. Then, even if they see us somewhere, they act as if they haven't seen us. I'm used to it. No matter who comes or goes, we will always be here. This is our world. But you are special to me, you know? Not like the others. You took me to a shop and bought me a saree and all. Even the one I loved didn't take me anywhere. I will think of you every time I see this saree.'

Ram did feel that their friendship was born out of sympathy. *And*, he thought, *when sympathy runs out, this friendship might also fade away.*

They didn't speak again until the train reached Nungambakkam.

Before getting off the train, he gave her the box of strawberries and said goodbye. She stood at the door, her gaze fixed on him. Ram couldn't quite decipher the emotions in her eyes.

Reshma, clad in a raincoat, pulled up beside him on her scooter as he walked towards the college holding his umbrella.

'Hey, Ram! Hop on,' she called out.

'Ah, so you're not mad any more, huh?' Ram said with a smile.

'I only asked for the money my useless brother borrowed to recharge his phone. I never expected you'd be shooting with other girls,' she complained playfully.

'Ha ha ha, that's hilarious. The girl in Vetri's project isn't exactly angelic. She's more like a parasite. Chances are, she'll soon swoop in and drain him of all his money.'

'Well, he deserves it. Instead of paying me one hundred and ninety-nine rupees, he ends up broke and standing on the street in his briefs,' Reshma chuckled, imagining the scenario.

'What a pair you two make! Come on, let's go. It's raining,' Ram said, folding his umbrella and settling behind her on the scooter.

Manoeuvring through the rain, they arrived at the college. Anandhi directed them to the mini theatre hall downstairs.

'What's happening there?' Ram asked.

'Principal Srinivas wants to see all your projects on the big screen,' Anandhi explained.

'Oh no! If the principal sees my work, he might just kick me out,' Reshma exclaimed nervously.

Anandhi led them to the hall, where the rest of the class, including Mr Shiva, had already gathered. As the bell rang at 9.30 a.m., Anandhi joined them in the hall.

The principal had assigned her the duty of uploading photos from the screening on the college website.

Once Principal Srinivas arrived, the screenings began.

Fifteen two-minute films played consecutively on the screen.

Reshma and Ram's projects were shown at the end since they were the last to enter the hall. When Ram's film ended, the principal and everyone else gave him a standing ovation. Ram noticed that Anandhi was among them, clapping enthusiastically, a camera hanging around her neck. The applause in the hall was a significant acknowledgment for him. Before leaving, the principal gifted a Parker pen to each outstanding student.

After the screening, everyone returned to the classroom. During the lunch break, Vetri informed Reshma and Ram that he was going to have lunch with Chinkavi at the restaurant.

'Cool, go ahead,' Reshma said and left.

'Looks like she's laying the groundwork,' Ram commented to Reshma as they headed downstairs.

As they approached the alley in front of the college, Ram and Reshma saw Anandhi helping with Karthik's neck, twisting and adjusting it. Soon, his discomfort seemed to ease, and he gratefully shook her hand. With a relieved smile, he continued walking, intermittently twisting his neck to maintain its newfound comfort.

'Is she practising some form of acupuncture or something?' Reshma asked sceptically.

'It's a very long story, my dear friend. If you really want to know, try invoking her father's name.'

'Right. So Karthik got involved, too, huh? Why does she consider herself superior to others? Didn't you also get into trouble for the same reason?'

'Yeah. Is her father deceased, or perhaps unwell? Maybe she's trying to earn money for his treatment or something,' he said.

'No way, Ram. Her parents visit Paatti's house sometimes. I don't think they were ever sick or in need of money,' Reshma replied.

When Ram heard this, he assumed that Anandhi was probably just a secretive person.

Anandhi was standing in the line when they arrived at the unavagam. Though they looked at each other, neither bared any expression.

As usual, she had curd rice, while Ram and Reshma opted for sambar rice. As they left the Unavagam after their meal, Anandhi walked up to Reshma and Ram.

'Ram, your short movie was really good,' she remarked as they walked back to the college.

'Thanks,' Ram replied.

The look on Reshma's face clearly suggested that she wasn't pleased to see them conversing like regular people.

'Did you get that story from Kalidas?'

'Kalidas? Who's that?' Ram asked Anandhi.

'I don't know his real name. He was with you in T. Nagar yesterday. I saw you,' she explained.

Ram realized that Anandhi was referring to Malli. 'How do you know Malli?'

'He once came to the college seeking admission. His certificate had a man's photo and name, but he appeared female. Even though Principal Srinivas told him to leave, he insisted on studying classical dance. There are no seats for male students in our dance academy, regardless of how they identify, and none of his documents classified him as female. Since then, the name Kalidas has stuck in my mind. I was reminded of it when I saw him again with you.'

'Did that really happen to her? I only met Malli yesterday. I don't know much about her.'

In his mind, Ram recalled the day when Malli had followed him to the college gate.

'As a form of protest, because Principal Srinivas didn't grant him admission that day, Kalidas danced in front of Principal Srinivas's car when he was about to leave the college. Everyone gathered around. Even the principal was surprised; his movements were so skilled and graceful. But rules are rules. He wasn't admitted,' Anandhi explained.

As the trio walked on, they spotted Vetri on his bike with Chinkavi. She waved to Ram.

'They're made for each other,' Anandhi observed.

'Do you know her?' Reshma asked, breaking her silence.

'Hello! I'm not just the receptionist at this college. I also manage the office affairs,' Anandhi replied.

'Maybe you fired the office staff to double up and take their salaries, too,' Reshma retorted sarcastically.

Anandhi threw a sharp look at her. 'Reshma, what do you think? You and your brother got admission here through some politician's recommendation? In fact, because of that, Principal Srinivas said he wouldn't accept you two. I strongly advocated for both of you. Paatti knows all about it,' she revealed.

Reshma was taken aback.

'There's no way that happened. Uncle is a close ally of the ADMK party,' Reshma said defensively.

'If you want, you can ask Principal Srinivas in person. He's not the type to be swayed by political recommendations. When the admissions process was about to end, two students cancelled and chose other courses. Sir felt thirteen students were enough for the batch, but I managed to persuade him to make room for both of you.'

Ram gauged Reshma's face as Anandhi elaborated. For a moment, Reshma seemed unsure about whether to befriend Anandhi or keep her distance.

'Sorry,' Reshma said, looking down without meeting Anandhi's eyes.

Ram burst out laughing and Anandhi joined in, soon followed by Reshma.

'Now, tell me about that girl,' Reshma said, trying to suppress her laughter.

'Sure. She's Chinkavi Subramaniam. She looks innocent, but there was a newspaper article about her once. She was arrested for growing weed in the balcony of her rented house in Velachery. She has a partner, who she lives with, and together they're the main weed dealers. They target mentally vulnerable rich men. Some girls in the dance academy, including Soumya, are also getting weed from her, it seems. The dance teachers are exhausted because she never gets even the basic mudras right and often complains of leg pain. That's how we ended up gathering all this information about her. You can't expel someone from the college just because of their past, right? So Principal Srinivas is waiting for the right opportunity to dismiss her,' Anandhi explained.

Reshma and Ram exchanged bewildered looks.

'Then what about Vetri?' Reshma asked.

'He's doomed. Soon, he'll become a weed addict, too,' Anandhi replied.

Hearing that, Reshma stared ahead blankly, and started daydreaming. She imagined Vetri and Chinkavi cultivating weed together. Vetri was watering the plants while Chinkavi plucked the leaves.

'Reshma! Reshma!' Ram shook her, snapping her out of her daydream as she walked absentmindedly down the street.

'Oh my dear brother! I have to save him,' Reshma exclaimed.

'Don't worry. It's just their first date, right? We'll discuss things with him in detail this evening,' Ram reassured her. And then he added, 'Soumya, who was with Chinkavi, didn't say good things about her either.'

'Yes, she must be under the influence. I've heard that when they smoke, they start blaming each other,' Anandhi said.

By then, they had reached the college. Soumya was standing near the gate.

'Are you Sriram?' she asked, approaching them.

Ram was stunned. The girl he had spent so much time with the day before was now speaking to him as if he was a stranger.

'Yes, what happened?' he asked.

'I heard you took some video of me and showed it to everyone. They all told me it was really good. I have no idea what it is about. Can you show it to me, please?'

Anandhi and Reshma looked at Ram in shock. He stood there, mouth agape.

11

One

While Ram was showing Soumya the video on his mobile phone, Anandhi said 'goodbye' to Reshma and went inside the college. After watching the video, Soumya asked him to send it to her. Ram complied, after which she happily ran off towards the dance academy.

When Ram and Reshma entered the classroom, they saw Vetri texting on the phone. Reshma noticed that the number he was exchanging messages with was saved as 'Chinku Baby'.

'Hey Vetri, I have something serious to tell you,' Reshma said.

Just then, Mr Thayalan entered the class. The students stopped talking and took their seats. Even during the cinematography lesson, Reshma and Ram noticed Vetri texting Chinkavi, with his phone hidden between his books.

After classes ended at 3 p.m., Vetri quickly gathered his things to leave.

'Machaa, why the rush? Reshma and I need to talk to you. Let's chat and then we can all go,' Ram said, holding Vetri back.

'Machaa, Chinkavi invited me for coffee. Her classed ended half an hour ago. She is waiting downstairs. You take the train today. We'll catch up tomorrow. Bye.'

With his bag slung over one shoulder, Vetri hurried out of the classroom, ahead of everyone else. Reshma and Ram watched him rush down the stairs.

Later, when they came down, Anandhi gestured to Reshma, asking for an update. Reshma signalled to indicate that she hadn't had the chance to talk to Vetri yet.

Ram and Reshma parted ways, agreeing that they would catch Vetri tomorrow and discuss everything.

Two

As Ram walked towards Nungambakkam railway station, Anandhi pulled up beside him on her Luna.

'Where are you headed?' she asked.

'Me?' Ram responded, surprised.

'Yes.'

'To Guindy.'

'Okay, I'll give you a lift till Guindy. Hop on.'

Ram was taken aback. He had never imagined that Anandhi would offer him a lift.

'Am I going to ride with you sitting behind me?' Ram asked nervously.

'No, no. Just sit at the back,' she said, revving the accelerator.

Ram carefully sat on the back of the Luna, making sure not to touch her. He placed his bag between them. As soon as he settled, Anandhi sped through the busy streets of Nungambakkam, honking continuously.

Ram was riding on a Luna for the first time and couldn't help but notice how well Anandhi had maintained it despite its condition. There was always a flower garland hanging at the front.

'Don't you have any events today?' Ram asked during the ride.

'Of course, I do. There's a birthday function at Iyyappanthangal. I'm heading straight there.'

'Iyyappanthangal? I'm going there, too.'

'Is that where you live, Ram?'

'Yes.'

'Aha, so you can get dropped off near your home.'

Ram smiled. Anandhi noticed it in the mirror.

'You're a good liar, aren't you?' she asked.

'No, I don't lie. Why do you ask?'

'You have dimples.'

Ram laughed out loud. 'If you promise not to tell anyone, I'll let you in on a secret. It's not a dimple. It's a "hen-ple". When I was young, I tried to kiss a hen. It pecked me.'

'What?'

Anandhi brought the Luna to a sudden halt and turned around. Ram grinned, proudly displaying his 'hen-ple'.

Anandhi covered her mouth and laughed.

As they continued their ride, Anandhi kept sneaking looks at him in the mirror, stifling her laughter. Seeing her laugh, Ram couldn't help but smile back.

Just before reaching the Iyyappanthangal bus depot, Anandhi received a phone call. She pulled over to the side.

'Hello, John. Have you reached?'

She got off the Luna and stepped away a little. Ram sat on the Luna, listening. The conversation sounded serious and involved some shouting. When she hung up, she looked visibly tense and desperate and proceeded to make several calls.

'What happened?' Ram asked.

'I'm in trouble, Ram. I have five regular workers for the catering jobs I manage. They recently demanded an extra three hundred rupees each. Right now, I'm paying them five hundred rupees each for a two- or three-hour programme. I don't take on big jobs that can pay the higher rates they're asking for. I told them I can't afford it. Now, at the last minute, they've called to say they won't be coming to work today. They know I am desperate. At such short notice, it's impossible to find replacements. God, what am I going to do? The function starts in less than an hour. The decorators have set everything up and are waiting for me in the auditorium. The food has also arrived.' Anandhi's voice was tense.

'Hey, don't stress. Do the catering staff have uniforms?'

'Yes, but they are with them now. Why?'

'Is it a problem if we don't use uniforms?'

'No, it's not.'

'Great. Let me see if I can find two people.'

Ram quickly dialled Bineesh's number.

'Hello Bineesh Etta, are you free? Get ready immediately and bring Kiran, too. I'll send you the location. Reach there in forty-five minutes maximum. It's for a function. I'll WhatsApp the details. Please don't be late.'

Before Bineesh could respond, Ram hung up. Anandhi looked at him in surprise.

'There are three of us now, including me. You'll help serve, right?'

'Of course.'

'Then let's head to the venue. We can set things up by the time they arrive.'

Anandhi, visibly relieved, hopped back on to her Luna. As they passed Oil Mill Road, Ram pointed out his apartment. He saw Bineesh hurrying inside, grabbing a pair of jeans from the balcony. Ram quickly looked away to avoid being seen.

They reached the front of the auditorium where the function was taking place. The decorators and caterers were waiting for Anandhi. It was a small auditorium, perfect for events like birthdays. Guests had already begun to arrive.

Anandhi parked her Luna, paid the decorators and sent them off.

'Ram, can you start pouring the welcome drinks? The guests are here. I'll deal with the caterers and be back quickly.'

Ram nodded and went to the welcome drink table, lining up glasses and pouring iced mango juice.

'What is this? Will you serve when you feel like it? About ten people are already here. Quickly take the juice to those already seated,' an elderly man scolded Ram and walked away.

Ram hurriedly filled the glasses and served the guests. Anandhi joined him soon, a dupatta tied around her waist. Together, they filled another one hundred and forty glasses. They then moved to where the food was set up in the hall.

They transferred the biryani and its accompaniments into the copper serving bowls.

'It's good that it's a buffet. Otherwise, we would have had a tough time, serving everyone individually,' Ram remarked, making Anandhi laugh.

More guests filtered in and the celebration of the first birthday of the twin girls, Yavanika and Yashika, began. As the cake-cutting began on stage, Anandhi and Ram kept an eye on the hall entrance.

'They will come, won't they?' Anandhi's face, which had been calm until then, bore signs of tension again.

'I have sent them the location. When I last spoke to them, they said they were close. Now they're not picking up their phones.'

Ram felt the stress mounting on Anandhi's face, which made him nervous, too. As the guests started moving towards the food area after the cake was cut, both Ram and Anandhi's hearts raced with anxiety. Ram sensed that the situation was slipping out of their control.

Just then, Kiran and Bineesh entered the hall hesitantly, dressed formally with their shirts tucked in. Ram called out to them and waved excitedly. Anandhi took a deep breath, momentarily relieved.

Kiran and Bineesh approached cautiously. Ram quickly directed them towards the bowls of biryani placed at each table, handing them serving ladles.

'You can beat me up, or whatever you wish, when we get back to the apartment. For now, please help us serve the biryani,' Ram pleaded urgently.

Anandhi also looked at them beseechingly.

Bineesh and Kiran exchanged a look. Bineesh clenched his teeth and gave Ram a stern look before taking the ladle and heading towards a table with biryani.

Kiran looked at Ram, silently asking if he should also start serving. Ram nodded. With one hundred and fifty guests eagerly awaiting a meal, Bineesh, Kiran and Ram worked tirelessly, serving like machines. Anandhi kept replenishing the biryani as the serving containers emptied.

The elderly uncle from the family frequently found faults and loudly scolded Bineesh and Kiran in front of the guests. Every time they were scolded, Bineesh and Kiran glared at Ram and clenched their fists.

Finally, when the last guest had finished eating, the four of them collapsed on the floor of the hall, exhausted. The irritable elderly uncle handed an envelope to Anandhi. After opening it and counting the money inside, she gave one thousand rupees each to the three men.

'Hey, I am liking this job now,' Kiran exclaimed.

'You'll earn money like this when you work. Unlike those who live off their parents' money. Well, dear, I don't need your money. If I take it, it'll lessen the strength of the beating I plan to give someone later at home,' Bineesh said, pushing back the money Anandhi had offered.

Ram frowned.

'I'm really sorry, chetta. Ram helped me out because I was in a tough spot. Please take this money. Otherwise, I'll feel bad,' Anandhi insisted. Eventually, Bineesh reluctantly accepted it.

'When I first started working in Chennai, I used to do a lot of catering jobs. When I entered and saw you, I immediately understood that you were in trouble. Anyway, since you've come all the way here, why don't you visit our apartment before you leave? Ram often talks about you. We've been curious to meet you,' Bineesh suggested.

'Did Ram mention me to you? What did he say?' Anandhi was inquisitive.

'That you're a tigress,' Kiran blurted out.

Anandhi shot a look at Ram, who responded with his trademark 'hen-ple' smile.

12

One

As they unlocked the door to the apartment, and Anandhi stepped inside, Kiran let out a traditional ululation, as though welcoming her warmly.

Ram and Bineesh gave Kiran disapproving looks.

'I mean, as far as I know, this is the first time a girl has ever visited our apartment. It's a joyous occasion,' Kiran tried to justify.

Anandhi smiled widely. All four of them settled in the living room.

'So, where is your house, Anandhi?' Bineesh enquired.

'It's in Vaniyambadi, chetta.'

'I've heard of that place. Who all are there at home?'

'I live with my father, mother and younger brother.'

This was new information for Ram too.

'Ah, sounds like a happy family,' he said with a smile.

'Ha ha ha, yes,' Anandhi agreed.

'What does your father do?' Bineesh quickly followed up with another question.

'Why do you want to know all that, chetta? You're only connected to my life, not theirs, right? Why not just focus on knowing about me?' Anandhi's unexpected response left Bineesh, Ram and Kiran shocked.

'Sorry,' Bineesh apologized, visibly embarrassed. 'I heard from Ram that you seem to face a lot of challenges every day to make ends meet. I was just trying to understand if you have any difficulties.'

'My struggles are not related to the situation at my home, chetta. Doesn't everyone have their own little secrets in life? Just think of it as something like that,' Anandhi replied calmly. 'Well, I should get going now. I have some garlands to deliver, which I should pick up before the flower shop closes,' Anandhi said, standing up.

The three of them walked her downstairs.

'Sharing certain aspects of our lives with others doesn't always benefit us. Sometimes, it can lead to losses. It's better to keep such things to ourselves,' she remarked, looking at Bineesh before mounting her Luna.

'There's something smouldering deep within her. Soon, it will be set ablaze,' Bineesh commented once Anandhi was out of earshot.

Ram didn't fully grasp the meaning behind Anandhi's words or Bineesh's statement.

That night, as he lay down to sleep, Ram pondered over what Anandhi had said until he eventually drifted off.

Two

The rain continued to pour the next day, but it was slightly stronger now. Ram saw Malli sitting on the first bench as he came down the steps of the railway overpass. Upon seeing him, she stood up with a smile.

'Malli has been waiting for you for quite some time,' the old lady who sold samosas said as she passed by Ram.

'Hello, good morning,' Ram greeted with a smile.

'Good morning. You're late. The train has already departed,' Malli informed him.

'Oh, really?'

'It's okay. Let's sit down. There's another one in fifteen minutes,' Malli suggested, settling back on to the bench.

Ram joined her. Both of them watched the raindrops fall on the railway tracks and the edge of the platform.

After a moment of silence, Ram asked, 'Who is this Kalidas?'

'What's the point of asking when you already know who it is, Ram?'

'I want to know about Kalidas, the one who wanted to join the classical dance course at our institute,' Ram said, looking straight into Malli's eyes.

'Do you really want to spoil your mood this early by hearing about Kalidas's past?'

'Aren't our moods something we control ourselves?'

'Ha ha ha! Exactly. We decide how we want to feel. That's why you met Kalidas as Malli.'

'Tell me, Malli. If you have a certificate listing you as a male up to the twelfth grade, then you didn't grow up on the streets. What's your story? I want to know.'

Ram's gaze was steady. Realizing he wouldn't leave without hearing an explanation, Malli turned towards the tracks and began to speak.

'Kalidas's home is in Salem. He has an alcoholic father, a noble mother and an innocent brother. They are still living there. When Kalidas was five, his mother often sent him to the neighbour's house to fetch his father, who would get drunk and pass out there. At that age, he only knew that a mother's breast could produce milk for her child. Later, it was his father's friend who taught him that men, too, produced a milky fluid. His father's alcoholism increased with each passing day, and along with it, his friend got more and more chances to satisfy his lust on Kalidas. As time passed, other adult men took advantage of that five-year-old's innocence and made him believe that when they touched or caressed him, it was a sign to release their milky fluid. They brought him sweets to ensure he would accompany them without hesitation. He never made friends with other kids his age. Many men in the village used to take Kalidas with them to quench their lust. When they exploited him, they would call out the names of many beautiful women from the village. Those moments made him believe that he, too, was like those women. His gait and mannerisms took on a feminine quality. Mentally and physically, he underwent significant changes, lacking the natural development of other children. His association with these adults familiarized him with every deserted corner of the village, like the narrow spaces behind walls, field ridges and the bases of trees.

'As he began to realize the true nature of what was happening, he understood that his life was far removed from the usual experiences of children his age. With that realization, he put an end to the arrangements that only served to satisfy others. But what is imprinted on a child's mind does not change quickly. While his peers were noticing girls, he found himself unknowingly falling in love with boys. He often chuckled as he realized that what his peers secretly discussed about sex was known to him since a very young age. One night, when he was in the tenth grade, Kalidas's father brought home a friend who had lent him money to buy alcohol, under the guise that he would offer his wife as a reward for helping him get drunk. The wife worked tirelessly to support the family, taking on numerous physically taxing jobs in the village, including working in the paddy fields. She poured boiling water on the head of the man the father had brought home. That night, a tumultuous fight broke out in the house. While Kalidas's younger brother slept soundly, Kalidas witnessed everything. His father stripped his mother naked and physically abused her. His mother, bruised, left the house that night with Kalidas and his younger brother. Afterwards, Kalidas was determined to focus on studying and caring for his mother and younger brother. Recognizing that the family couldn't sustain itself on his mother's meagre earnings from working in the fields, he also sought employment to contribute to their livelihood.

'He faced limitations in finding work due to the ridicule and mockery aimed at his femininity. That's how he began dressing as a dancer girl for festivals and celebrations, where he met many others who faced similar challenges. His family's survival depended on the income he earned from this. Both his and the younger brother's studies progressed. Throughout his higher secondary years, sometimes even a day before exams, he would dress up and dance until dawn. His sole wish was to ensure that his mother and brother never starved, and that his brother didn't experience the lack of anything. He passed his higher secondary exams with ninety per cent marks. By then, his younger brother had reached high school. He felt ashamed of Kalidas's feminine demeanour and was often ridiculed by his friends.

'During this time, their father returned after years of absence, apologized and took the family back home. Kalidas had no desire to return to the village that had caused him so much pain. However, when his mother and brother expressed their interest in rejoining the father, he reluctantly went along. As his father quit drinking, the family's financial situation improved. Kalidas wanted to pursue higher education and enrolled in a degree course with his own earnings.

'Both his father and younger brother disapproved of his night-time outings as a dancing girl for local events, forcing him to stay home to avoid embarrassing them. Kalidas continued to study and perform, but his mother, who initially supported him, grew silent when his brother sided with their father and began taunting Kalidas. He felt profoundly lonely in that house.

'At this point, a handsome bearded man came to stay near Kalidas's house for a month, as part of his company's training. He listened to and seemed to understand Kalidas, providing much-needed support. A love relationship blossomed between them. He provided Kalidas shelter during uncomfortable times at home. Sometimes, Kalidas would cook his favourite dishes. Eventually, after his training, the man decided to move back to Chennai and invited Kalidas to join him. That invitation meant the world to Kalidas, who was weary of his life's struggles and was starved for love. He knew he couldn't let go of the love he had finally found. Trusting love, Kalidas left his home in Salem, without informing even his mother, and took a train to Chennai. Sadly, this man and his friends, whom Kalidas trusted with his life, exploited him as much as possible before abandoning him on the streets of aruvanis. However, with the assistance of the aruvanis, Kalidas was reborn as Malli. Now, Malli is sharing old stories with another bearded man on platform 2 of Guindy railway station,' Malli recounted with a smile. 'And the train is here,' she added, patting Ram on the shoulder as he listened intently.

'You don't have to come with me today, Malli. I can't bear to see people sneer at you, or you begging in front of them,' Ram said as the train slowed down on the platform.

Malli laughed and ruffled his hair. 'Okay, you go. I'll take the next train.'

Ram looked into her eyes again. There wasn't any trace of tears in them, but his own eyes were watery.

When the train stopped, he boarded and found an empty seat. A minute later, as the train began to move, he looked out of the window once more. Malli was nowhere in sight. The train gradually picked up speed and pulled out of the station.

It was 9.45 a.m. when Ram reached college that day.

When Anandhi spotted Ram, she asked, 'You're late, huh?'

'Was talking to Malli,' he replied in a monotone.

Anandhi gestured upstairs and said, 'Mr Shiva isn't here yet. Hurry up.'

Ram smiled at her and headed upstairs.

The classroom was buzzing with noise. Ram scanned the room and noticed Satish sitting on the seat adjacent to the one where he usually sat. Vetri was sitting on Satish's seat, lost in his phone. Reshma appeared visibly upset.

'What's going on? Why did he move there?' Ram asked as he approached the back of the class.

'We had a spat over that Chinkavi.'

'Didn't he believe it?'

'Not at all. Now he claims that Anandhi, who gave us this information, is the one who has smoked up. Let it be, Ram. Let him face his own problems.'

'You can't just leave it like that. Let me talk to him.'

With resolve, Ram walked to the front row and snatched Vetri's phone from his hand mid-text.

'What's this, machaa? Give me my phone back,' Vetri demanded.

'What Reshma said is true. If you doubt it, ask Anandhi.'

'Aha. So now you're all in cahoots, huh? Just leave,' Vetri snapped, reclaiming his phone just as Mr Shiva entered.

Ram returned to his seat. Reshma moved to sit beside him, vacating her seat for Satish. During the afternoon break, Vetri didn't join them at the Unavagam. Since it was still raining, Ram and Reshma walked together under an umbrella.

'I never expected him to be so henpecked,' Ram commented as they strolled.

'All he attracts are people with some kind of disorder. Before this, he had a girlfriend—during his engineering days—named Faroochi. He got to know her after offering her a lift on his bike. She was a bit crazy. She loved water so much that she would skip class every day to go swimming in all the pools and check dams around. One day, she went to Marina beach to swim and never came back. After that, Vetri grew his hair long and wandered around for a while, listening to that sad song from Suriya's Tamil movie, *Vaaranam Aayiram*. Eventually, he stopped when no one paid attention to him.'

'But what happened to the girl who went swimming in the sea?'

'Who knows? When I checked, there were no reports of an accident at sea during those days. But she wasn't the type to drown easily. My strong suspicion is that she was swallowed by a whale. Or we would have at least found her body, right?'

Ram stared at Reshma after hearing her casual reply.

When they reached the Unavagam, Anandhi, who had already arrived, was in front of them in the queue. Ram and Reshma bought curd rice and approached her to talk about Vetri.

'We'll find a way to sort it out soon,' Anandhi replied after listening to them.

Just then, the lady serving food started a noisy argument with a woman who had come to buy food.

'One day, I want to pour boiling sambar over her head,' Reshma said, glaring at the lady.

Ram and Anandhi exchanged amused looks, trying to suppress their laughter.

The rain had subsided by the time the three of them started walking down Nungambakkam Street after lunch.

'What's up with Kalidas, Ram?' Anandhi asked Ram.

'Kalidas is dead. Now it's Malli who is alive. Well, I didn't say this, she did.'

'Um ...'

'Anandhi, can't you help her get admission in the next batch at the dance academy?'

'I've been thinking about it, Ram. We should talk to Principal Srinivas and emphasize that admitting an aruvani student will enhance the college's goodwill and reputation.'

Ram was pleased to hear that.

'Tomorrow is Saturday, isn't it? Are you coming to Paatti's house, Ram?' Reshma asked.

'Yeah, yeah. I can't go a week without getting stung by a bee,' he joked.

'After showing a property to a party tomorrow morning, I will be free,' Anandhi said. By then, they had reached the college where a crowd of the dance academy students had gathered.

They were shocked to see some policewomen taking Chinkavi away, carrying ten large plastic bags of weed.

'You cheat! Fuck you!' Chinkavi yelled, looking at a corner.

They saw Vetri showing his middle finger to Chinkavi while talking to a police officer. Principal Srinivas, Mr Shiva and a few other teachers were standing nearby.

After Vetri finished speaking with the officer, Ram, Reshma and Anandhi made their way through the crowd towards him.

'What happened?' Ram asked.

'I've been waiting to trap her for two years, machaa. She walked right into it.'

'For heaven's sake, could you please explain what's going on here?' Reshma asked anxiously.

'Reshma, remember the girl who supposedly drowned in the sea? Faroochi! She and Chinkavi are part of the same gang. Yesterday, when I dropped Chinkavi at her apartment, she introduced me to Faroochi. Imagine! While I was mourning back then, thinking Faroochi was dead, it was Chinkavi who had consoled me and offered me weed to smoke and forget my sorrow. That was fine, but one day she told me, "Chetta, it's a loss to buy weed-stuffed cigars in small packets; it's more profitable to buy large party packs." She took seven thousand rupees from me that day, and then she disappeared. After that, I saw her in college. Since I've cut my hair and changed my looks, she didn't recognize me. But Faroochi? I thought she might remember me, but she didn't. She just asked if we had met before. I said "no". If they forgot me so quickly, how many people must they have dealt with in these two years? But I didn't forget. I've been watching Chinkavi for the past few days. Although she is enrolled here, she is actually selling weed disguised as a student. When she comes in the morning, there is weed in her bag. Her stash is hidden in the ceiling of the ladies' toilet in our college. If someone calls her, she heads to the toilet immediately. Yesterday, during the lunch break, she went to the toilet eight times. Each time she came out, different people came to meet her immediately after. When I asked, she said they were her cousins. Early this morning, I checked out the ladies' toilet and found weed packets of various quality. I reported this to Principal Srinivas. He said he would catch her red-handed with the weed during the lunch break. When the police came and checked, they found a couple of weed sticks in the toilet's waste bin. Doesn't that mean some girls in this college are smoking weed in there? Anyway, she was caught. Now, I want to see that mermaid, Faroochi,' Vetri explained.

After the police left, the students dispersed.

'Have you seen my partner, bros?' Hearing this, Ram turned around and saw Soumya, who looked evidently stoned.

Anandhi and Reshma looked at her, scrutinizingly.

'Aunties, have you seen my partner?'

'Hey! How dare you call me "aunty"?' Reshma snapped.

'Now we know where those weed sticks were coming from, right?' Ram said to Vetri.

Soumya continued to look at them expectantly.

'If you go straight from here, there's an Amma Unavagam. Ask the lady serving food there. She'll show you your partner,' Reshma said.

Anandhi, Ram and Vetri burst into laughter as they watched Soumya walk down the road.

'Either she finds her partner, or that lady does. A decision will be made today,' Reshma declared, crossing her arms and watching Soumya leave.

Just then, Vetri received a call from an unknown number.

13

One

The call lasted only a minute before it was abruptly cut. Vetri looked at Ram, Reshma and Anandhi nervously.

'It was the annan from the bakery. When he went home to buy sweets, he found Paatti unconscious in the front yard. She's been admitted to Sri Ramachandra Hospital in Porur.'

All three were shocked by the news.

'Vetri, head to the hospital right now. I'll inform Principal Srinivas and join you,' Anandhi said, quickly walking towards the office.

'Hey! Don't waste time. Get the bike quickly,' Reshma urged.

Vetri sprinted towards his parked bike.

'Ram, you tell Mr Shiva and then come to the hospital,' Reshma said, handing the Luna's key to him and jumping on to Vetri's bike. The two of them sped away.

After informing Mr Shiva, Ram returned to the parking lot and saw Anandhi starting her Luna. Not knowing where Sri Ramachandra Hospital was, he quickly approached her.

'Anandhi, can I come along, too?'

'Hurry up.'

Ram hopped on to the Luna and it zoomed out of the parking area and on to the road.

Nungambakkam Street was lightly crowded, but the main road was packed with vehicles. Anandhi expertly navigated the Luna through every small gap, while Ram, seated behind her, heard curses from the several people they passed. Each time Anandhi squeezed the Luna through tight spaces, Ram clung to the rear bar for support.

Due to the heavy traffic, Anandhi veered on to a side road she spotted on the left. She sped through alleyways, between houses and down narrow paths where people stopped to urinate. Ram marvelled at both Anandhi's knowledge of these shortcuts and the speed of the Luna scooter.

When they finally reached the parking at Sri Ramachandra Hospital, Ram's ears were slightly numb. In the observation ward, they found Paatti dozing on a bed, an IV drip attached to her left arm. A very short man, who seemed to be in his thirties, sat next to her.

'Balaji Annaa, what happened?' Anandhi asked as she approached the bed, evidently familiar with the man.

'Paappaa, when I got there, Paatti was lying unconscious in the yard. We brought her here immediately. The doctor said it was due to high blood pressure. Thankfully, she didn't hit her head when she fell. Her blood pressure was very high when she was admitted, but now it is normal. When she regained consciousness, she asked to call that boy who lives with you—Vetri. She even knew his number by heart. That's how I called him. I changed my old phone, so all the numbers were lost. Otherwise, I would have called you right away, Paappaa,' Balaji explained.

Anandhi approached Paatti and gently touched her forehead.

Reshma and Vetri arrived ten minutes later. They were delayed because their bike had run out of petrol. As soon as they reached, Balaji got a call from the shop and had to leave. Paatti was still asleep. Ram and Vetri met the doctor, after which they returned to the ward.

'What could have caused Paatti's blood pressure to spike so suddenly? She was all smiles and waved at me when I left this morning. The doctor said her BP was high enough to burst a blood vessel in her head. If that had happened, she could have died,' Vetri said, worried.

Anandhi looked at sleeping Paatti with concern.

'Vetri, I need to tell you something. You may eat the food Paatti makes, and she might wave goodbye to you, but have you ever sat with her to understand how she lives, or what thoughts she has every day? Have you ever hugged her with love or kissed her on the forehead? When you order clothes online, Paatti is the one who collects them for you. Have you ever bought her anything to wear for a celebration?' Anandhi's questions were heartfelt.

Seeing Vetri's silent, she continued.

'This isn't just about Vetri. It's for all of you. Paatti is completely alone in this city. Just because she's old doesn't mean her feelings and desires have vanished. Like us, she has many desires and emotions. If not, would she live alone at this age, in that house with the Padmini car, surrounded by memories of Thaathaa? I realized that she makes and sells all those sweets just to keep herself busy. It doesn't seem like she's doing it for the money. When Vetri and I entered Paatti's life, she felt like she had someone. Every meal she cooks for us every day is worth much more than the rent we pay her. If you think about it, you'll understand. It's about a woman who's been left alone in life without children or a husband, who cares for us like a mother, or even more, wishing her loved ones never left her. She desperately wants her loved ones to always be with her.

'I don't have much time to spend with Paatti, but whenever I can, I sit down and listen to her patiently. She always reminisces about how happy Thaathaa and she were back then. Paatti used to go out every day until Thaathaa passed away. She's a woman who loves to travel, but now she's alone at home all day. She wants someone to take her by the hand and share stories with her. Last Pongal season, I bought Paatti a saree for the first time. The poor lady hugged it and cried for a long time. That's when I realized how much pain she hides behind the happy front that she puts up in front of all of us.

'No matter how many times Vetri and I argue, I can never think of driving him away because I know Paatti likes him more than me. Whatever she cooks, she sets aside a portion for Vetri. She loves him like her own child. But I've never felt that even a fraction of that love has been returned by Vetri. You come home after eating from outside and don't even taste what Paatti has made for you. Vetri, you need to understand that what she makes for you is not just food. It's her care and love for you. Even though you don't touch the food, she continues to set it aside for you, hoping you'll appreciate it someday. Now, when she met with this accident today, her first thought was to call you, not me. If an elderly woman can remember someone's phone number without looking it up, imagine the love she has for you.'

Vetri's eyes welled up as Anandhi finished speaking.

'Anandhi, I don't know how to show love. Ever since I can remember, my parents have been fighting. Eventually, they both remarried and had other children. I've never felt such affection for anyone. I only saw Paatti as a landlord until now. But she's clearly much, much more than that. I promise, I will take care of her like my own mother from now on,' Vetri said, tears streaming down his face.

Seeing her brother cry, Reshma was also misty-eyed. She hugged Vetri tightly.

Just then, a drowsy Paatti opened her eyes and looked around. When she saw the four of them together, she smiled innocently. Vetri turned away to wipe his tears and then looked at Paatti with newfound love.

'Oye, little girl! Is there no place to sleep at home that she came to the hospital for a nap?' Vetri hugged Paatti lovingly and kissed her forehead.

Anandhi smiled, happy at the sight. Anandhi, Reshma and Ram joined Vetri by Paatti's bedside, surrounding her with warmth.

'When you have four children with you, what can this sweet granny be tense about?' Anandhi said.

Paatti's eyes were brimming with love for all four of them.

'What's going on here? Are you all trying to smother the patient with affection? I've been listening to all this drama for a while now,' the duty nurse shouted.

Reshma glared at her for intruding into their moment.

'What are you staring at, girl?' the nurse asked Reshma.

'You nosy lady! You ...' Reshma was about to utter a profanity when Anandhi swiftly covered her mouth to silence her. Vetri, Ram and Paatti burst into laughter.

Paatti was discharged at 6 p.m. and taken home in a taxi, accompanied by Anandhi and Reshma.

'Take care of my Luna, okay? It's the first time I'm giving it to someone,' Anandhi said, handing the key to Ram as she got into the taxi.

'You speak as if this is a brand-new vehicle, straight out of the showroom. This thing looks older than Paatti,' Vetri mocked.

Anandhi winked mischievously at him.

Ram grinned.

While riding Anandhi's Luna to Guindy, Ram felt a special fondness for it, one that he hadn't felt for any other vehicle. He tapped one of its metres, smiling to himself. He plucked petals from the garland hanging in front of the Luna and tossed them into the air.

Vetri, who was riding his bike beside Ram, noticed this and looked at him in surprise.

After giving Paatti food and medicine, and ensuring that she fell asleep, Ram and Reshma headed home. While on the bus to Iyyappanthangal, Ram called his mother and shared every detail. By now, his mother knew all the new people in his life, even though she'd never met them.

After the call, Ram reflected on the recent additions to his life. Except for Bineesh, everyone had come into his life unexpectedly. He realized how fond he had grown of his life in Chennai, the city full of surprises. He was also glad to have so many interesting characters as inspiration for the story he had begun writing.

14

One

Four months went by. During this time, not much changed in their lives, except Ram, Anandhi, Vetri, Reshma and Paatti had grown closer. Most evenings, they hung out with Paatti at Besant Nagar beach, Marina beach or Semmozhi Poonga, a botanical garden.

Whenever they visited Besant Nagar beach or Marina beach, everyone except Anandhi joined in to play a game introduced by Ram.

Ram, who grew up in the coastal area of Kerala's Alappuzha district, used to play this game with his friends. They would stand apart on the beach and write 'kadalamma kalli' in the sand, which meant 'the sea goddess is a fraud.' They would then watch to see whose words were erased by the waves last. The person whose writing lasted the longest was the winner.

When Ram told them about this childhood game, Paatti and the others were eager to try it. When they asked Anandhi to join, she pointed to the fishing boats in the distance and said, 'You write like this and mock the one thing that many people believe in the most in life.'

In response, the four of them jokingly bowed to her with folded hands and then started the game, writing 'kadalamma kalli' in the sand.

It was during one of these playful evenings at Besant Nagar beach that Paatti mentioned the temple festival celebrated in her hometown—Alligramam in Thanjavur district. Every year, she returned to her hometown for this special event. Most members of her family, too, travelled from all over to gather at their ancestral home and participate in the festivities. Last year, Paatti had taken Anandhi to Thanjavur. Anandhi was thrilled when she heard the festival was approaching again. Despite having visited Paatti's native place only once, those days held a special place in her heart.

Hearing Paatti's stories, Reshma, Vetri and Ram were also eager to visit Alligramam and see the festival at Kaliyamman Temple. Since the festival was on the following Saturday, they decided to head to Paatti's hometown on Friday. Their plan was to take the Tiruchendur Express from Chennai Egmore station at 4 p.m. on Friday and return by Sunday night, ensuring they didn't miss any classes. Paatti was overjoyed.

That same day, Ram informed Bineesh and Kiran about the trip. He was worried Bineesh might object, but since Ram had been transparent about his daily activities, there were no issues.

The days passed one by one. Anandhi continued juggling her jobs as a real estate and rental broker, the owner of an event company organizing small ceremonies and a garland supplier.

Vetri and Reshma collaborated to create short music videos, resembling those of young couples, which they shared on Facebook and Instagram to gather likes.

Meanwhile, Paatti was busy making extra sweets and packing them in boxes to ensure the local bakeries wouldn't run short during her absence. She also intended to carry some to her hometown.

Ram's thoughts were also focused on the upcoming weekend. Every morning on his way to college, he would meet Malli who had introduced him to all her friends. One day, Malli mentioned that she planned to buy a bike for her younger brother with the money she had been saving. After speaking to her mother on the phone many times, she had realized that her brother had been persistently asking for a bike. Ram understood that this was another reason for Malli to visit home.

All five of them eagerly awaited Friday.

Two

On Friday, Ram packed his travel bag and took it to college. In the afternoon, the four friends went to Amma Unavagam for lunch.

While they were eating, Anandhi received a phone call that slightly altered their plans. Originally, they had planned to leave the college at 3 p.m., take a taxi to pick up Paatti and head to Egmore station together. However, Anandhi had to meet a client who had seen a property the day before. She informed the group that she would join them at the railway station after the meeting. Anandhi asked them to take her bag, too, which she had packed and kept ready at home.

Finally, at 3 p.m., Ram, Vetri and Reshma left the college and headed to Paatti's place.

'Where is she?' Paatti asked, standing in front of the gate with Murukan Annan's taxi, an acquaintance from the next street, ready to go.

'She'll come straight to the railway station, Paatti,' Reshma replied.

'Shall we go? It's half past three. We'll be there just in time if we leave now,' Murukan Annan said, glancing at his watch.

After locking the scooter and securing it, Reshma ran inside and brought Anandhi's bag. On the way to the station, Ram called Anandhi. She said she was already near the station and expected to arrive at the same time as they would.

Murukan Annan got them to the station with five minutes to spare before the train's arrival.

'Anandhi, we are here. The train is about to come. Where are you?' Ram called her again.

'I'm here, Ram, parking my scooter. Aren't our tickets for the S-1 compartment? Go ahead, I'll be there soon,' Anandhi replied.

Ram was speaking to her while walking towards the S-1 compartment with a bag hanging from his shoulder. Paatti, Reshma and Vetri reached the door after placing their bags on the seats. Vetri got down on the platform with Ram.

'Why did she have to do this now? She'll never change her ways, always greedy for money. Why else would she change the plan we all made and go to show someone some property? Reshma and I had a thousand things to do too. We left all those, didn't we? I even had to beg Reshma's mother, whom I despise, to let her go so far away. All for the sake of being together. But then one of us has to go to trade a property at the most crucial minute,' Vetri said angrily, glaring at Paatti.

Paatti didn't reply. She was peering at the far end of the platform. The train was about to leave. Reshma was also visibly tense. Ram called Anandhi again.

'Anandhi, where the hell are you?' he demanded.

'I'm here, Ram,' she replied just as the train honked loudly.

'Stop this nonsense! I called you when we left the house and before we got here. You said the same thing both times. If money is more important to you than us, just say it. We won't bother you any further,' Ram said angrily and hung up.

Vetri and Ram were fuming, but their eyes stayed fixed on the far end of the platform.

'The train is about to leave. Should we get off?' Paatti asked Vetri and Ram, standing at the door. Reshma stood beside Paatti, unable to decide.

'If she doesn't come, let's forget her. Come on, Vetri, let's go ahead' Ram said, patting Vetri on the shoulder.

After one last look down the platform, Vetri jumped on to the moving train. Ram followed him inside.

'Reshma, take Paatti and go to the seat,' Ram said harshly.

Paatti's face showed the distress caused because of starting this journey in such an inauspicious manner. She walked to her seat with Reshma, looking at Ram and Vetri in despair.

'Machaa, I'll just go to the loo and be back. You settle into your seat,' Vetri said to Ram.

Vetri entered the toilet and shut the door behind him. Ram turned in the direction Paatti and Reshma had gone. The train had started to pick up speed, its carriages gliding past the passengers on the platform. As Ram walked to his seat, his phone rang. It was Anandhi.

'Ram, the train has left,' she said, panting.

Ram hurried back to the door. By then, the train was halfway down the platform. He saw Anandhi standing at the far end, one hand supporting her back and panting.

'Ram, can you hear me?'

'Yes, tell me,' he replied, watching her from the door.

'I can see you. I also want to come to Thanjavur.'

'What can I do? Indian Railways isn't your father's property. Why will it wait for you!' Ram retorted.

Anandhi fell silent. Neither spoke for several seconds.

'Anandhi, if I jump off here, will you cover my travel expenses to Thanjavur?' he asked.

'Of course, yes! Jump, Ram, jump!' she exclaimed excitedly.

The S-1 carriage was nearing the end of the platform. Ram hesitated briefly, realizing he would have barely any space to land after jumping off at that speed. However, summoning all his courage and praying to every god, Ram extended his left leg towards the platform and jumped from the train. He landed awkwardly and scrambled to grip a railway post, breathing heavily. Had the railway police seen it, they would definitely have registered a case against him.

It took almost a minute for Ram's leg cramps to subside and the tightness in his chest to ease. He took out his phone and dialled Vetri's number.

'Hey, why are you calling me on the phone?' Vetri asked suspiciously.

'Vetri, have you come out of the toilet?' Ram's voice was urgent.

'Yeah, just coming out now. Let me come to you.'

'Okay, then pass the phone to Paatti.'

'What? Pass the phone to Paatti? Where are you?'

'Just do it. Pass it to Paatti.'

Vetri handed the phone to Paatti quickly.

'Hello?' Paatti's voice came over the line.

'Paatti, I got off the train. Anandhi is with me. We'll be there soon. Don't worry, Paatti. You're going home after a year. I'll bring your beloved daughter safely,' Ram reassured her.

Paatti burst into a happy laugh upon hearing Ram's words.

'Both of you travel safely, okay?' Paatti said warmly before Vetri snatched the phone from her.

'Oh, you cheat! You left us for her, huh? You wicked fellow! Give her two whacks on my behalf,' Vetri said.

'You want me to get stabbed, huh?' Ram replied with a smile.

'Anyway, just come. I'm already wondering how I'll put up with this monster for another six and a half hours,' Vetri joked, looking at Reshma.

Ram chuckled and hung up, hearing Reshma's voice and then Paatti scolding both her and Vetri.

Anandhi stood by the side of the track with a small smile, her side bag dangling from her finger. Ram solemnly walked towards her, stroking his moustache and puffing out his chest. Anandhi followed him, puzzled by his behaviour.

They walked across the platform to the ticket counter, where they inquired about the next train to Thanjavur. The person at the counter informed them that the Kollam Express, heading to Kerala in less than an hour, would stop at Trichy, which was roughly fifty kilometres before Thanjavur. From there, they could take a bus to Thanjavur.

'Let's take a bus straight from here. That way, we'll get there when they arrive,' Ram suggested, turning to Anandhi.

'Oh, I can't handle a long bus ride. I'll get sick,' Anandhi said, making a vomiting gesture.

Ram then bought two tickets to Tiruchchirappalli, popularly called Trichy, and approached Anandhi, who was looking around as if she couldn't see him.

'Don't look around. Two hundred and forty rupees. Pay up,' he said, holding out his hand.

She opened her bag, counted out exactly two hundred and forty rupees and placed it on his palm.

'Ha ha ha, I'm going to have a blast today,' he said, laughing as if he had achieved something great.

At 4.45 p.m., they heard an announcement that the Kollam Express was now at platform 2. Ram walked towards it, with Anandhi following closely behind. He looked back occasionally, stroking his moustache every time.

Puzzled, she wondered what he was up to.

Finally, they managed to get into the crowded unreserved compartment. As it was almost 5 p.m., the train was packed with commuters returning from schools, colleges and offices, all scrambling for seats. Anandhi argued with a north Indian guy, who was napping on an upper berth, and eventually got him to move.

'Hey, climb up!' she shouted to Ram, who was navigating through the crowded aisle below.

'Up?'

'No, down,' she teased. 'If you want to sit, come up.'

Ram quickly removed his shoes and stowed them under the seat before climbing up to join Anandhi. The north Indian guy glared resentfully at her for inviting Ram, too.

'What are you staring at? If you stroke your moustache one more time just because we're travelling together, I'll knock your teeth out. Got it?' she warned Ram in Tamil.

The north Indian guy stared back, clearly not understanding her words. Ram looked around innocently, whistling as if he hadn't heard her, and adjusted his moustache downwards.

With a blaring whistle, the Kollam Express began its journey from Egmore station.

15

One

When the Kollam Express arrived at the Trichy railway station, it was past 10.30 p.m.

In the meantime, Paatti had called Anandhi and Ram many times. She was relieved to know that Anandhi remembered the way to Alligramam.

Paatti's village was two hours by bus from the Thanjavur railway station. Since the train was on time, Paatti and her group had managed to catch the last bus to Alligramam at 11 p.m. Paatti had offered to wait at the Thanjavur station for Anandhi and Ram, but considering her health, Ram and Anandhi had insisted that she go home and rest.

Vetri had found out at the station that the Antyodaya Express left Trichy at 10.50 p.m., but it reached Thanjavur only by midnight. If Ram and Anandhi missed that train, the only option left would be to catch the first bus at 7 a.m.

After assuring Paatti that he would safely bring Anandhi to Alligramam, Ram ended the call. Then, he and Anandhi went to a shop in front of the railway station to have dinner.

Anandhi ate a single dosa, while Ram had four parottas, two fried chicken legs and a double omelette. After washing his hands and wiping his lips, he grinned widely at Anandhi, displaying all thirty-two teeth. Anandhi looked at him sternly and paid the bill.

Two

The Antyodaya Express arrived at 10.50 p.m. Most of the passengers inside the compartments were asleep. The vacant seats were mostly occupied by elderly women, and weak or tired people, all of whom were sound asleep. Ram was worried that Anandhi might wake someone up in a quarrel. However, after taking a look inside, she stopped at the door. As the train left the station, she sat on the steps, holding on to the handrails on the sides of the door. There was room for him to sit beside her, but he remained standing, watching her.

Her hair fluttered in the wind. She caught it every now and then, laughing as the breeze blew against her face.

The train passed through a village. The wind was very cold. Ram rolled down the sleeves of his denim shirt and buttoned them. Anandhi continued sitting at the door, playing with the wind.

'If it were daytime, we could have enjoyed the beautiful scenery, right?' Ram asked, moving a little closer to the door.

'Um,' Anandhi looked up.

'Are you mad at me?' he asked.

'Why would I be?'

'Because I ate so much food on your dime.'

'Not at all.'

'Then why are you so quiet?'

'Come, sit here,' Anandhi said, moving aside to create more space.

Ram sat down immediately, as if he had been waiting for an invitation.

'How were the fried chicken legs?' she asked as soon as he settled beside her.

'They were great.'

'Then why didn't you consider sharing with me?'

'Well, they weren't that great to share,' Ram said with a chuckle.

'Ha ha ha! I thought you would eat up the entire food stall out of spite,' Anandhi laughed.

'I have no grudge against you,' he said, looking straight into her eyes.

'Well then, fine,' she replied, turning her head to look out again.

'Anyway, I dodged a bullet today,' Ram said after a minute's pause.

'A bullet? From whom?'

'Actually, I managed to invoke someone's father in the middle of it all.'

'Ha! I remember you saying that to me on the phone, right? I just stayed quiet, waiting for an opportunity when no one else would be around.'

'Oh no. Well then, okay, bye,' Ram said, starting to get up.

'Hey, sit down. I was just kidding.' Anandhi grabbed his jeans and pulled him back down. As he had forgotten to put on his belt, his pants slipped, revealing his Playboy underwear.

'Oh, sorry, sorry,' Anandhi said, covering her eyes with one hand.

Ram sat down, embarrassed, and pulled up his pants. They avoided looking at each other for a while, but Anandhi couldn't help covering her mouth and laughing.

Ram noticed her quiet laughter and gazed at her.

'You pulled my pants down and embarrassed me, and now you're laughing?'

'No, no. I was laughing thinking about the Playboy's face,' Anandhi replied with a mischievous smile.

Ram blushed and turned his face away.

Antyodaya Express arrived at Thanjavur station around 1 a.m. The cold wind hinted at imminent rain. Ram disembarked and dialled Vetri's number, but before he could do so, he received a call from a local landline.

'Hello machaa, it's Vetri. We've reached. It's a small village. Only BSNL phone numbers have network here. This is the landline number. Where are you guys?'

'We just reached Thanjavur,' Ram replied.

'Ah, good. What's the plan since there are no buses now?'

'What plan, machaa? We can't stay on the platform all night. We'll find a lodge and get some rest. Very tired,' Ram replied.

Anandhi, who was listening, frowned. 'No way we're staying in a lodge. Let's take a taxi.'

Ram paused to look at Anandhi and then resumed his conversation on the phone.

'It seems we are yet to reach a consensus on this. You go rest. I'll call you back on this number if needed. Inform Paatti and Reshma that we are here. Goodnight,' he said, ending the call and putting the phone in his pocket.

'From here, I'm only going to Paatti's house. Go find out how much a taxi will cost to get there,' Anandhi passed instructions before Ram could say anything.

He gave her a stern look and walked towards the front of the railway station. About ten autorickshaws were lined up in a row. On the right side, a tea shop was open; a cluster of people had gathered about to drink tea and chat.

He scanned the area for a taxi, but found none. He approached the first autorickshaw. Inside sat a short, stout man in his forties, engrossed in a movie on his phone, earphones plugged into his ears. Noticing Ram, he removed the earphones.

'Annaa, how much to Alligramam?' Ram enquired.

The man eyed him suspiciously for a moment.

'Is this your first time here?'

'Yes.'

'Alligramam is a remote village at the far end of Thanjavur district. Most rickshaws won't go there, especially at this hour. The roads through the paddy fields are rough. People usually take the government bus, which will leave at 7 a.m. tomorrow. It's better you take that.'

'Okay, annaa, thank you.'

Ram returned to the platform where Anandhi stood, observing people sleeping under blankets.

'No taxis or rickshaws go there at this time. It's safer to wait for the morning bus,' he informed her.

'Why is that?' she asked.

'You have been here before, right? No one wants to go to such remote villages.'

'So, what do we do now?'

'What else? Let's get a room at a lodge and rest.'

'Ugh! I'm not going to any lodge,' Anandhi retorted, moving to a steel chair on the platform and sitting down.

Nearby, a man surfaced from under a blanket upon hearing their conversation. Peering at them, he asked, 'Who's luring girls to lodges at this hour?'

Ram glanced at the man and then at Anandhi, surprised by this intervention.

'Are you coming or not? If not, we'll meet at the bus stand tomorrow morning,' Ram said, ignoring the man and addressing Anandhi.

'You useless fool! It's night-time and creeps like you invite girls to lodges and bus stands.' He paused and then continued looking at Anandhi, 'Don't give in to temptation, and don't worry. You have me to look out for you, dear,' the man declared, tightening his dhoti as he stood up.

Anandhi felt queasy because of the smell of alcohol emanating from him.

Despite everything, Anandhi remained seated, prompting Ram to storm out of the station. He approached the autorickshaw driver he had spoken to earlier, interrupting his movie.

'Annaa, where can we find low-budget lodges around here?'

'What's your budget?'

'Five or six hundred at most.'

'Just for one person, right?'

'No, for two,' Anandhi's voice echoed from behind.

The autorickshaw driver looked suspiciously at Anandhi before turning his attention to Ram, who seemed oblivious to her.

'Finding a room at this hour for couples is really tough, especially with the rain coming. Let's give it a try. Get in,' he said.

Anandhi hopped into the autorickshaw first. Giving her a sceptical look, Ram followed suit.

'Don't go with that creep, my dear,' the drunk man called out.

Ram turned towards the station's entrance and saw the drunk man gazing forlornly at the departing autorickshaw. When he turned to Anandhi, she flashed him a toothy grin.

The autorickshaw travelled down a road leading towards the Thanjavur bus stand.

After covering a short distance, it halted in front of an average-looking lodge. The driver honked twice at the locked grill door. A man wrapped in blankets, sitting at a long table, glanced up.

'The rooms are all occupied, Satya Annaa,' he mumbled before covering himself up again.

'It's tough to find rooms in Thanjavur on Fridays, Saturdays and Sundays. Tourists flock to see the city and the temple on weekends. Let's try somewhere else,' the driver said.

He restarted the autorickshaw. Anandhi looked at Ram and then at the road ahead.

Four more lodges later, they had not found a vacant room. Eventually, they decided to return to the railway station.

On another road leading back to the station, the auto driver halted upon seeing a lodge adorned with numerous string lights.

'Do you mind if the lodge is a bit below average?' he asked.

Anandhi and Ram exchanged a glance.

'What do you mean by "below average"?' Anandhi asked suspiciously.

He gestured across the road towards the faintly lit building.

'It's an old lodge.'

Anandhi instinctively pushed Ram back and peered across the road at the sign that read 'Dhanashree Lodge', adorned with colourful string lights. She estimated the two-storeyed building to be at least fifty years old.

'Annaa, are you sure there will be rooms available?' Ram asked cautiously.

'They might have rooms. But the issue is that many people book rooms here to end their lives. Most of the rooms have witnessed suicides. We don't usually recommend this place to guests. I mentioned it only because there are no rooms anywhere else. The decision is yours,' the driver explained.

Anandhi glanced at the lodge once more. In that moment, Dhanashree Lodge seemed eerily reminiscent of a haunted mansion.

'No, Ram. Let's just go back to the station,' she suggested.

'Why? Are you scared?'

'Not scared, just have a bad feeling about it.'

'Annaa, are the rooms secure?' Ram redirected the question to the driver.

'Yes, they are.'

'Then we'll get off here,' Ram decided. He stepped out of the autorickshaw.

Anandhi remained seated in the autorickshaw for a moment, contemplating her decision. Eventually, she took out money from her bag, as if agreeing with Ram, but by then he had already paid the fare.

'Alright then, take care,' Ram said to the driver.

'Okay, see you,' the driver said as Anandhi and Ram headed towards the lodge on the other side of the road.

Occasional lightning accompanied by strong winds greeted them as they ascended the long, cracked red oxide-coated steps to the lodge. Anandhi turned to Ram once more, a hint of uncertainty flashing in her eyes. He gave her a reassuring look and moved ahead.

At the end of the stairs, Ram saw an elderly man with a beard and long hair at the reception. His skin bore patches of white, and he was clad in a black shirt and black dhoti, reminiscent of those undertaking penance for the Sabarimala Temple pilgrimage.

Seeing Anandhi and Ram, he picked up a blue Cello gripper pen from a steel glass on the counter and uncapped it. Without waiting for them to inquire about room availability, he opened a closed register and turned it towards them.

'Write your name, address and phone number,' he instructed briskly.

'Wait, what about the rate?' Ram asked.

'Three hundred and ten rupees. Ten rupees for water. Check out by 10 a.m. Take the key for room number one hundred and eleven,' he replied, pointing to a row of keys hanging on the wall to their left, each labelled with a number.

While Ram jotted down the address, Anandhi reached for the key marked '111'.

'You should also provide the number of someone you know,' the old man added once Ram finished writing.

'Why is that necessary?' Ram asked.

'It's our policy,' came the curt response.

After observing the old man briefly, Ram found Vetri's number on his phone and wrote it down in the register. He then took out three hundred and ten rupees from his wallet and handed it over. The old man accepted the money and placed it in the drawer close to him. He then gestured towards the stairs on the right.

Ram looked at the old man once more before leading Anandhi upstairs, turning right towards room 106. Room 111 was situated at the far end of the corridor.

Opening the door, Ram entered first and switched on the light. The bed was neatly made with a fresh white and green checked bedsheet. A wooden table, accompanied by an old-fashioned iron folding chair, stood next to it. Across the room hung a large wood-framed mirror on the wall.

Anandhi stepped in and inspected the attached bathroom. It featured an Indian-style toilet and a bucket for bathing, both appearing clean and well-maintained. Ram opened the water bottle kept on the table and took a sip.

'Despite its dull exterior, it's cool, serene and very homely,' he remarked.

Anandhi walked over to the window beside the mirror and pushed it open. Peering through the window, she took in the view. The street was illuminated by a halogen lamp that cast light on a road flanked by numerous mayflower trees. Crimson flowers adorned the road and its sides, creating a picturesque scene, akin to a red carpet amidst the tree-lined path. The flowers danced in the wind, continuously swirling around.

'Ram, I want to take a stroll along that road,' she said.

Hearing that, he joined her at the window and looked outside. With no crossbars, they had an uninterrupted sight of the road adorned with red flowers.

'Shall we go in the morning?' Ram asked wearily.

'If we wait until the morning, all the traffic will choke the road and these flowers will be trampled. Such views should be enjoyed in the moment, before they fade away forever. Please, Ram, let's go for a night walk,' Anandhi pleaded.

Ram considered her request for a moment, looking at her standing there expectantly.

'Okay. Let's go,' he agreed finally.

16

One

Ram and Anandhi locked their room and headed down to the reception. The elderly man was eating from a steel container.

'Uncle, we're going for a walk along the road behind this building,' Anandhi explained.

Hearing this, the old man cast a look at the round clock on the wall. It was 1.45 a.m.

'We'll be back soon.'

As they turned to leave, the old man called them back, pointing them towards another route down the road, advising them not to stray too far.

Anandhi and Ram strolled along the road lined with the mayflower trees.

'Isn't this amazing?' Anandhi asked Ram, her voice joyful.

'We have plenty of these trees back at our place. So, this isn't particularly new to me,' Ram replied casually.

'But for me, all of this is new!' Anandhi exclaimed, scooping up a handful of fallen flowers and playfully tossing them at him.

He caught one flower that landed inside his shirt and examined it cursorily.

'You're so boring!' Anandhi remarked with a hint of disappointment.

'Why do you say that?'

'I mean, usually in such situations, a guy would try to throw flowers back at the girl. But here I am throwing flowers at you, and you seem least bothered.'

'Ugh, such a cliché! Besides, we're not exactly lovers to be doing cheap romantic stuff like that.'

'Oh my goodness! Please forgive me,' she said, pretending to apologize with folded hands.

He chuckled. 'Well, I have a question for you, if you don't mind. I've been noticing this since yesterday. Do you have any issues with your parents?'

'Why do you ask?'

'I mean, usually if a girl is away from home, either her mother or father would call. But for you, all I have heard are calls from customers and Paatti.'

'Shall we sit here for a while?' she suggested, pointing to an iron bench in front of a closed workshop.

Although he didn't get a direct answer to his question, Ram joined her as they walked towards the bench. There were several red flowers on it, which they brushed aside to make space.

'I do call them sometimes. But lately, they haven't been calling me that often,' Anandhi replied after a moment's thought.

'Why is that?'

'I'll share that some other day. So, who all live in your house?'

Ram sensed that she didn't want to dwell on the topic and decided not to press further. Instead, he took out his phone and showed her his wallpaper.

It was a family photo of Ram, his younger sister and their parents.

'You have a nice family. What does your sister do?'

'She's in higher secondary.'

'And her name?'

'Padma.'

'She looks just like you.'

Ram didn't respond immediately. Suddenly, he grabbed a handful of flowers from the bench and tossed them at Anandhi. She laughed and threw some back at him. When he repeated the gesture, she sprang up with a laugh, scooped flowers up from the ground and tossed them at him. Unfortunately, there was soil mixed in, which hit his mouth, shirt and face. He spat out the dirt. Anandhi, realizing he was about to retaliate, bolted, laughing loudly.

'I'll get you for that!' Ram shouted.

He grabbed another handful of soil-laden flowers and chased after her.

Anandhi ran back up the road and entered the lodge, dashing to the reception where the old man was seated. She hid under his table, signalling for him to keep quiet.

The old man looked at her in surprise. When Ram burst in, soil still streaking his face, he figured out what might have happened.

'Uncle, has the girl who came with me gone upstairs?'

The old man subtly gestured towards the table. Ram mouthed a 'thank you' and moved to the other side.

'Oh no! I'm going to be killed!' Anandhi cried from under the table.

Ram reached down with his strong hands, pulled Anandhi out from her hiding spot, dragged her outside and dumped the soil-laden flowers over her head. They both re-entered the lodge, panting, and collapsed into steel chairs.

The old man's grave expression softened into a smile. Anandhi and Ram smiled back. He went to a nearby cupboard, fetched two freshly washed white towels and handed them over.

'You're both covered in dust. Go have a bath.'

'Thanks,' they said in unison.

Anandhi noticed the key stand just then and realized that all the keys were there except for room 111.

'Uncle, are we the only ones staying in this lodge?' she asked.

He shrugged, indicating a yes.

'I heard that this lodge is where people come to end their lives.'

Ram, wanting her to be respectful, gave her a quick nudge without the old man noticing.

'Only one person has committed suicide here, and that was my son,' he said without any emotion. Anandhi and Ram were shocked.

'People say all sorts of things, don't they? When I bought this building, there wasn't a single lodge around. Now there are many. Autorickshaw and taxi drivers bring guests only to those lodges where they get a commission. When other hotels are full, they bring some guests here and spread such stories so that people don't come back. I'm not going to scold anyone or fight for the truth. By God's grace, I've managed to get by and will continue to do so. Otherwise, why would you be here today?' he said confidently.

'Why did he commit suicide?' Anandhi asked.

'He had brain cancer. We found out too late. The doctor said there was a fifty per cent chance of survival. But he, like his mother, preferred shortcuts. He knew I would sell everything I owned to get him treated. Maybe he thought about what would happen if I sold this lodge, our last asset, and things didn't improve. So, he went into a room upstairs and ended his life.'

As she listened, Anandhi casually glanced upstairs.

'Don't worry. I don't rent out that room. During the day, when my wife is here, I go to that room and take a nap,' he said with a smile.

'Do you have any other kids, Appa?'

Ram appreciated Anandhi calling him 'Appa' instead of 'Uncle'.

'No, he was my only child.' He fell silent.

'Why are you wearing this black outfit, Appa?' she asked.

'I had promised to go to the Sabarimala temple if his health improved. It was during that time he committed suicide. After that, I didn't feel like changing out of this outfit. I'll change when I go to Sabarimala, after my heart has healed.'

Hearing this, Anandhi got up, went to him and gently touched his cheek.

'We'll come back here again. Next time, you'll be here with a healed heart and wearing stylish clothes,' she said with a smile.

Seeing his eyes fill with tears, she turned to Ram.

'Shall we go?'

'Yeah, let's go.'

Ram got up from his seat. They both wished him good night and went upstairs. The old man opened the guest register and marked them as 'special guests' in red ink.

After reaching the room, they both bathed. By then, it was 3.30 a.m. Since they had to catch the bus at 7 a.m., they decided to go straight to sleep.

'Madam, hope you don't mind if I sleep here next to you,' Ram teased.

'I don't mind. Just make sure you don't get yourself beaten,' she replied with a grin.

She turned off the light and got into bed. Ram lay down on the other side.

Exhausted, they both fell asleep almost immediately.

Anandhi drifted into a dream. She was on a train speeding over a bridge across the sea. Standing at one of the doors, she held on to the handles, watching the waves below. The wind whipped through her hair. She looked at her hands and slowly let go of the railings, preparing to jump into the roaring sea below. Just then, a familiar, hairy hand grabbed hers firmly. She struggled to break free and jump, but the hand pulled her back into the train. Realizing it was Ram who saved her, she pulled her hand away from his grip. After staring into his eyes for a moment, she jumped into the sea. As she plunged into the turbulent waters, she began to drown. Suddenly, a small hand, resembling that of a child, grabbed hers.

Anandhi woke up with a start, as if from a nightmare.

She heard the patter of rain outside. The window was open, letting the wind flow freely. Light from the halogen streetlight shone into the room. In that light, she saw Ram's face.

He was sleeping like a baby. She lay next to him, watching him for a while. His moustache seemed to amuse her.

Quietly, she moved closer and sat up on one arm, facing him. With her little finger, she lifted the ends of his moustache, careful not to touch his face.

Just then, some of her hair accidentally fell on his face. His breathing changed. She quickly lay back down and peeked with one eye to see if he woke up. Realizing he was still asleep, she relaxed and eventually fell asleep watching his face.

Two

'Ram, get up! Ram!'

Ram woke up with a start to Anandhi calling him.

'It's already past seven,' she said, worried.

'Oh no!'

He jumped up, rubbed his eyes and checked his phone.

'I set an alarm. What should we do now?' he asked.

'You get ready quickly. I'll go downstairs and ask Appa when the next bus is.'

Anandhi tied her hair and left. Ram quickly went to the bathroom.

When he came out after freshening up in five minutes, Anandhi was back.

'What's the update?' he asked anxiously.

'The next bus to Alligramam is at eleven.'

'Oh no! If we wait for that bus, we'll be late.'

'Yes, but Appa had a suggestion. Trucks that come to the market with goods to sell are there until eight o'clock. They often go back empty and might let us hitch a ride. The market is close, so if we get there before eight, we can catch a ride to Alligramam.'

Ram checked his watch. It was 7.30 a.m.

'Get ready quickly. We'll head there as soon as possible,' he said.

Within ten minutes, they had locked the room and left.

When they reached the reception, the old man was standing at the door, as if expecting someone.

'Appa, we're leaving,' Anandhi said, hanging the keys with the others.

'Can you please wait a couple of minutes?' he asked.

Anandhi and Ram looked at him, wondering why.

'My wife will be here in a couple of minutes. She has reached the adjacent street. When she called this morning, I told her about you two, and she wants to meet you,' he explained.

Ram smiled. 'Sure, why not? Anandhi, let's sit here.'

Ram sat in a chair while Anandhi stood near the door with the old man.

The flowers and mud Ram had thrown on her head the previous night were now wet on the ground from the rain. The flowers still looked fresh. Anandhi picked one up and placed it in her bag. The old man noticed and looked at Ram, who was engrossed in his phone.

'You two haven't confessed your love for each other yet, have you?' he asked Anandhi quietly.

'I don't understand,' she replied.

'Don't try to fool me. I can see these things. The person we're waiting for and I have been in love for seventeen years.'

'Seventeen years! Wow!' she exclaimed.

'Ha ha ha, yes,' he winked and laughed.

Exactly two minutes later, a lady appeared at the end of the road. She wore a light blue saree and had a stone-studded nose pin. Her smile was bright. She was carrying a steel container, which Anandhi guessed had food for the old man. Anandhi turned and called Ram, who came to the doorstep and stood with them.

The lady walked up to them, her smile showing her beautiful teeth. Anandhi stepped forward and hugged her. Ram also hugged her gently, like he would hug his own mother.

Suddenly, her smile faded a bit. Ram worried he had hugged her too tightly.

'When my son felt affectionate, he would hug me tightly like this,' she said and gently brushed Ram's hair from his forehead, kissing it softly. Ram's eyes filled with tears.

Ram and Anandhi didn't really know who this old couple was, or why they had crossed paths with them, but they felt a strong affection for them.

Before leaving Dhanashree Lodge, they marked their memorable stay there by writing their names and the date on the wall with a red marker pen, after getting the old man's approval.

17

One

By the time Ram and Anandhi reached the Thanjavur bus stand, it was almost 8 a.m.

Shops were just starting to open, and the market was getting busy. There were about five vehicles waiting to leave the market, but none were going to Alligramam. However, one vehicle was heading to Chinnapuram, which was close to Alligramam. They told Ram and Anandhi that they would be going via Periyapuram, which would take about half an hour longer than the usual bus route. Relieved that they would at least get closer to Alligramam, they got into the vehicle. It was a pickup truck with a few bundles of cattle fodder in the back, some of which were dotted with patches of cow dung.

Anandhi and Ram found some clean bundles to sit on.

In the front of the truck was a man wearing a local dhoti and an old shirt; he looked like he was about thirty-five years old. The other person was a woman they assumed was his wife, though she seemed older than him. She had a long scar on her forehead. She told Anandhi and Ram that they had to pay two hundred rupees each. Though she seemed unfriendly, they agreed since they had no other option.

Within ten minutes of them getting on the vehicle, it left the market. Since there wasn't much traffic, the vehicle went fast. Ram and Anandhi enjoyed the view from the back. Sometimes, Anandhi glanced through the glass window into the cabin, where the couple sat silently, their eyes fixed on the road.

After about twenty minutes on Thanjavur's main road, the vehicle turned on to a side road. Soon, they saw signs of villages approaching. The buildings gave way to fields of sugarcane, paddy, mulberry, corn and coconut groves.

Continuing to drive, the man took out his phone, called someone and gave details about their route. Then the woman took the phone and talked, mentioning a new route.

Anandhi felt this was unusual but decided not to tell Ram, who was still enjoying the countryside.

'That road,' the lady said, pointing to a road with tall grass on both sides. The man made an abrupt turn. As they moved forward, they saw five people standing, as if waiting for them.

'Look! Them!' the woman said aloud.

Ram and Anandhi, who were enjoying the scenery, heard the woman's voice and grew suspicious. They peered through the glass window. Right in front of them, five people stood blocking their way.

'Don't stop the vehicle. When they realize we won't brake, they'll get out of the way,' the lady said, leaning forward.

'Whether they move or not, I'm going to hit them,' the driver said.

He sped up. The five people jumped out of the way at the last moment. Ram and Anandhi, completely clueless, looked at each other and gasped. Suddenly, a stone came out of nowhere and shattered the rear windscreen. Glass pieces fell on Ram and Anandhi, missing their heads by just centimetres, shocking them.

They looked back in fear. The people who had tried to block them were now following on three bikes. One of them, sitting on the back of one of the bikes, had thrown the stone that smashed the glass.

They started throwing more stones from their cloth bags. One stone hit the mirror on the right, almost breaking it. The lady in the front told Anandhi and Ram to lay low and then called someone. Anandhi and Ram obeyed, kneeling down and covering themselves with bundles of grass.

After finishing the call, the lady screamed for the driver to turn on to the unpaved road on the right. He did so, driving on to a rough road lined with sugarcane shrubs.

'Oh God! Damn!' the driver yelled as soon as they turned.

Hearing that, Anandhi and Ram, who were still kneeling, managed to peek through the glass window. Almost twenty men stood in the distance, armed with farming tools, ready to fight.

At that moment, the lady turned around and pointed to the grass bundles that had patches of cow dung. Ram and Anandhi were unsure of what they were supposed to do.

'There's something inside that bundle. Get it. Quickly,' she commanded.

Upon hearing this, Ram cautiously moved forward, using the grass bundles as shields, and began searching through the bundle she had indicated. When his hands reached the bottom, his hands found something. He pulled it out.

It was a locally made double-barrelled gun. It was the first time Ram had ever seen a gun. It made him tremble.

'Give it to me. Fast,' the woman demanded angrily through the window.

Ram pushed aside his thoughts, crept back and handed the gun to the lady through the window. He returned to sit next to Anandhi.

The lady lowered the window on her side, leaned out halfway and brandished the gun.

Seeing the gun, the people standing on the road scattered in fear, running off in different directions.

Taking advantage of the situation, the driver sped up.

As they drove past the now-scattered group, the people who had gathered started hurling stones, sticks and whatever else they could find at the truck, but none of them came close to the mark.

They soon got on to a road that cut through fields of sugarcane and corn.

'What's going on?' Ram asked the lady who held the gun.

'Didn't I tell you we were going via Periyapuram?' she snapped angrily.

'How do we know what kind of a place it is! Stop the vehicle. We need to get out,' he shouted.

At that moment, Anandhi looked back and saw several people following them on bikes. She turned to the lady.

'Akka, they're right behind us.'

Upon hearing this, the lady cast a look at the bikes behind them. She then took out a locally made bomb with a long wick from a cloth bag nearby. She also grabbed a cigar lighter from the dashboard and handed both to Ram through the window. Ram stared at her, unsure of what to do.

'Light this and throw it at them,' she instructed.

Ram and Anandhi gasped in shock.

'Anandhi, it seems we hitched a ride on a terrorist's vehicle,' Ram said fearfully, looking at the bomb.

At that moment, another round of stones hit the back of the vehicle.

'Oh no!'

Ram and Anandhi knelt and took cover behind the grass bundles.

Peeking through the grass, Ram saw the pillion riders continuously throwing stones from cloth bags at them. Most of them hit the grass bundles and landed inside the truck.

Ram and Anandhi sat close together, wondering what to do next.

The pickup truck sped through the sugarcane fields, closely followed by about ten bikes. The riders assumed Anandhi and Ram were with the truck's crew and kept attacking. At one point, a stone bounced and hit Anandhi's little toe, causing her pain. In anger, she picked it up and hurled it back. It struck a lone rider on a motorcycle, causing him to fall off the bike and into the sugarcane field.

Ram looked at Anandhi with surprise.

'I threw it because it hurt me,' she said, rubbing her toe.

Stones continued to rain around them.

'Anandhi, shall we start throwing these stones back at them?' Ram asked as the pelting became relentless.

She picked up a stone that had landed nearby and looked at Ram, as if to answer his question. They shielded themselves with grass bundles and retaliated with equal force. The man and the woman in the front exchanged pleased glances.

Anandhi and Ram kept throwing stones competitively. Most of the bikes stopped halfway. The others were knocked down by Ram and Anandhi.

Finally, ten minutes later, the speeding pickup truck reached a residential area with houses and shops. Ram and Anandhi tossed the grass bundles on to the truck's floor and looked ahead.

'Don't worry. We've passed Periyapuram. This is Chinnapuram, our village,' the woman said with relief.

Ram and Anandhi sighed and lay down on top of the grass bundles, exhausted and relieved. Just then, Ram's phone, which was in his pocket, rang. Without checking the caller ID, he answered it. It was Vetri.

'Hey, where are you guys? I've been trying to call you. What's going on?' Vetri asked urgently.

'We couldn't answer the phone earlier. We had quite a situation,' Ram replied, exhausted.

'Alright, just get here soon. What happened?'

Before Vetri could say more, Ram lost signal on his phone.

'Hey kids, where are you headed?' the driver, who had been silent all this while, asked.

Ram sat up on the bundles and looked around. The road they were on was lined with shops selling parts of old vehicles. Many of the shop owners waved as their pickup truck passed by.

'We need to go to Alligramam, sir,' Ram replied after observing for a moment.

'You mentioned that when you got in. I meant, where exactly in Alligramam? Maybe we can drop you there,' the driver suggested.

The woman in the front seat looked at him confused. He gestured to say that it was okay.

'I'll tell you the way,' Anandhi eagerly spoke up.

18

One

In about half an hour, they reached Alligramam. Anandhi knew the way to Paatti's home from the main junction and gave directions to the man through the window.

They travelled along a road next to an irrigation canal. Green paddy fields stretched on endlessly, with workers tending to them here and there.

Finally, the truck drove through a road lined with coconut groves, which ended at a two-storeyed house built with red stones. Ram and Anandhi, through the truck's front screen, saw that right in the middle of the front yard was a sacred tulsi plant in a stone pot smeared with cow dung. At one end of the yard was a heap of coconuts. Kids were playing around, and some people had set up a makeshift stove and were cooking. Women were chopping vegetables on a platform in the front. Some men were chatting and laughing. Reshma and two other girls were sitting by a big pillar, while Vetri gazed outside.

When the truck entered the courtyard, everyone stopped what they were doing and carefully watched the two people in the front seat. When the vehicle stopped, Ram and Anandhi stood up in the back.

This was a complete surprise for Vetri and Reshma. They hadn't expected them to arrive this way. They hurried to the front yard as Ram and Anandhi got down.

Moments later, when the pickup truck was leaving, the man and woman sitting in the front smiled. Ram and Anandhi stood there, watching them drive away.

By then, the men who had been sitting nearby had gathered around them. An old man among them asked, 'How come you were in that vehicle?'

'We got a lift,' Ram started to say.

Anandhi quickly spoke up. She moved closer to Ram and whispered, 'That's Paatti's younger brother. Better we don't tell him everything that happened. He'll get worried. We'll explain to Paatti later.'

'Do you know who they are?' the old man asked.

Ram and Anandhi looked confused. 'Do you know them, uncle?' Anandhi asked anxiously.

'They are top criminals being hunted by the Tamil Nadu Police. Vathikkutchi and Selva. They're siblings,' he said, his expression grim.

Hearing this, Vetri and Reshma were as shocked as Ram and Anandhi. The old man continued, explaining all he knew about Vathikkutchi and Selva.

'Have you heard of the village of thieves? Well, they own one such village. Even the small kids there are skilled robbers. Their main job is stealing luxury vehicles, disassembling them and selling the parts. Vathikkutchi and Selva are their leaders. Chinnapuram is their village. There's another such village nearby; it is called Periyapuram. Those people are worse. Though both villages engage in the same trade, they are deadly enemies, much like India and Pakistan. Chinnapuram residents have to pass through Periyapuram to reach Thanjavur if they don't want to get caught by the police. Usually, both villages avoid Alligramam because of the police station here. Yet, Periyapuram has set strict rules for the people of Chinnapuram who pass through. They must not stop or stare at anyone. If a Chinnapuram vehicle stops in Periyapuram for more than five minutes, it will be attacked.

Some years ago, the government even set up a police station between the two villages.'

He hadn't finished his story about the thieves' village when Paatti emerged from inside, interrupting him.

'Oh, my children are here! Madan, look! This is my other son in Chennai. And you know Anandhi,' Paatti said warmly, holding Ram and Anandhi close.

'Yes, we were just getting to know each other, akka,' the old man replied with a smile.

Ram realized he had been listening to stories without properly introducing himself. He shook hands with Madan.

'I'm Madan, your Paatti's younger brother,' the old man said.

'Both of you, come inside. I want to introduce you to everyone,' Paatti said excitedly.

'Paatti, please wait a minute. Madan uncle, could you finish the story about them?' Ram asked.

Though Paatti had no idea about what was being talked about, she waited to hear the story.

'Yes, yes. The officers at the police station set up between these two villages started their operation soon after. First, they arrested Selva, the leader of Chinnapuram village. His sister Vathikkutchi tried to bail him out, but she herself was an accused in many robbery cases. The inspector and other policemen arrested and physically abused her. She fought back, and the scar on her forehead is from that day. Eventually, both Selva and his sister were jailed. The jail time and abuse they faced changed their appearances drastically. After their release, they, along with the entire village, attacked the police station. They beat up the eleven men on duty and threw them out of the village. They even demolished the police station. That day, even the people of Periyapuram supported them. They still have pending cases against them for attacking the police and destroying the station. Since then, the people of Chinnapuram have focused on stealing police vehicles. Many come to these villages to buy vehicle parts. The police have attempted to enter these villages on numerous occasions, but the villagers have consistently put up strong resistance at their respective borders. Nowadays, the Tamil Nadu Police largely leave them alone. Selva and Vathikkutchi are heroes in their village and rarely leave except for important matters. Lately, things have been peaceful, but I have heard that Selva and Vathikkutchi attacked the leader of Periyapuram village in Thanjavur. The workers here told me about it. You both took a lift in their vehicle. They likely avoided Periyapuram, given the current conditions, and might have come through Alligramam. It's sheer luck that you didn't get caught by the police, else you too could have been framed as their partners,' he said with relief.

'We came through Periyapuram, uncle,' Ram added with a sigh.

Anandhi explained what had happened to everyone. As she talked, the workers stopped what they were doing and gathered around her. By the time she had finished describing their adventurous journey through Periyapuram, everyone from the house had come together to listen.

Paatti was frightened by their story but relieved that they had reached safely.

'Did the stone you threw hurt anyone?' another woman asked, her hand on her chin.

'Even if it did, who cares?' Madan said lightly.

'I'm Saraswathi, his wife,' the woman said.

Other family members rushed to introduce themselves, too. Almost everyone from the family was there that day, about forty people in total.

'Now, both of you freshen up and come back. Then we'll have some food. Come, I'll show you your room,' Paatti said.

Anandhi and Ram followed her inside. Reshma and Vetri came along as well.

Two

They climbed up a wooden spiral staircase and reached a room on the first floor, where Ram and Anandhi's bags were already placed.

'Is it okay if the four of you share this room?' Paatti asked.

'You say that as if you'd give us another room if we said no,' Reshma joked, sitting on one of the beds.

'I'm amazed that villages like Periyapuram still exist, Paatti,' Ram said, still excited from their adventure, as he sat down.

'Many such villages exist in Tamil Nadu, dear. In most places, the situation is similar. They create their own little empires. But don't worry, it's safe here. Take a quick bath and come downstairs. Everyone is busy preparing lunch, and we have four varieties of payasam, too. Come, join us. It will be fun. I'll head back down now,' Paatti said, tucking her saree's pallu into her waist as she went downstairs.

Seeing Paatti so delighted and at peace filled Ram and Anandhi with happiness.

Anandhi opened her bag, took out a fresh set of clothes and went to the bathroom. Ram lay flat on the bed. Vetri took out his phone, went near the window to check for mobile network, and, finding none, came back to sit on the bed.

'Did you really throw stones at them? I'm jealous,' Reshma said to Ram.

'Of course, we did. If not, they would have got us with their volley of stones,' Ram said, recalling the events.

Reshma looked disappointed that she hadn't been part of the stone-throwing.

After a while, Anandhi came out of the bathroom, wearing a half saree with a pink, long and flared skirt, a black short blouse and a light green pallu. Ram and Vetri stared at her with their mouths wide open. It was the first time they had seen her in such an outfit.

Water droplets dripped from her hair as she smiled and towel-dried her hair before putting the towel out to dry in the corridor.

'Aren't you all coming down? I'm going,' Anandhi waved her hand.

'I want this outfit too!' Reshma exclaimed like a child.

Anandhi opened her bag, took out another half saree in red and yellow and handed it to Reshma. 'I thought you might need this.'

'Come on, let's all go down. I'll be waiting,' Anandhi said before heading downstairs. Ram went to freshen up while Reshma began to drape the half saree with Vetri's help.

By the time the three of them reached downstairs, the kitchen was abuzz with festival-like fervour. The women were cooking on one side, the men were chopping vegetables on a table on the other and some kids were sitting on a floor mat, peeling onions and garlic. Two women were sitting with their infants, and next to them, two old ladies, probably in their nineties, were enjoying their betel nuts. Ram saw Anandhi standing with Paatti and others, stirring pink-coloured rice payasam in a large uruli.

'What are you staring at? Go help!' Vetri nudged Reshma forward.

She tucked the edge of her half saree into her waist and went to help Paatti and Anandhi. Ram and Vetri joined Paatti's brother and the others who were chopping vegetables.

One of the two elderly women began singing a Tamil folk song while grinding betel leaves. Gradually, everyone in the kitchen started humming and singing along. Ram and Vetri grabbed a steel plate and a spoon and joined in to add to the rhythm. Reshma and Anandhi smiled at each other.

The two elderly women sang nearly five lively songs. By the time they finished, rice with ten different dishes, four types of payasam and several snacks were all ready.

Tender banana leaves were spread out in the long corridor in the front of the house. Elderly people, children and those who had been working outside were served first. Ram, Vetri, Reshma and Anandhi helped serve the food.

Everyone eagerly enjoyed their meal.

After lunch, they took a group photo, post which the men and women split into teams and started playing antakshari. Like the previous years, the women won again. It was an unforgettable day for Vetri, Reshma, Ram and Anandhi.

19

One

In just one day, all four of them felt like a part of Paatti's family. In the evening, they went to the Kaliyamman Temple for the festival. They walked down the country roads and along the ridges of paddy fields. Vetri and Ram happily carried small kids on their shoulders.

'A few years ago, we wouldn't have been able to walk this way during this time,' Madan told Vetri and Ram while they walked. 'This used to be the time when Karuppasamy went to the temple.'

'Karuppasamy? Who is that?' Ram asked.

'He's a god, the protector of every village. On the day of the temple festival, there used to be a special ceremony under a banyan tree a little distance from here. During the ceremony, Karuppasamy would enter the body of one of the men there. The sickle, mace and chain are considered his weapons. The man possessed by Karuppasamy would tremble continuously and move towards the temple, through some random path. If anyone accidentally got in his way, he would either cut them with the sickle or hit them with the mace.'

Ram looked at Madan in surprise. 'And then?'

'Well, in 2001, a man possessed by Karuppasamy chased four women working in the fields and injured them using the sickle. It became a big legal issue. After that, the courts intervened and stopped the worship of Karuppasamy,' he explained.

'Ugh! That's weird for a protective god,' Ram quipped.

After walking for half an hour, they reached the Kaliyamman Temple. The scene was much more intense than what Madan had described. One part of the temple was filled with embers, and men were running over rows of burning cinders. In another area, women were circling the temple holding clay pots filled with embers. Some women, with their hair loose, were shaking vigorously, carrying branches of neem trees.

Seeing all this for the first time, Ram's curiosity was stoked.

The rest of the festivities were happening in a large field near the temple, which had been cleared after the harvest. There were fireworks, people dressed as gods, amman kudam (a ritual with pots), mayilattam (peacock dance) and thakiladi melam (a type of folk performance involving drums). There was also a giant wheel and playthings for children.

Anandhi and Reshma walked around with girls their age. Ram and Vetri joined those who were dancing near the thakiladi melam. When the beats intensified, everyone, including the women who had been watching, started dancing together.

Paatti called Anandhi, Reshma and the other girls who were eating ice sticks and pushed them into the celebration. They threw away their ice sticks and joined in. Ram, Anandhi, Vetri and Reshma danced in circles with their arms on each other's shoulders. They included Paatti in their circle. Soon, Madan, Saraswathi and all the aunts, uncles and their children joined in. The locals came in, too, making it a big human circle. The musicians and drummers stood inside this circle, playing their instruments. Little children and some girls danced in the middle, sharing the joy of their parents. The fair became lively and full of energy. As the music picked up, the energy levels soared. When the fair finally ended, everyone expressed their joy with loud shouts, hugging and kissing each other. As the initiators of the dance, Ram, Anandhi, Reshma and Vetri were very happy.

Two

'Do you want some sundakanji?' Madan asked Ram and Vetri.
'What is that?' Ram asked.

'The preparation is similar to that of wine. They make sundakanji by burying porridge in the soil. I've never tried it, just heard about it. Let's give it a shot,' Vetri suggested.

'Deal,' Ram said to Madan with a smile.

Madan and another man named Suman took them both through the sugarcane field near the temple to a grass hut. Inside, five or six people wearing white shirts were drinking sundakanji from small clay pots.

'Hey Paatti, four sundakanjis, please,' Madan said aloud.

An old lady, almost eighty years old, wearing only a saree and no blouse, with large gold ear studs on her dangling ears, came out and looked carefully at Madan. Then she grinned with tobacco-stained teeth, seemingly recognizing him, and walked back inside.

The four men sat on a charpoy in the courtyard. As Ram looked down, wondering if that old bed would break, Paatti returned, holding four small pots close to her. She handed them over. Vetri and Ram clinked their pots together and took a sip. The drink was slightly sour but with a distinct flavour.

Madan had expected that they would consume only one pot each of sundakanji, but he soon realized he was mistaken. Suman and Madan ended up drinking two pots each, while Ram and Vetri consumed four pots and then asked for a fifth.

Lost in time, they didn't notice the hours passing. Family members began calling Madan to return home from the temple with them. He told them to go ahead and stayed behind, watching Ram and Vetri lie on the charpoy, inebriated. Suman and the Paatti who sold the sundakanji also stayed, sitting with their palms on their chins.

Back at the house, Paatti, Reshma and Anandhi were sitting on the verandah with the rest of the family members, casually discussing family matters. Suddenly, Reshma and Anandhi saw something that made them cover their mouths with their palms.

Madan and Suman were approaching, supporting Vetri and Ram on their shoulders and panting heavily. They laid them down on the verandah. Everyone gathered around, looking concerned, worried some unfortunate accident had occurred.

Before anyone could ask, Suman reassured them, 'Don't worry. They just had some sundakanji.'

Madan was fearful of his sister, Paatti. But to his surprise, Paatti was the first to laugh out loud.

'Saraswathi, bring some buttermilk, quick,' Paatti instructed her sister-in-law.

Saraswathi and another lady brought buttermilk out in two vessels.

Reshma, Paatti and Anandhi managed to get Ram and Vetri to drink some. Within fifteen minutes, they regained consciousness.

As they opened their eyes, they noticed everyone around them stifling their laughter. Not entirely sober but still aware, they felt embarrassed. Nevertheless, they managed to eat with everyone else before retiring to their room.

Still a little inebriated, they couldn't stand straight and barely managed to climb the stairs, bending to grab each step for support.

Anandhi and Reshma slept on the bed, while Ram and Vetri slept on a mattress on the floor.

Three

The next day, as dawn broke, people started to leave one by one. Ram, Vetri, Reshma, Anandhi and Patti's return journey was booked on the Rameswaram–Bhubaneswar Express at 2:30 p.m. By 11 a.m., they bade farewell to the remaining family members and headed to the station. Their relatives urged them to return the next year with Paatti.

Madan drove them in his tractor to the bus depot, from where they were supposed to catch a bus to Thanjavur at 11.30 a.m.

Before boarding the bus, Ram and Vetri hugged Madan tightly.

'There's another treat like sundakanji waiting for you next year,' he said with a smile.

'Oh no! Please spare us!' Ram and Vetri playfully folded their hands.

Soon, the bus from Alligramam began its journey to Thanjavur. They waved to Madan until he was out of sight.

By 1.45 p.m., they had reached the Thanjavur bus stand. From there, they took an autorickshaw to the railway station.

Vetri wondered if they should have lunch at the bus stand before proceeding, but remembering the delay on the onward journey, Paatti suggested they go straight to the station and eat at the canteen there if time allowed.

As their autorickshaw passed by Dhanashree Lodge, Anandhi leaned over to peek inside. She saw the old man's wife at the reception, seemingly expecting someone.

The autorickshaw travelled down the same road lined with the mayflower trees. Upon reaching that familiar stretch, Anandhi turned towards Ram. He met her gaze and smiled. Then they both looked at the iron bench where they had sat together that night.

Navigating through the traffic, the autorickshaw arrived at the station just before 2 p.m.

Having enjoyed delicious meals at Paatti's house, Ram, Anandhi, Vetri and Reshma found the bland food at the railway station canteen disappointing.

Soon, they heard an announcement informing them that the Rameswaram–Bhubaneswar Express was running twenty minutes late. They checked their coach position and sat on a bench close to where their compartment was expected to stop.

'So, how do you like my hometown?' Paatti asked, looking at Ram, Vetri, Anandhi and Reshma.

'We should have come last year,' Vetri sighed.

'From now on, we'll come with you every year, Paatti. Okay?' Reshma said excitedly.

'I was about to say the same. The one thing that binds the four of you together is me and my house in Chennai. In the future, you might go your separate ways. But I want you to promise me something now. No matter how busy you get, every year, all four of you should come for the temple festival at Alligramam. Even if I'm not alive, all my four children must gather at least once a year and remember me. That's my biggest wish. Promise me that wherever you are in the world, you'll meet at Alligramam every year.'

Paatti stretched out her hand. Ram was the first to hold it, followed by Vetri, Reshma and, finally, Anandhi. Paatti hugged them all with joy.

When their train's arrival on platform 1 was announced, they all rose and gathered their bags.

The long journey, nearly half a day by bus and train, had left them exhausted. Upon reaching Egmore station by 10 p.m., Vetri booked a taxi online. Since Anandhi's Luna was already parked there, Ram took the keys from her and headed to get it.

Given it was Sunday, Chennai's traffic was at its peak even at that hour. It took them nearly an hour to reach home.

By the time they arrived, Ram was waiting outside the gate with the Luna.

Given the late hour, Ram and Reshma decided to stay the night at Paatti's house and go to college from there in the morning, returning to their own homes in the evening.

And so, after two days, all five of them slept in Chennai.

Ram and Vetri slept in Vetri's room upstairs. Reshma, Anandhi and Paatti slept in Paatti's room.

It was past 1 a.m. when Reshma woke up, startled. She tried to get back to sleep but noticed Anandhi wasn't beside her. Slowly, she sat up. Paatti was sleeping soundly. Reshma looked at the bathroom and then towards the main door, which was open. She got down from the bed.

The light in the verandah was off. Quietly tiptoeing to the sit-out, she saw Anandhi talking to someone outside the gate. Anandhi received a large, covered object from the person while conversing.

What is she doing here at this hour? Reshma wondered.

Suddenly, Anandhi turned back. Reshma immediately hid behind the cushioned chair on the verandah. When she was sure they hadn't seen her, she peeked at the gate again. The face of the person talking to Anandhi wasn't very clear, but Reshma felt that his body structure was very familiar.

She saw Anandhi giving the person a small packet in return. She sensed something fishy. She got up and switched on the light from behind the chair.

As soon as the light came on, Anandhi turned around to see Reshma. Her face went pale with shock. The man standing at the gate quickly walked away.

Reshma walked briskly to Anandhi, who stood there with the packet in her hand.

'What are you doing here at this odd hour? Who was that person?' she asked suspiciously.

In response, Anandhi opened the packet and showed her. It contained two garlands.

'Need to deliver these early in the morning,' she said with a smile.

Reshma felt bad about doubting Anandhi.

'Why are you working so hard, Anandhi? You earn enough money from your job as a receptionist at the college. Why are you pushing yourself to make money like this?'

Anandhi smiled and looked down. Reshma tenderly lifted her face and found her eyes welling up.

'Anandhi, you are beautiful. Way more beautiful than me, even though I'm the one dreaming of becoming an actress someday. If I had your looks and figure, I'd have become a superstar by now. I'm telling you this because I care. Don't work so hard and risk losing your beauty. I really like you, and that's why I'm saying this. If you have any financial difficulties, let us know. The four of us are here for you. Why sacrifice your sleep for a garland that earns you barely ten or twenty rupees in commission?' Reshma said, running her hand through Anandhi's hair.

'Thanks, dear.' Anandhi hugged Reshma tightly. In that deep embrace, Reshma felt the warmth of sisterhood.

After placing the garland in her room upstairs, Anandhi went with Reshma to Paatti's room.

Unbeknownst to them, the man who had walked away earlier was standing next to the compound wall, carefully watching them until they went inside.

20

One

The next day, by the time everyone woke up, it was almost 8 a.m. Anandhi had already left for her routine tasks.

Since the Padmini was all dusty, Paatti started cleaning it early in the morning.

Reshma made some coffee and handed it to Vetri and Ram. The three of them sat on the first floor, legs dangling through the iron railings, sipping their coffee and watching Paatti clean the car.

'She's totally obsessed. She spends so much time cleaning that car, but she never takes it out. Except for the staff at the car service centre, none of us are allowed to even touch it,' Vetri said unhappily.

'Well, what's the story behind it?' Ram asked.

'Machaa, Thaathaa bought this car, second-hand, decades ago. He married Paatti and brought her to his house in it. Later, when he got a job in Madras, Paatti and Thaathaa left Alligramam with their belongings and came here in this very car. Since then, almost every important milestone in Paatti's life has involved this car. If you ask her, she could probably tell you a thousand stories about it. When Thaathaa was alive, if they had a fight, Paatti would lock herself in the car. If Thaathaa was angry, he would do the same. When the person inside the car cooled down, they would honk. Then the other would come and join them, and they would go straight to Besant Nagar beach together. It seems Paatti sometimes picked fights just to have an excuse to go to the beach.'

When Vetri finished speaking, Ram smiled widely and looked at Paatti, who diligently washed the car, like a mother tending to a small baby.

Reshma continued the story where Vetri left off. 'One day, Thaathaa had a fight with Paatti and locked himself in the car. Paatti, dressed in a new saree and ready to go to the beach, waited inside the house for the horn. Even after a long time, she didn't hear the horn. She went to check and found Thaathaa dead inside the car from a heart attack. Since then, Paatti hasn't sat in the car. Some nights, she stands near the car, crying and honking. She's determined that she will only enter the car again when her body is taken for cremation. She keeps it spotless just for that.'

Ram realized the profound significance the Padmini car held in Paatti's life.

'Aren't you going to college today? Go and get ready,' Paatti called out from below.

Before long, all three of them were ready to go. Paatti served them idlis and mint chutney.

Two

As the three of them left home, Ram mentioned that he wanted to be dropped off at Guindy railway station.

Vetri and Reshma teased him, asking if he was on some mission to woo someone at the station. However, respecting his privacy, they didn't pry further and dropped him off. It was almost 9 a.m. by then.

When Ram reached platform 2, he saw Malli, as usual chatting with the elderly samosa vendor. He approached her and playfully covered her eyes from behind.

'Hey, Ram,' she said, laughing.

Ram stepped in front of her. 'Wow, that was a brilliant guess. How did you know it was me?'

'The only man in all of Chennai who dares to cover my eyes on this platform in broad daylight is you.'

Ram laughed out loud. He then recounted all the details of the interesting events from his journey to Malli.

'My hometown is similar. It's total fun during the temple festival time. But since I'd always be dressed up and dancing, I never got the chance to enjoy it all,' Malli said, a bit disappointed.

'Next year, come with us to Alligramam. It'll be so much fun.'

'Me? Ha ha ha,' she burst into laughter.

'By the way, did you spend a night with that girl at the lodge? Is some romance brewing?' she winked and asked.

'Oh, Malli! You ask because you don't know her well.'

'But I know you well, right? You jumped off that train because you like her. Am I right?'

'Oh no, Malli. She's not interested. She's always so focused on her work and making money.'

'That's good, isn't it? In the future, you'll be busy making movies. It's good to have someone responsible in the family.'

'You've already thought about us having a family, huh? But I'm serious, Malli. She doesn't have those feelings,' Ram said firmly.

'I think she's just not expressing it. Let me tell you a secret, Ram. Among all the people around us, at least one person is secretly in love with us. They just don't express it for some reason. Similarly, we also love someone secretly without saying it. Why do you think people check their reflections when they accidentally see a mirror? Why do they carefully choose clothes that suit them instead of wearing anything random? It all comes down to one reason: the secret love within us. Without it, no one would spend even a minute caring about their appearance. Time flies, Ram. Many secret admirers surround the ones we love, too. Before she moves on to someone else, ensure she stays in your life. If we lose some people, it's forever. You should propose to her without any delay.'

Though Malli said a lot, Ram just listened silently without objecting. When the train arrived, they both boarded and stood near the door, facing each other and looking outside.

'What's the latest on your brother's bike?' Ram suddenly remembered.

Malli untied a knot in her saree's pallu, took out a yellow slip from a small purse and showed it to him, as if she had been waiting for the question. Ram looked at it—it was a booking slip for a Royal Enfield Bullet 350.

'Oh my God! A Bullet?' he asked in surprise.

'Yes. He has loved Bullet bikes since he was small. He used to run after them whenever they passed by. I couldn't make enough money to buy one, but my friends chipped in from their savings. His wish should be fulfilled. If this can mend things between us, maybe he'll call me back home. If he's by my side, I won't fear anything or anyone,' she said hopefully.

'What's your brother's name?'

'Kavidas.'

'Okay. When will the bike be delivered?'

'They said it might take up to a week. A dealer here called the showroom in my hometown and made all the arrangements. When the showroom staff go to deliver the bike as a surprise, I'll go with them,' Malli said happily.

'Wow. So, if you go back home, we won't be seeing each other any more?'

'Oh, I just realized I don't have your phone number. I wanted to call you yesterday, but I didn't have your number.' She took out an old-fashioned keypad phone from her purse and handed it to Ram. He gave her a missed call. Both of them saved each other's numbers.

Ram said goodbye to Malli and got off at Nungambakkam. After a brief halt, the train started moving again. Malli walked through the train, clapping her hands and asking for money.

Vetri and Reshma were waiting for him in front of the Nungambakkam station. When the three of them reached college, Anandhi smiled at them.

That day, Mr Shiva showed them an English movie titled *The Help*. Afterwards, he told everyone to write a detailed review and bring it the next day.

During lunch at Amma Unavagam, Ram kept stealing looks at Anandhi. Every time he did, Malli's words echoed in his mind. As they finished lunch and walked back to the college, his eyes remained fixed on Anandhi.

She was dressed in a modest, sky-blue cotton salwar-kameez, accessorized with a simple black dupatta draped over one shoulder. Ram had never seen Anandhi in expensive outfits. Her routine involved only combing her hair neatly and tying it back tightly after bathing. She didn't seem to be interested in enhancing her appearance further. Anandhi didn't fit into any of the categories Malli had described. She appeared uninterested in letting anyone into her life.

'Why are you looking at me like that?' Anandhi asked Ram with a smile.

He simply closed his eyes in response.

Reshma and Vetri were walking ahead, engaged in a discussion about an upcoming movie audition.

'What movie audition is it?' Ram asked Vetri.

'Machaa, it's for a new movie by director Mani Ratnam. Just to be considered for the auditions is really big. I registered Reshma's name, but now she's saying she won't go,' Vetri replied, turning back to include Anandhi and Ram in the conversation.

'Reshma, what's your ambition in life?' Anandhi asked.

'To be an actress,' Reshma replied.

'Then why are you turning down such a great opportunity that your brother is bringing to you?' Anandhi enquired.

'It's not that, Anandhi. I've never given an audition before. I'm scared. How can I focus on acting when so many people are staring at me? And in these auditions, they make you stand on a big stage and all. I don't think I can handle it. I might even faint,' Reshma explained honestly.

'Okay, just imagine you are selected for a movie without any auditions. In the first scene, you have to stand on a big stage, facing a thousand junior artistes, and act as someone who is there for an audition. What will you do? Will you faint while acting or run through the back door?' Anandhi asked.

Reshma didn't respond. By then, they had reached the front of the college.

'When we focus on something with all our sincerity, it will drive us forward. The path to our dream might be frightening, but if we retreat, we will always have to run back in fear. Fear is as fragile as an ice cream, while our dreams are as valuable as diamonds. We should never let go of our dreams. Imagine this audition is the first scene of your movie and go for it. Let's face whatever comes our way.'

As Anandhi finished speaking, Ram and Vetri noticed a newfound confidence in Reshma's eyes.

'The audition is at Vadapalani tomorrow evening at five. You three should come with me,' Reshma said.

'Oh, I can't. I have a small birthday event to organize in a nearby auditorium. But if you help me blow up balloons and do the decorations, I can join you afterwards,' Anandhi said.

'How long will the decorations take?' Vetri asked.

'If we all work together, an hour maximum.'

'So, as soon as classes end at three, we get out of the college, go there, put up the decorations and then head to Vadapalani with Reshma. Okay?' Vetri suggested.

'That's a deal,' they said in unison.

The bell signalling the end of the lunch break rang. Later, when Ram returned to the apartment with his travel bag, Bineesh and Kiran were eagerly waiting to hear stories from his Thanjavur trip.

After taking a bath and a change of clothes, he recounted the trip in detail. When he finished, Kiran clapped his hands together. 'Chetta, why don't you become a storyteller? I could vividly imagine everything you just described. It was like watching a movie. Or did you spice it up like those film-makers?' Kiran asked, somewhat suspicious.

'Can you please keep quiet? If something happened to you, Ram, how would I face your family?' Bineesh asked, concerned.

'Nothing happened, Bineesh Etta. Though it was dangerous, it was a lot of fun,' Ram reassured them with a smile.

'Hey, aren't this Selva and Vathikkuchi from Chinnapuram? There are news articles about their attack on a police station on Google,' Kiran interjected, searching on his mobile to confirm his suspicions.

Bineesh also looked at his screen.

'Well, was she scared during all of this?' Bineesh asked.

'Who? Anandhi? Ha ha ha! She was the one who threw stones and got rid of most of the bike riders. I was the one who got scared.'

'Hmm,' Bineesh murmured.

'Why did you ask that, bro?'

'Nothing. Just curious.'

'Tomorrow, we're helping Anandhi with the decorations for one of her events. Are you guys joining?' Ram asked.

'Oh no! That means standing in front of a giant pot of biryani, drooling. Count me out,' Kiran said, folding his hands in a mock plea before heading to the balcony.

Later, as he was about to go to bed, Ram sent a goodnight message to Anandhi. He waited for a while, hoping for a reply. When none came, he put his phone on charge and went to bed.

21

One

The next morning, Ram went with Kiran to a nearby street to buy dosa batter.

While he was making dosas in the kitchen, chatting with Kiran, he noticed a 'good morning' message from Anandhi at 5 a.m. Ram immediately replied with a 'good morning' himself, to which she responded with 'Thanks'.

'Hi, Anandhi. What's up this morning?' he asked.

'I'm delivering garlands at various places. On the way, I need to meet the people for whom I'll be organizing a birthday party this evening.'

'Okay. I'm making dosas here. Did you have breakfast?'

'Just had a coffee. Most days, breakfast isn't possible. I have to go. See you at college, Ram. Bye.'

'Bye, Anandhi.'

It was the first time Ram had chatted with a girl on his phone. When he left for college that day, he took two dosas and some tomato chutney in a small container.

When the bus reached Guindy, he saw Malli standing with the elderly samosa vendor, talking to her.

'Hey, what's up? Did you tell that girl you love her?' Malli asked excitedly as soon as she saw Ram.

'Hey, no.'

'Huh?'

'Malli, I need to first confirm that I have feelings for her. Give me some time,' he said and sighed.

The samosa vendor handed them each a samosa and walked away. The train arrived. As usual, they stood on opposite sides of the door, facing each other, slowly eating their samosas.

'Only six more days until I go to my hometown,' Malli said, her voice brimming with happiness.

'Are you really going?' Ram asked.

'Yeah, I have to, right?'

'Will you be happy if you go home, Malli?'

'Happiness isn't meant for me, Ram. But if I go home, I won't have to fear the lustful advances of the policemen here. I'll be safe at home.'

'I'll miss you, Malli.'

She laughed at that.

When they reached Nungambakkam, Ram looked into her eyes once more.

'Bye,' she said.

After bidding her goodbye, Ram walked to the station's exit. When he reached college, Anandhi was typing some information into the computer from some papers. Ram took out the container with the dosas and placed it on her table.

'I made this.'

Anandhi opened it, curious.

'Wow, Ram, may you be be blessed abundantly. I was starving. I had to bargain a lot with those people over finances. It drained all of my energy. By the time I finished, it was really late. If not, I would have had another coffee. Thanks for the dosas.' She pinched a piece and put it in her mouth.

'Alright. See you at noon,' he said, turning to go upstairs.

When Ram reached the classroom, everyone was discussing the reviews they had written about yesterday's movie. Reshma and Vetri snatched Ram's review to read.

A message popped up on Ram's phone: 'Thanks for the care.'

Reading Anandhi's message, he felt a surge of positive energy.

That afternoon at the Unavagam, Anandhi, Vetri and Ram helped Reshma prepare mentally for her audition. Vetri played her musical and Dubsmash videos, highlighting the huge applause she had received, to boost her confidence. Despite all their efforts, a slight fear was still visible in Reshma's eyes.

In the evening, after college, they went to Vighneshwara Auditorium in Nungambakkam. Paatti was waiting for them at the entrance.

Seeing Paatti there, Reshma looked at the three of them in surprise before rushing ahead to hug her.

'How can our team be complete without Paatti?' Anandhi said with a smile.

'This is your first audition, and you will rock it. I am sure of it,' Paatti assured her, holding her close.

'Come on, we need to finish our work quickly and get to Vadapalani,' Ram urged.

While Ram and Vetri blew up balloons, Paatti, Reshma and Anandhi quickly decorated the stage.

Soon after, the catering vehicle arrived, followed by some college girls wearing white T-shirts printed with the words 'Anandhi Decorations and Catering'. Anandhi gave some suggestions to one of the girls.

'When did you name your company?' Ram asked.

'I had the name ready for a while. When the boys, who came for catering, started causing problems, I replaced them with these girls. They work much better and are more organized. Plus, they manage their studies and take care of their families. The raise those boys wanted, I'm giving to these girls. They're happy, and I'm happy. The T-shirt idea was from the girl I just spoke to,' Anandhi said confidently.

'That's brilliant. So, your company does not need our help any more?' Ram teased.

'Who said that? If I get a big job, I'll call you. You should come flying with your roommates, Chettan and that boy.'

They watched in awe as Anandhi carved shapes and flowers into the watermelons brought for decoration. Within an hour, they had finished all the decoration and handed over responsibility to Malini from the catering team. The five of them then headed to Vadapalani in three vehicles, with Paatti riding with Reshma.

Two

Reshma was relieved to have everyone with her. She felt that Vetri, her brother from another mother, was her biggest blessing. When they arrived at the audition hall, they found a moderate crowd, most of whom were heavily made up to impress the judges. Anandhi glanced around before walking over to Reshma and wiping the sweat from her face with a handkerchief. She adjusted Reshma's hair, pulling it forward on both sides of her face. Still, something seemed missing. Anandhi took off the small sticker bindi from her own forehead and placed it in the centre of Reshma's.

'You are such a ravishing beauty,' Anandhi said with a bright smile.

Reshma started to look at her reflection in the mirror of a nearby vehicle, but then she stopped and turned towards Anandhi instead.

'Do I look okay to you?'

'You are more than okay. Now you just need to perform well on stage,' Anandhi smiled.

Vetri and Ram went to the registration counter, provided Reshma's online registration number and collected her tag. She put it around her neck, took a deep breath and smiled at Paatti, Vetri, Ram and

Anandhi, who were watching her. The care and concern on their faces fuelled her confidence. Then she walked towards the area designated for the participants.

Paatti, Anandhi, Vetri and Ram found seats among the chairs arranged for the audience.

The five-member judging panel, including director Mani Ratnam, was ready in front of the stage. A male anchor announced that the audition would consist of three rounds. Nearly three hundred participants were seated on one side, with Reshma one of them. The first round required each participant to introduce themselves in Tamil within thirty seconds.

Participants lined up according to their registration numbers and delivered their introductions on stage. Some struggled to complete the task within the time limit. Those who couldn't finish, performed poorly, or appeared diffident were eliminated. Much to the surprise of Paatti and the team, Reshma gave her introduction by mimicking Tamil actress Kovai Sarala. All the members of the judging panel, including Mani Ratnam, applauded.

By the end of the first round, the number of participants was down to one hundred and seventy-three.

In the second round, the participants were asked to reenact the climax scene performed by actress Jyothika in the Tamil movie *Chandramukhi*. Hearing this, most of the participants became anxious. It was, after all, an intense scene. Each participant came on stage but many couldn't complete the dialogue and were eliminated. However, those who did manage to finish the dialogue gave marvellous performances.

Reshma requested a volunteer to excuse her and came running towards where Paatti and the others were seated.

'Anandhi, things are out of my hands. I don't think I can do it,' Reshma said, looking tense.

Ram and Vetri exchanged disappointed looks. Seeing the tension on Reshma's face, Paatti held her hand tightly. It was ice-cold and damp because of sweat.

'Reshma, in every competition, there is only one winner. But that doesn't mean those who don't win are not talented. The scene given to you is challenging, and even established actresses might struggle if asked to perform it suddenly. But does that mean they are not talented? Everyone is unique in their own way. It's not about imitating someone and doing things exactly as they did. Have you seen the Malayalam version of this scene? In that, actress Shobana performed it differently. Here, you saw Jyothika's style. But the public welcomed both styles. Both Shobana and Jyothika made their mark. Now, the future actress Reshma is going to do that scene in her own unique way. You don't need to imitate anyone. Just think about how beautifully you would perform if you were the one originally doing this scene. And then, just do it! All other thoughts about success and failure can wait,' Paatti encouraged.

Reshma's eyes were moist. She hugged them tightly, kissed their foreheads and walked back to the other participants. After sitting down, she turned around and looked at them. Anandhi, Vetri and Ram gave her a thumbs-up and silently wished her good luck.

Those who had been eliminated stood on one side of the stage, disappointed.

When Reshma's turn came, she walked up to the stage hesitantly. She closed her eyes for a moment and took a deep breath.

Though she was the one standing on the stage, the hearts beating fast belonged to Paatti, Vetri, Ram and Anandhi.

'Can you please give me the mic for a moment?' Reshma asked the anchor before starting her performance.

The anchor looked a bit confused but handed her the mic.

'Dear judges, I will perform the task you've given me with all my might. It may not be exactly like how actress Jyothika did it because what Jyothika did was not an imitation of actress Shobana's performance in the Malayalam version of this movie. Both movies were superhits, and I believe that performing a scene in one's own style, without losing its intensity and importance, is more crucial than copying someone else's style. Thank you.'

She returned the mic and looked at Paatti and her friends. In their minds, she was already victorious. When Reshma finished her one-minute performance, the first applause came from the eliminated participants. It was for a girl who had resurrected herself from the brink of failure.

Reshma cried with happiness upon hearing it.

All five members of the panel gave her a standing ovation. As the entire hall echoed with cheer, Paatti and her friends hugged each other, proud of Reshma.

22

One

The audition wrapped up close to midnight. The final round involved quickly changing expressions based on the emotions announced by the judges. Finally, before wrapping up the audition, they said that the selected participants would receive a phone call shortly. Some of the participants who admired Reshma's performance approached her to offer congratulations.

'Shall we head to Besant Nagar beach?' Reshma asked as they walked towards the parking lot.

'At this hour?' Anandhi asked, a little sceptical.

'I'm ready,' Paatti responded enthusiastically.

'Then I'm in too,' Ram chimed in.

'Don't you need to get back to your apartment?' Vetri asked Ram.

'I've informed Bineesh Ettan that I'll be late,' he said with a wink.

'Then let's go,' Vetri agreed. Anandhi followed suit.

Reshma started her scooter with Paatti on the backseat. Ram was on Vetri's bike, while Anandhi kick-started her Luna. In a line, the five of them rode through the streets of Vadapalani, towards Besant Nagar.

After a while, Anandhi sped ahead and overtook the others, turning back to grin mischievously. Reshma and Paatti chased after her, with Ram and Vetri close behind.

Soon, Ram surged ahead on the Thunderbird bike, leaving

Reshma and Paatti on their scooter and Anandhi's Luna trailing behind. Vetri, riding pillion, turned to make faces at them.

'Gear up!' Paatti urged Reshma.

'Just be quiet! This is just a 110-cc scooter. How do you expect me to keep up with a bike?' Reshma scolded her.

'Listen, it's not about winning or losing. It's about participating in the race. Success and failure are—'

'You're crazy, Moodevi! Just stop talking, or I'll kick you off,' Reshma cut her off.

Paatti blushed with embarrassment, realizing her motivational words had little effect.

Besant Nagar beach was mostly deserted, with only a handful of people scattered around.

'Would you like some coffee?' asked an old man standing there, his bicycle equipped with a large flask on the carrier.

'Yes, please. Five coffees, annaa,' Paatti replied as if she knew him well.

He looked at her curiously, lines of doubt creasing his forehead. Then, suddenly, he smiled as recognition dawned.

'How have you been, lady?' he asked affectionately.

'I'm fine, annaa.'

'It's been a long time since I saw you. By the way, who are they?' he enquired, looking at Vetri, Reshma, Anandhi and Ram.

'They're my kids, annaa,' Paatti said, holding them close with a smile.

'Children of God, aren't they?' the old man asked with a smile, a smile that spread to Paatti's face as well.

The old man served coffee to all five of them.

'He's been a coffee vendor in this area for many years. Thaathaa used to bring me here some nights for coffee. That's how I know him. After Thaathaa's passing, this is the first time I've come here at this hour,' Paatti explained.

'Forget all that. Shall we play "kadalamma kalli"?' Ram suggested, changing the subject.

'Yeah, perfect for midnight. Let's go,' Reshma said eagerly.

After disposing of their empty coffee cups in the dustbin, they headed towards the sea.

Except for Anandhi, all four of them wrote 'kadalamma kalli' at different spots on the beach. They turned on their mobile flashlights and waited to see whose writing would be erased first by the waves. Anandhi sat at a distance, observing them. While keeping an eye on them, she removed her phone's battery, swapped out the SIM card, inserted another SIM card and dialled a number. After two attempts, she switched back to her usual SIM card, disappointed.

Meanwhile, the others were completely absorbed in the game. The waves erased Vetri's writing first, followed by Paatti's and then Reshma's. Ram cheered and whistled happily, declaring himself the winner.

After the game, all four of them joined Anandhi and sat on the slightly damp sand. Reshma and Vetri began sculpting a mermaid in the wet sand, with Paatti offering to create the mermaid's face after observing their progress. Ram glanced at Anandhi, who was gazing up at the stars.

'Oye, Anandhi,' he called out.

'Oye, what's up?' she replied.

'What are you looking at?'

'Ram, look at those two stars,' she said, pointing towards a spot in the sky.

'Yeah, but there's only one there, right? What's so special about it?'

'No, they're twin stars. Their names are Sirius A and Sirius B. Since one of them is brighter, the other becomes less noticeable. I've been gazing at them like this for almost ten years now. I never get tired of watching them. Even if the clouds hide them on rainy nights, they always peek out eventually.'

Listening to her, Ram was reminded of an old friend.

'I had a friend whose husband was in the army. Sometimes they wouldn't be able to talk for days. When she really missed him, she would sit staring at a star like this. When he missed her, he would do the same from some other corner of the country. She once told me that they communicated silently through the stars. Now, hearing you talk about these stars, I get the same sense. Who is this person you miss every day?' Ram asked, looking deeply into Anandhi's eyes.

'That's a secret,' she said with a wink.

'If I ask you something, will you answer honestly?'

Hearing Ram's question, her eyebrows furrowed.

'You just need to say "yes" or "no".'

'I'll answer if I know, Ram.'

'Do you have a lover?'

Anandhi looked down and smiled.

'Tell me, please,' Ram urged.

'Well, no.'

Ram's face lit up. He turned to the side, made a triumphant fist pump and then looked back at the stars. 'Those stars have a unique beauty. I, too, never get tired of watching them.'

Hearing this, she alternated gazing at Ram and the stars. He was pleased that she understood his state of mind and moved closer to her. When she looked at him questioningly, he grinned. She nodded with a hum of understanding.

'Come quickly! You've got to see our gorgeous mermaid,' Vetri called out loudly.

Ram and Anandhi hurried over. They gasped when they saw the mermaid. Paatti had done a decent job with the face, but below that were two uneven mounds of sand, humorously claimed to be breasts. Adding to the amusement, they had adorned the mermaid with a pair of unclaimed briefs from the beach.

Seeing the comical shape, Anandhi and Ram couldn't stop laughing.

'Hey, you! What's going on here?' a serious voice called out.

'Oh no! It's the police!' Reshma said.

Two policemen approached. They gave the mermaid and the group a stern look. Vetri quickly used his toe to remove the briefs from the mermaid and tossed them aside.

'Why are you all here at this hour?' asked the younger policeman, who was more than six feet tall.

'She had a movie audition. After that, we just came here,' Paatti explained, pointing to Reshma.

'It's not safe here at this hour. If you come to the beach at night, you should stay near the road and avoid the sea. Okay?' he advised.

The policemen then walked towards another group of youngsters nearby.

'Shall we leave?' Paatti asked the group.

The younger policeman returned just then with a notepad and pen and said, 'Just share your names, addresses and phone numbers.'

Ram was the first to provide his name, Chennai address and phone number. Reshma followed, and then Paatti gave details for herself, Vetri and Anandhi, stating they all shared the same address.

'Alright, you can go,' he said.

'Why do they need all this information?' Ram asked as they walked back to the road.

'It's part of their duty,' Vetri replied.

'I gave a slightly altered phone number. He's so young. And he's a policeman, too. He might become a nuisance later,' Reshma remarked with a smile.

'Oh, as if they have nothing else to do! If anyone starts calling with that intention, just trap them and get married,' Vetri joked, laughing.

'Just wait until I become a movie star. Then boys will be lining up for me,' Reshma retorted.

'If that's your ambition, you might as well work at a beverage stand. Men will surely line up all the time,' Vetri teased.

'It's my fault for talking to a kummanamoonji like you,' Reshma said angrily as she took the helmet that was hanging on the side-view mirror of her scooty and put it on.

'What's a kummanamoonji?' Ram asked, puzzled.

'Who knows! It's one of those swear words she makes up,' Vetri said with a scornful laugh.

'So, what's our next plan?' Anandhi asked as she sat on her Luna.

'Please take this idiot with you and drop her home on your way. I'll drop Ram off and come. Don't lock the gate. I'll be back soon,' Vetri said, looking at Paatti and Anandhi.

'Ram, why don't you sleep in Vetri's room tonight?' Paatti suggested.

'No, Paatti, sorry. I already told the chetta at my apartment that I'd be back tonight.'

'How nice it would be if we all lived together. Anyway, let's get together this coming Saturday,' Paatti said.

As soon as Reshma, Paatti and Anandhi left, Vetri took Ram to his apartment. Ram entered the apartment through the balcony, just like Kiran usually did.

Two

The next morning, when Ram woke up, he saw a missed call from Anandhi, along with a message asking if he could call her back when he woke up.

Kiran was already in the kitchen, preparing something.

Ram dialled Anandhi's number.

'Hello, Anandhi. Good morning. Just woke up.'

'That's okay. Can you do me a favour, Ram? I have a booking for an event in your area. Can you go there if I send you the address?'

'Okay. But why me?' he asked, puzzled.

'Relax. They'll give you some money. Just collect it and give it to me. My Luna is being repaired. I'm at the workshop now. Even if I take a bus or auto to come there, I'll be late for work. Hope you don't mind,' Anandhi explained.

'Not at all. Send me the address. See you at college,' Ram replied.

'Thanks, Ram. Bye.'

Ram washed his face, went to the kitchen to wish Kiran good morning, quickly got ready and headed out on Bineesh's bike.

Finding the address Anandhi had provided was challenging and took a lot of time. When he reached Guindy, his usual train had left and Malli was nowhere to be seen.

'Malli left?' Ram asked when he spotted the elderly samosa vendor.

'She's not well, mone,' she replied sadly.

'What? What happened all of a sudden?'

'These things happen. The police took her yesterday. Her friends said she was badly tortured.'

'Do you know where she lives?' Ram enquired.

'That's easy. They all live under the Kathipara bridge.'

'Alright.'

He hurried up the railway overbridge.

The Kathipara bridge was just a five-minute walk from Guindy railway station. Ram navigated through the street vendors and reached the lower part of the bridge.

Multicoloured sarees were used to create 'rooms' all around, but they were all empty. As he looked around, he noticed someone lying in a saree-tent near a pillar. Next to the pillar, black residue and waste from drainage were piled up. Despite the ample space, the proximity of the trash to the makeshift tents struck him as deeply unfair. The stench was unbearable.

When he approached the occupied saree-tent, he saw Malli lying on a plastic mat. Photos of Lord Ganesha, Tamil actor Vijay and actress Nayanthara were stuck on the pillar next to her.

'Malli,' he called softly.

Seeing Ram, Malli smiled weakly from her position. Her lips were bruised and her cheeks were swollen—all the signs of brutal beatings.

'What happened?' he asked, kneeling beside her, concern evident in his voice.

'Maybe I'm more beautiful than the policemen's wives, Ram. Why else would they come after me when they have them?' she said, forcing a smile.

'Come on, let's go to a hospital.'

'For what? This is routine for us. It'll get better in a couple of days,' Malli replied nonchalantly.

'Why don't you file a complaint against them?'

'You mean complain to them about them, huh?'

'Not to the police. Maybe you could go to the district collector or a minister or someone higher up.'

'Listen, Ram, even if one of us is found dead on the streets, we won't get any more attention than a stray dog. We have no one to speak for us. Even if someone raises a voice, no one cares to listen or pay attention. The only way out is to live like this.'

Ram fell silent, unable to find words.

'Anyway, I'm leaving Chennai soon. Maybe this will be my last memory,' she said with a sad smile.

Ram spent some more time with her before leaving for the railway station, making sure to buy her food to last till the evening.

It was past 10.30 a.m. when he reached the college.

'Hey, how come you're late? What happened? You didn't answer my call either,' Anandhi asked as soon as she saw Ram.

'Did you think I ran off with your money?' Ram teased, handing her the envelope.

'Never!' she replied, placing the envelope in her bag.

'Malli was tortured by the police yesterday. I went to check on her.'

'Oh no! How is she now?'

'She's managing. Anyway, I need to get to class. See you during the break,' he said, heading up the stairs.

'Wait, it's Mr Thayalan's class now. Don't mention this. He might not take it well and might misunderstand.'

He nodded and went upstairs.

Mr Thayalan was lecturing on modern cinema when Ram entered. He immediately asked Ram why he was late.

'Sir, I went to check on an aruvani friend who was unwell.'

'Are you mocking me?' Mr Thayalan retorted.

'No, sir. She's my friend, and I heard she wasn't well, so I went to see her.'

'Alright. It's my session until noon. You can join after that,' he said sternly.

Reshma and Vetri, seated at the back, watched the exchange intently.

'Okay, sir,' Ram replied and left without further protest.

Seeing him come down the stairs so soon, Anandhi understood what had happened.

'I expected this,' she said with a smile.

'And he's teaching about modern cinema. What an irony!'

'The printer here is faulty. I need to get some printouts done and am heading to the next street. Want to come?'

'Yeah, why not?'

Before heading to Nungambakkam Street, she informed the woman who was watering the plants in the garden to call her if anyone came to the reception.

The street was bustling. Street vendors and buyers had created quite a commotion, and the constant blaring of horns from those trying to move through this chaos only added to the noise. At the printing shop, an elderly man was working. Anandhi handed him her pen drive and then gave him the envelope containing the money that Ram had delivered. He told her to come back in fifteen minutes for the printed copies.

She led Ram to a nearby public park.

'Why did you give that money to him?' Ram asked as they walked.

'He's coordinating today's food arrangements. The money is for that.'

They reached the park and sat on a yellow bench. In the shady corners of the park, couples were nestled together.

'I come here sometimes. For some reason, no one ever picks this bench. So, it's always available for me,' she said.

Ram looked around. Directly opposite their bench was an autorickshaw stand. Some drivers were discreetly glancing at Ram and Anandhi, perhaps hoping for some drama. He chuckled at the thought.

'Look, there's that cop we met yesterday at the beach,' Ram pointed out.

Anandhi turned and saw the same young, tall policeman, now in civilian clothes, walking along the road in front of the park, carrying some vegetables.

'Seems like he lives nearby,' Ram observed. 'He's even doing some grocery shopping.'

Anandhi suddenly took out her phone and made a call. 'Hello, it seems the weather is hot today. I'm heading out. I'll collect the prints tomorrow,' she said and hung up. Looking at Ram, she got up from the bench and said, 'Let's go.'

Ram was puzzled.

As they walked back towards the college, he noticed that the shop where they had left the pen drive had its shutters down.

23

One

Malli was both excited and nervous about seeing her mother after five long years, especially since she would be meeting her in her new avatar, one her mother had not seen before. That evening, she and Ram went to T. Nagar to buy clothes and sweets for her family.

Later, as they walked back from the Guindy railway station towards where Malli was staying, Ram asked, 'Do they know you've changed your gender?'

'I sent a photo to Amma,' Malli replied. 'She later told me that she showed it to Dad and my brother.'

'What did they say?'

'It seems they laughed a lot.'

'Well, what if they don't accept you?'

Malli's smile faltered for a moment, but she quickly regained it.

'Don't say so, Ram. I know my mother will support me, no matter what. And when I give my brother the new bike, he'll be on my side, too. After that, I'll do whatever it takes to convince my father to let me be at home. Even if they say I can never leave the house again, I'll agree. I'm so tired of this place, Ram. All my friends here feel the same. We all live in temporary shelters under the bridge and dream of having a safe place to stay. None of us want to be forced into trading our bodies or living as slaves. We wish we could have regular jobs, but that still feels like a distant dream. Though my friends are sad to see me go, they're happy that at least one of us will get a better life. And, Ram, I hope you don't mind if I ask you to visit them and spend time with them, even after I'm gone. Most people avoid us and don't bother to talk, but you're different. Some nights, when we all sit together for dinner, we often talk about you. They all like you, Ram.'

Ram nodded, and they continued walking in silence for a while.

As they neared the Kathipara bridge, Ram asked Malli, 'If I come with you, to where you're staying, will you have enough food for one more person?'

Malli's face lit up with a wide smile.

That evening, Ram had dinner with Malli and her friends. Even though their jokes and way of talking were different than what he was used to, he joined in.

He thought to himself that if he owned even a small piece of land in Chennai, he would build a little house as a safe haven for those thirteen friends. By 9.30 p.m., he said goodbye and caught the bus to Iyyappanthangal. Malli showed her friends the things she had bought to take home.

She had two days left before she returned to her hometown, Salem.

Two

The next day, a Saturday, Vetri convinced a family he knew to let Anandhi organize their upcoming birthday party. Ram, Vetri and Reshma took charge of setting everything up. Paatti made all the sweets, including laddus and jalebis, for the event, which had over two hundred guests.

For Anandhi, this was a trial run. She realized she could earn more profit by doing the event herself instead of hiring outsiders.

Plus, by using Paatti's homemade sweets instead of bakery ones, she hoped to improve her margins even more. That evening, after paying the catering team, they all gathered in Paatti's living room. Anandhi divided the day's profit into five shares, with each person receiving three thousand rupees.

'Not bad! How about making us your partners?' Vetri asked, folding the money and putting it in his pocket.

'Oh no! Please spare me! I'm not a machine that can churn out sweets in bulk. I barely slept an hour last night and still have to finish making sweets for the bakery. I quit this partnership!' Paatti said, getting up and heading to the kitchen.

'That's okay, we'll convince her later. No worries. But seriously, this partnership idea is working out well for me, too,' Anandhi said, laughing.

Just then, Reshma got a call. She covered her mouth in disbelief as she listened, then said thanks and hung up.

'I've been selected as a supporting actress in Mani Ratnam's movie. It's a comedy role,' she said, beaming with excitement.

Anandhi jumped up, ran to Reshma and hugged her tightly. Vetri and Ram cheered loudly. Paatti came running from the kitchen.

'No matter how much noise you make, I'm not joining your business. Period,' she said firmly.

'Hey, oldie! I got selected for a movie!' Reshma pushed Anandhi aside, who was hugging her, and announced.

'So, you're not joining the business either, right? Well done!'

All four of them burst into laughter at that.

They decided to celebrate Reshma's big news. While Vetri and Ram went to buy beer, Anandhi and Reshma went out for food and snacks.

Ram called Bineesh to let him know that he would be staying at Paatti's house that night. Reshma called home, too. By 9 p.m., they had gathered on the open terrace on the second floor.

Except for Paatti and Anandhi, who had wine, the other three enjoyed beer. Reshma had half a beer, while Vetri and Ram had two each.

'So, she's the first among us to achieve her dream,' Ram said as he set down his second empty bottle.

'Well, what about your dreams? You haven't shared them yet,' Paatti asked, looking at Anandhi, Ram and Vetri.

'Now that Reshma's in the movies, Ram and I will be her assistant directors,' Vetri said with fake modesty. 'As for Anandhi, who knows!'

'Yeah, right. As if Mani Ratnam is eagerly waiting to hire you two,' Reshma teased.

'Look, how haughty she is! True to her newfound tribe! Let me tell you, those who trust you are fu—,' Vetri started, but Ram cut him off before he could finish.

'I want to write a novel set in Chennai, Paatti. If possible, I'd like to turn it into a movie, too. That's my goal,' Ram said.

'Then I'll be the co-director of that movie. Starting today, that's my new goal,' Vetri said, adopting his humble act again.

'Vetri, please!' Reshma said, folding her hands, as if begging.

'What about you, Anandhi?' Paatti asked, noticing her quietly listening.

'I don't have any specific goals, Paatti,' Anandhi replied, trying to dodge the question.

'That's not true! I'm sure you're saving every penny with a plan in mind. Tell us,' Reshma urged.

'Yeah, I want to know, too,' Vetri chimed in.

'Now that we're all so close, why not share it?' Ram added.

Anandhi glanced at Paatti, unsure. Paatti wasn't pushing her like the others, but her curiosity was evident.

'Oh, I really don't have any specific goals. Trust me!'

Though not convinced, the others didn't press further.

That night, Ram slept in Vetri's room, while Reshma and Anandhi shared Paatti's room.

Three

Around midnight, Reshma woke up, startled by a noise. As her eyes adjusted to the dark, she saw Anandhi tiptoeing out of the room. Curious and suspicious, Reshma got up without waking Paatti and followed her. Anandhi headed towards the main door, switched off the front yard light and quickly walked towards the gate. Reshma hid behind a cushioned chair in the corridor.

Suddenly, a figure appeared near the gate. Anandhi opened the gate just a crack and the person slipped inside. Anandhi led him upstairs to her room, closing the door behind them. Reshma's heart pounded as she realized what was happening. She panicked, realizing that someone she cared about deeply might be doing something wrong. She even considered waking the others, including Paatti, to catch Anandhi in the act. She was torn between the two thoughts. But then she thought about Ram, who clearly had a special fondness for Anandhi, and how shocked he would be if he found out.

While Reshma was lost in thought, the door to Anandhi's room opened, snapping her back to reality.

Anandhi came down the stairs first, quickly scanning the surroundings before signalling the man to follow. As he descended, he lifted his shirt and tucked the packet he was carrying securely between his pants and his stomach.

Reshma desperately wished for just a bit of light to fall on his face so she could see him clearly.

After he left through the gate, Anandhi opened the back of her phone, swapped the SIM card and made a call, speaking in hushed tones. Then, she replaced the SIM with her usual one and headed back into the house.

Reshma quickly crawled back to the room, ran to her bed and lay down just in time. Anandhi turned the front yard light back on, closed the door and lay down to sleep.

While Anandhi quickly drifted off to sleep, Reshma couldn't do the same. She kept glancing at Anandhi's face in the faint light that filtered into the room.

The next morning, when Reshma woke up, Anandhi had already left. Paatti was busy preparing breakfast in the kitchen.

Reshma washed her face, freshened up and went to the kitchen. 'Paatti, when will Anandhi be back?'

'Around ten.'

Reshma glanced at the clock. It was just past 7 a.m.

'Paatti, do you have a spare key to Anandhi's room?'

Paatti, who was placing fresh, hot idlis into the casserole, looked at her. 'What are you up to?'

'I want to give her a surprise, Paatti. Come on, do you have another key?' Reshma asked, playfully insisting.

'Yes, I have a spare key. But if you're planning to cause any trouble, leave me out of it. Understood?' Paatti warned.

'Never, Paatti. Please, just give me the key,' Reshma said, tugging on Paatti's pallu with a grin.

'There's a red bag inside the small drawer of my cupboard. The key's in there.'

Reshma hurried to Paatti's room.

She found the red bag in the cupboard and emptied it on to the cot. The key to Anandhi's room fell out along with a few papers. Reshma noticed it was Anandhi's rental agreement and higher secondary certificate. She quickly took a photo of the certificate with her phone, put everything back in the cupboard and headed upstairs.

The door to Vetri's room was closed, so she assumed Vetri and Ram were still fast asleep.

Before unlocking Anandhi's room with the spare key, Reshma peeked out at the road one last time. She then carefully opened the door, slipped inside and locked it behind her. It was her first time in Anandhi's room. As she turned on the light, her heart skipped a beat. The walls were covered with photographs of various sizes of actress Trisha. What shocked her even more was that Anandhi had never mentioned this actress in any of their conversations.

The room had a cot, a wooden cupboard, a table and a chair, just like Vetri's room. Reshma scanned everything without touching anything. She noticed that one corner of the bed seemed slightly raised. Slipping her hand underneath, she found a small diary hidden there. It was a diary with a lock, the kind often advertised during the New Year season, bound with a leather strap and secured with a small padlock. She searched the room for the key but couldn't find it. A million questions about Anandhi flooded her mind.

Just then, she then heard the door to Vetri's room open. Quickly, she put the diary back in its place, turned off the light and stood still, holding her breath. Listening closely, she realized that someone had gone downstairs, entered the toilet, closed the door behind them, come out after a couple of minutes, returned upstairs and closed the room again.

Once everything was quiet, Reshma quickly left Anandhi's room.

24

One

Ram and Vetri woke up at 9.30 a.m. After freshening up, they headed to the kitchen, where Paatti and Reshma were feasting on idlis.

'Oh, so you two are enjoying idlis without waiting for us? How unfair! By the way, where's Anandhi?' Vetri asked.

Reshma gave him a firm look just as they heard the Luna's familiar sound outside.

'There she is!' Ram said, turning towards the courtyard.

Anandhi parked the scooter and waved to Ram and Vetri.

'I'll take a quick shower and be right back,' she said, heading upstairs.

'Is she going to be surprised now?' Paatti asked Reshma in a low voice.

'Not yet. I've just started working on it. Soon,' Reshma replied.

Although Paatti didn't fully understand, she smiled.

'Come, join us. We have delicious coconut and groundnut chutneys with the idlis today,' Paatti invited Ram and Vetri.

While they were eating, Anandhi joined them with a wet towel wrapped around her hair, freshly bathed.

Reshma, usually full of jokes, was unusually quiet, which didn't go unnoticed.

'What's got into you?' Vetri asked, nudging her with his shoulder.

'Amma gave me an earful this morning, so I need to go,' Reshma said, coming up with a quick excuse.

'She's impossible,' Vetri said angrily.

'Should I talk to her?' Paatti asked.

'No, it's better if I handle this myself. I haven't told her about the movie yet. Once I do, she'll calm down,' Reshma replied.

Just then, Ram received a call from Malli.

'Hi, Malli. What's up?'

'Ram, the showroom executive called. They said the bike can be delivered tomorrow morning. I'm leaving early morning tomorrow too, so if you're free today, could you come to Guindy? I'd like to see you.'

'Of course! I'm nearby. I'll be there soon.'

'Okay, Ram. Bye.'

As the call ended, Ram turned to Reshma. 'I'm coming with you. Malli is leaving for her hometown early tomorrow, and I need to see her.'

As they left the house after breakfast, Reshma glanced at Anandhi, who was standing there with a warm smile. Reshma smiled back before hopping on the back of the scooter that Ram had started.

As they drove away, Paatti and Anandhi waved goodbye. But a hint of doubt had started to creep on to Vetri's face.

Ram parked the scooter near Guindy railway station and got off.

'You all right?' he asked, handing Reshma the helmet.

'There's something, but I'll explain later. Bye for now.'

She put on the helmet and sped off. Watching her leave, Ram had an inkling of some sort, but he brushed it off and called Malli.

When she mentioned she was under the bridge, he went to her. When he arrived, all thirteen of them were there. Malli handed him a carry bag in front of everyone. Inside, he found a pair of jeans and a shirt.

'Oh no! Why did you spend money on this?' he asked.

'What if this is our last meeting? You should have something to remember me by,' Malli replied.

For Ram, just like Malli, it was the first time someone had gifted him clothes.

Malli noticed his silence and asked, 'Shall we take the train to T. Nagar?'

'Sure. Should I wear this outfit?' he responded.

She gestured towards a room set off by plastic sheets, next to a pillar. 'We change in there.'

He went inside with the carry bag, which held sky-blue jeans and a black shirt.

Even though Malli wasn't sure about the size, when Ram came out, everyone agreed that the clothes fit him well.

After saying goodbye to her friends, they walked together to Guindy railway station.

Since it was Sunday, the station wasn't crowded. The elderly samosa vendor hugged Malli tightly and kissed her forehead. After she left, Malli turned to Ram.

'Ram, I want to show you something. Come.'

She led him to the cement bench where Ram always waited for the train. Next to his name, which he had written with a marker pen some time earlier, Malli's name was now added.

Ram looked at her, touched by the gesture.

'Let me have a place beside your name, at least on this cement bench.'

As soon as Malli said it, a train pulled in, its horn blaring. Malli and Ram boarded the compartment and took their usual spots at the door, facing each other.

Ram's mind was occupied with Malli's words. He glanced at her from time to time, realizing that beneath her self-assured exterior was hidden affection.

They got off at Mambalam railway station and strolled casually through the bustling streets of T. Nagar. When the crowd thickened, Ram held Malli's hand tightly.

'It's easy to get lost in this crowd,' he said, echoing the words Malli had once said to him. She squeezed his hand and smiled.

People around stared, but Ram ignored them. He walked with her to the end of the street, enjoying the view, before they entered the old man's shop that sold lassi—the same place they had visited before. After finishing their drinks, they headed back to Mambalam station. They caught the next train and returned to Guindy.

'So, from tomorrow, you won't be here on this platform with the samosa vendor?' Ram asked as they walked towards the Kathipara bridge.

Malli remained silent.

When they reached a fork in the road—one path leading under the Kathipara bridge and the other to the bus stop—they stopped.

Ram looked at Malli. Malli looked back at him. Then Ram hugged her.

'Listen, Kalidas. Wherever you are, in whatever form or style, always be happy. That's all I want for you. I'll pray to God that you become my child in the next life, and then I'll protect you as my dearest, keeping you safe from all harm,' he said.

With that, he turned away and hurried to the bus stop without looking back.

Malli stood there, watching him walk away. She had thought about going with him to a studio to take a photo together, but then she had decided it was better to keep his smiling face and their fond moments safe in her memory.

When Ram returned to his apartment, it was already past 2 p.m. Bineesh and Kiran were heading to the supermarket, so he joined them. Thus, his Sunday passed.

Two

It took a long five and a half hours for the train to reach Salem. Malli's house was in a place called Attur in Salem. As she stepped on to the platform, memories flooded back—of a dawn five years ago when she had left for Chennai with her beloved.

She pulled out her phone and called Mani, the showroom executive who had been in touch with her. He arrived at the station with a car from the showroom within fifteen minutes. Attur was nearly sixty kilometres from Salem railway station. Being a small, underdeveloped village, they relied heavily on Salem city for trading vehicles.

When Malli had shared her plans with Mani, he had promised to do everything he could to help surprise her younger brother.

'How was the journey?' Mani asked as he placed her luggage in the car's boot.

'It was fine. But where's the Bullet?' she asked, glancing around.

'Two guys from the showroom have already taken it to Attur. They'll add some small decorations before arriving at the village. I'll bring them with me on the way back,' Mani replied humbly.

Malli had already confided in Mani about her worries—fearful of how her father and brother might react when they saw her. Her heart raced as they neared the village. Mani parked the car by the roadside, about a kilometre from Attur.

Malli spotted a black Bullet then, adorned with orange ribbons and garlands. She stepped out of the car. Two guys wearing black T-shirts with Royal Enfield logos stood beside it. When they saw Malli with Mani, their senior executive, they looked at her in awe. Mani discreetly signalled to them not to stare.

'Thank you, brothers,' she said, smiling at them.

They smiled back. Once Mani saw that Malli was pleased with the bike, he invited her to get back in the car so that they could go ahead.

Though the alleys had changed slightly, the untarred road next to the Vinayakan Temple and its pond was still familiar. Malli gave directions to Mani as they drove. The two guys followed slowly on the Bullet. When she stepped into the courtyard of her home after five long years, a wave of emotions hit her.

The small two-room house looked even older, with layers of fungus and smoke staining the walls.

Seeing a car approach the house, children and elderly neighbours stepped out to watch. The guys on the Bullet parked it in front of the house, set it on its central stand and moved aside.

'Well, you may leave,' Malli said to Mani as she got out of the car.

'Usually, when we deliver vehicles, we take photos,' Mani said, pulling out a digital camera from his pocket.

'You know my concerns. I have no idea what to expect here. If anything goes wrong, please leave immediately,' Malli replied.

As they spoke, Malli's mother came out of the house. Though she knew that Malli was coming soon, the sudden arrival caught her off-guard. She wasn't mentally prepared. She looked at her child, now dressed in a woman's attire, getting out of the car. Then she looked around and saw both surprise and scorn on the faces of those who recognized Kalidas.

Mani also got out of the car and retrieved Malli's luggage from the boot. Malli smiled broadly as she saw her mother. Her mother rushed towards her.

Malli hugged her.

'Why did you come during the day?' her mother asked, pulling back from the hug.

The smile on Malli's face faded.

'Hey Kali, how are you, girl?' a man her age who lived across the street called out teasingly, holding his son in his arms.

The mild commotion on the road drew more neighbours out of their homes, including Malli's younger brother, Kavidas. As soon as she saw him, she gestured to the boys from the showroom, indicating that he was the one.

Five years have turned him into a handsome man with a beard, Malli thought as she gave him a warm smile and walked towards him.

Mani pulled out a large cardboard cutout, shaped like a bike's key, from the backseat of his car.

'Kavi, I've got a gift for you. Come and give it a try,' she said, pointing to the decorated Bullet.

Kavidas looked around and noticed that he and his mother had become a subject of ridicule for the neighbours and passersby. He turned his gaze to Malli.

'Take this and leave,' he said coldly. Malli, however, kept smiling, her expression unwavering.

Their father, fresh from his bath and still wearing a towel, emerged from the toilet in front of the house. He, too, noticed everyone staring at them.

'I'm not going back, Kavi. I have come to stay with you. I bought this bike for you, after fighting many odds,' she said, her voice full of love.

'What odds?' he asked, his teeth clenched.

Malli fell silent, unsure of what to say.

Mani and his staff stood awkwardly, unsure whether to stay or leave, still holding the cutout of the key.

'How dare you come here dressed like an aruvani?' her father shouted as he entered the scene.

Malli lowered her head. The crowd began to murmur and pass comments about Kalidas, now Malli, standing before them. A quick look later, Malli recognized many of them as the same people who had abused her as a child.

Malli looked at her father. 'Appa, may I come inside? You can scold me all you want in private. Please,' she pleaded.

He didn't respond, his body trembling with rage.

Mani's staff glanced at him, silently asking if they should leave.

Kavidas, enraged by the humiliation his family was facing, suddenly kicked Malli in the chest with all his might. She hadn't expected such an attack from her own brother and fell on to the road, landing on her back. The cardboard cutout slipped from the staff's hands as they watched in shock.

Kavidas stormed into the house, seemingly out of his mind. Malli, who had believed her mother would stand by her, was crushed to see her more concerned about the onlookers than her child. Tears welled up in her eyes.

'You go around pleasuring men who undress in front of you, don't you? You filthy hooker,' her father spat, lifting the towel he was wearing.

'If we stay here any longer, we'll be no better than these people. Let's go,' Mani said to his staff.

They gave Malli a sympathetic look before getting back into the car.

Kavidas returned from the house, wielding a long iron rod. The sight of it made Malli realize his intent. She knew his habit of smashing anything he disliked since he was a child. Scrambling to her feet, she ran after him.

Kavidas charged toward the Bullet, smashing its headlight and speedometer. Shards of glass flew as he relentlessly attacked the bike. Mani and his staff, who were reversing their car, were stunned.

'Chettan bought this for you after working and begging for days. Please don't break it,' Malli pleaded, trying to stop him.

'You want me to ride something you earned by selling your ass, you filthy bitch?' he spat, before slapping Malli hard across the face and shoving her to the ground. Then he pounded the petrol tank, denting and disfiguring it.

Mani and the two other men jumped out of the car and rushed to stop Kavidas from causing more damage. Malli's mother and a neighbour, who was a friend of her father, also intervened and tried to restrain him.

Malli, who had managed to sit up, watched her brother unleash his fury in despair.

Finally, they managed to drag Kavidas inside the house.

Mani helped Malli to her feet and guided her to the car, but his words of consolation seemed to fall on deaf ears. One of the staff members kick-started the Bullet and found it was still running. They assured Malli that they would follow with the bike.

Without delay, they left Attur and headed to Salem railway station with Malli.

25

One

Ram and his friends were heading to Amma Unavagam during their lunch break, when Ram said with a smile, 'Malli must have reached home by now.'

Anandhi, Vetri and Reshma took a quick look at him as they walked on.

'Why is she so special to you, machaa?' Vetri asked.

'Why are you three special to me? It's just like that. Beyond explanation.'

'Anyway, I'm glad she escaped from those aruvanis,' Reshma said, relieved.

'You shouldn't call them "aruvanis". The proper term is "thirunangai". That's what they should be called,' Anandhi corrected her.

Reshma looked at Anandhi and gave a small smile.

'Thirunangai ...' Ram repeated softly to himself.

By then, they had reached the unavagam. As they started eating, an alarm went off on Reshma's phone. She quickly turned it off and pretended to take a call.

'Yeah, Amma, tell me.'

Hearing that it was Reshma's mother on the line, Vetri scoffed and continued eating.

'I promise I'm not with Vetri. I'm with Anandhi. Here, I'll call you back from her phone right now,' she said, pretended to end the call, and then looked at Anandhi.

'Anandhi, can you please lend me your phone? Yesterday, my silly brother stuck a beer bottle sticker on my dress, and Amma spotted it right away. She warned me that I won't be allowed to go to college if I keep hanging out with him. If I call her from your number, she'll be relieved. She still thinks you two are enemies,' Reshma explained, stretching out her hand.

Anandhi pulled out her keypad phone from the side pocket of her bag and handed it to Reshma.

'I swear I didn't put any sticker on your dress,' Vetri protested, trying to defend himself to Anandhi.

'Whatever, I'm the one who's in trouble,' Reshma sighed.

She dialled her mother's number from Anandhi's phone. 'Hello, Amma, can you hear me? Hello?'

Reshma pretended that the noise around her was making it hard to hear anything and moved towards the door.

'Amma, hello,' she repeated from the doorway of the unavagam, making sure her friends could hear, before stepping outside.

'Reshma, is that you? I can hear you. Whose number is this?' her mother asked.

'Amma, I'm just testing a call. Please don't hang up. Hold on for a minute.'

She quickly licked the food off her fingers and pulled out another keypad phone from her pocket. She opened the back flap of Anandhi's phone and, and as expected, found a BSNL SIM card.

Reshma glanced back inside the Unavagam to make sure no one was watching and then did a quick Google search on her phone: 'How to find my BSNL number.'

Seeing the result '*888#' on her screen, Reshma quickly inserted Anandhi's SIM card into her keypad phone and waited for the signal to appear.

'Amma, just hold on a bit longer, don't disconnect,' she said, keeping Anandhi's phone pressed to her ear.

As soon as the SIM card caught signal, she dialled the code she had found on Google. Within seconds, the number of Anandhi's secret SIM appeared on the screen. Reshma quickly typed the number into her smartphone. Then she carefully removed the SIM card and placed it back into Anandhi's phone, just as it was before.

'Amma, the phone was under repair. I was just testing it. You can hang up now. And please don't call back on this number, okay?'

'You troublemaker! You could only think of me for your testing, huh? Get lost!' her mother scolded before disconnecting the call.

Reshma, feeling triumphant, sent the number to a contact saved as Simba. Satisfied with her achievement, she walked back into the unavagam.

Two

That evening, as soon as classes ended, Reshma headed straight to St Thomas Mount, a hilltop spot near Chennai International Airport, without waiting for Vetri and Ram. The location was popular for watching sunsets and aeroplanes take off and land.

Reshma joined the crowd that had gathered to watch the sunset and took out her phone, dialling the contact saved as 'Simba'. After a few rings, the person on the other end disconnected the call.

Reshma had visited St Thomas Mount some time ago with a friend, but since the friend had managed all the arrangements that day, she was unaware of the details. Now, needing assistance, Reshma had managed to get the contact information from that same friend.

'Hi,' came a voice from behind. Reshma turned around.

A lean young man, wearing sunglasses, a black jacket and a cap, stood there.

'Simba?' she asked, uncertain.

'Yes,' he replied.

Without hesitation, Reshma discreetly handed him three five-hundred-rupee notes clenched in her fist. In exchange, he passed her a folded piece of paper before disappearing into the crowd.

Hurrying to her parked scooter, Reshma unfolded the paper to find a one-month call history of Anandhi's secret number. She noticed that, aside from the call Anandhi had made the previous night, all calls were to just two other numbers. Calls made during the day were to one number, while calls past midnight were to an international number.

She quickly opened the Truecaller app and searched for the two numbers. The Indian number was listed as 'Sudha Akka', suggesting it was a common contact. The foreign number, however, returned no results. Feeling that something was off, Reshma decided not to linger at the church and went home.

As soon as she got home, Reshma called Vetri.

'Vetri, where are you?'

'I'm at Koyambedu right now. What's up?'

'Take the day off from college tomorrow. We need to go to Vaniyambadi.'

'Vaniyambadi? Wait, isn't that Anandhi's hometown? What's going on?'

'Yes, it's her hometown. We need to go there. And, most importantly, don't mention this to anyone, not even Ram. I'll text you after checking the train schedules.'

Vetri was puzzled, unsure of Reshma's intentions.

Three

At the apartment in Iyyappanthangal, Ram was sitting on the balcony with Kiran, his phone in his hand, debating whether to call Malli.

'She probably just got home. She has your number, so she might call when she gets a chance,' Kiran suggested.

Ram agreed that it made sense.

When Bineesh called them in for dinner, they both went inside. The evening passed uneventfully.

The next morning, as Ram descended the stairs to platform 2, he was shocked to see Malli sitting on the bench he usually occupied, staring blankly at the railway tracks.

Alarmed, he hurried over to her. Even as he approached, her gaze remained fixed on the tracks. Ram sensed something was very wrong.

'Malli.' He gently placed his hand on her shoulder and called her name. Her eyes, brimming with tears, finally overflowed. She wrapped her arms around his waist and cried uncontrollably.

'What's wrong, Malli? If you cry like this, people will start thinking something else is going on. Tell me what happened, then you can cry all you want,' Ram said, looking around and gently lifting Malli's face.

Through her sobs, Malli recounted everything that had happened during her visit home. Ram was at a loss for words, unsure of how to comfort her.

'I've never sat behind someone on a bike, Ram. Whenever I saw people riding close together, I always wished I could do that. When I bought the bike, I dreamed of riding with my brother. But he destroyed it right in front of me. What he destroyed wasn't just the bike, Ram. It was … it was …' Malli clutched her chest, unable to finish.

Though his usual train had arrived by then, Ram didn't board it. 'I'm not going to college today,' he said firmly.

Malli stared blankly at the platform, as if her dreams and hopes had been completely shattered. As the train left without them, Ram made up his mind and turned to Malli.

'I'll be back in an hour. Don't go anywhere. I'm leaving my bag here,' he said, pressing her hands and placing his bag next to her. Then he hurried out of the station.

The samosa vendor on platform 1 noticed Malli and rushed over to her.

Instead of heading to the bus stop, Ram, for the first time, asked someone where the auto stand was.

Four

Vetri and Reshma stepped off the train at Vaniyambadi and took an autorickshaw towards their destination.

'Can you please tell me what's going on now?' Vetri asked in a low voice, ensuring the driver wouldn't overhear.

'Just wait a little longer. I need to confirm something first. Once I do, I'll explain everything,' Reshma replied.

Vetri felt a surge of frustration at her tone but kept it to himself, staring at the passing scenery.

Vaniyambadi was a semi-rural area. In some places, it felt as though parts of the town had simply been dropped into a village setting. Vetri noticed that the small canal by the road had water that looked milky white, piquing his curiosity.

'Why is the water so white?' he asked the driver.

'This area has a lot of small shops that make chemicals like phenyl. That's the residue,' the driver responded disinterestedly.

Lean stray dogs were drinking the polluted water from the canal. Roughly thirty minutes later, the driver pulled over.

'This is the street you asked for,' he told Reshma, pointing down a long road.

'Vetri, get out,' Reshma said as she stepped out of the autorickshaw. Vetri followed, looking around.

'You might have trouble finding a ride back, and I probably won't get another passenger to the station either. Should I wait here? I won't charge you for the wait. Will you be long?' the driver offered.

'Can't say. You don't need to wait. You can go,' she replied, taking money out of her bag.

'I can wait for an hour if you need. You don't have to pay extra,' the driver offered again, almost pleading.

'That's okay. How much is the fare?' Reshma asked.

'Two hundred and fifty.'

'Here you go.'

She handed him two hundred rupees and a fifty-rupee note. He tucked the money into his pocket, gave a quick salute with his hand as a farewell and then turned his autorickshaw around.

Reshma walked over to a small vegetable shop nearby. An elderly woman, probably in her sixties, was sorting through tomatoes, separating the fresh ones from the rotten.

'Excuse me, do you know where Anandhi's house is on this street? She works in Chennai now,' Reshma asked.

The old woman glanced at Reshma, and then at Vetri, who was still standing on the road.

'There are a lot of Anandhis around here. Do you know her father's name?' the woman asked.

Reshma quickly checked the photo of Anandhi's school certificate on her phone.

'R. Ramaswamy,' she replied.

'Oh, that Ramaswamy? The one who's part of Sudha's group? They moved away a long time ago. Now they live in the same area as her. What's the matter?' the woman asked.

At the mention of 'Sudha', a flood of questions filled Reshma's mind. She figured this must be the same 'Sudha Akka' that Anandhi frequently contacted.

'Nothing in particular. I just need to visit them. Where does this Sudha live?' Reshma enquired.

'It's near the school. Walk straight for about fifteen minutes, then take a left.'

'Thank you so much,' Reshma said, folding her hands in gratitude before returning to Vetri.

'We should have kept that autorickshaw,' she muttered, looking at the road ahead.

'What happened?'

'The family we're looking for has moved further down the road.'

'Reshma, can you please tell me what's going on now? Enough with the suspense!' Vetri said, irritated.

'It's nothing, Vetri. Just a little surprise for our Anandhi. Come on, let's head in the direction the woman pointed.'

Reshma began walking. Vetri followed, clearly disinterested.

Five

Ram returned to Guindy railway station a while later. Malli was still sitting on the same bench, staring ahead blankly, with his bag on her lap. Next to her, the samosa vendor sat on the platform.

'Malli, come with me,' Ram said. She looked at him with a vacant expression.

'Please, just come,' he urged, gently pulling her hand like one would with a child.

Malli stood up with a deep sigh and then followed his lead like a machine.

The samosa vendor followed them, carrying her basket along. When they descended the foot overbridge and reached the main road, Ram pointed to the side.

Malli's eyes followed his hand to a black Royal Enfield Classic Bullet.

'You said that you haven't had a chance to ride on a bike with anyone. Let me be the first. I will take you on a bike ride,' he said, gripping her hand firmly.

The samosa vendor smiled at them. 'What are you thinking? Go with him, dear. He's inviting you, isn't he?' she said gently, nudging Malli, who was hesitant.

Malli looked at her and then at Ram, realizing that his eyes were filled with genuine concern for her.

'Who are you to me, Ram? Why are you spending your precious time and money on me?' she asked, her eyes brimming with tears once more.

Seeing her on the verge of crying again, Ram gently pulled her towards the bike. Malli, unfamiliar with sitting on a bike, awkwardly climbed on it, trying to mimic what she had seen others do, her hands resting on Ram's shoulders.

'Settled?' he asked.

'Hmm,' she replied.

Noting that Malli wasn't sure about how to sit on a bike, Ram guided her right hand around to rest on his chest.

'Don't be scared. Hold on tight,' he instructed as he started the bike.

The old woman watched them leave, smiling.

As they rode, Malli clung tightly to Ram's chest, observing the passing vehicles. It was hard for her to distinguish whether she felt happiness or sorrow. The pain from her brother's actions still lingered heavily, both physically and emotionally.

Ram took Malli directly to his college. Anandhi eyed them suspiciously as they came through the stairs and into the reception area.

'I need to see Principal Srinivas urgently. We agreed on something that day, didn't we? I need to discuss it. You should come with me for support,' Ram said in one breath.

Anandhi stood up from her chair. They helped Malli into a seat in the reception area before heading to Principal Srinivas's office.

Though Malli had no idea what was happening, she waited as instructed. After about twenty minutes, Ram and Anandhi emerged from the office and looked at Malli. Unsure of what was going on, Malli approached the desk. Anandhi opened a drawer, took out a small packet and handed it to Malli.

Malli looked at both of them anxiously before opening the packet.

Inside were a pair of ghungroos.

'A new batch is starting at the dance academy next week. I won't let you enter the classroom without these, understand?' Anandhi said with a smile.

The ghungroos tinkled in Malli's hands. Her trembling palms betrayed her sheer joy.

Six

Vetri and Reshma stood facing each other in front of a locked house in Vaniyambadi.

26

One

'Vidyananda Higher Secondary School, Vaniyambadi,' Reshma read out from the arched entrance in front of her.

After discovering that Anandhi's home was locked, Reshma had brought Vetri back to the school they had seen earlier. Since Anandhi's certificate had mentioned this school, Reshma headed inside and told the peon she needed to see the principal. He asked them to wait for five minutes.

'Reshma, I still don't understand what you're trying to do. I have a bad feeling about this. What if Anandhi finds out?' Vetri said, sitting on one of the steel chairs outside the office.

'Why are you worried about Anandhi? We just had some questions and came to her village to get answers. That's all.'

'If we have questions, we can ask her directly. Is she doing anything that could harm us? No, right? So, why are we playing detective?'

'Vetri, my doubts might turn out to be right or wrong. We've come this far, so why not wait a little longer? Please?' Reshma pleaded, folding her hands.

The peon signalled that they could enter. Before going inside, Reshma motioned to Vetri that she would handle everything.

The office was a spacious, air-conditioned room. On the desk was a nameplate that read: Dr Kanaka Thilakam Perumal MA PhD (Tamil). The principal had a private library in the room. Upon

Reshma's arrival, she set her book, *Aasai Tilaka Aasai* by Tamil novelist Ramanichandran, face down on the table.

Reshma greeted Principal Kanaka Thilakam Perumal, who had a distinguished salt-and-pepper hairstyle and a warm smile.

'Vanakkam, madam.'

'Vanakkam. Please, have a seat,' the principal said, gesturing to the chairs.

Reshma sat down and said, 'We're here to speak with the class teacher of Anandhi Ramaswamy, who was in the Class XI and XII science with biology batch from 2010 to 2012. Is it possible to arrange that?'

The principal's eyebrows shot up in surprise.

'So, you didn't study here?' she asked.

'No, madam. We have come from Chennai to learn more about this particular student,' Reshma explained.

The principal removed her glasses, looking intrigued.

'We just need to clarify a small doubt. We went to her house, but it was locked. We thought someone here might know her, so we decided to come to the school. Since she achieved around 98 per cent in her Class XII board exams, there is a possibility her class teacher might remember her.'

The principal paused for a moment and then pressed a button. A peon hurried in.

'Chinna, go and fetch our Botany teacher.'

'Ms Amritha?' Chinna asked.

'Isn't she the only Botany teacher in this school, Chinna?' the principal replied, turning back to Reshma and Vetri. 'He's like that. No matter what we tell him, he always has more questions.'

Soon, Ms Amritha, a stout woman in her forties, entered the room.

'Madam, you called me?'

'Yes, yes. These people have come all the way from Chennai to inquire about one of your former students,' the principal said, gesturing towards Reshma. 'Ms Amritha has been the class teacher for our biology batch for the past ten years. You can ask her whatever you need to know.'

Reshma turned to Ms Amritha, eager to get some answers.

'Madam, do you remember Anandhi Ramaswamy? She graduated in 2012 with around 98 per cent marks.'

A smile of recognition immediately replaced the look of doubt on Ms Amritha's face.

'Of course, I remember! How could I forget? Anandhi was the top scorer in that batch and excelled in all activities. She's one of my favourite students.'

Hearing this, Vetri shot a look at Reshma, as if to ask whether she was satisfied with the response.

'Do you know her personally, madam? I mean, did she ever mention any issues at home—financial problems or anything like that?' Reshma probed further.

Ms Amritha's eyebrows furrowed at the question. 'When she was here, she never mentioned any such issues. But now ... her mother's condition is quite dire. Ever since Anandhi's sudden demise in that accident, I haven't seen a smile on her mother's face.'

'What!' Vetri and Reshma exclaimed in unison, shocked.

'Oh, that's the girl who passed away ...' the principal murmured to Ms Amritha, as if trying to recall the details.

Reshma quickly composed herself and pulled out her phone, opening Anandhi's certificate. She zoomed in on the photo and showed it to Ms Amritha.

'Are you sure you're talking about this person?' Reshma asked.

Ms Amritha looked at the photo, confused. 'Who is this?'

'This is the Anandhi we were asking about.'

'This isn't the Anandhi I was referring to. But there was only one Anandhi Ramaswamy in that batch,' Ms Amritha said, visibly puzzled.

The principal was also bewildered. 'Let's check this. Give me the registration number on the certificate you have. We keep copies of all certificates issued in our system,' she said and woke up her computer.

Reshma read out the registration number from her phone, which the principal carefully entered into the system. Ms Amritha watched the screen anxiously. Vetri and Reshma, growing more nervous, moved closer to the desk.

When the search result appeared, the principal double-clicked on it, bringing up the full certificate on the screen. The name, details, registration number and marks all matched the certificate Reshma had. The photo, however, was different. Vetri and Reshma were stunned.

'Oh my God! Someone has dared to forge a certificate in the name of a deceased person. That too under my watch as principal! This cannot be tolerated,' she said, reaching for the phone.

'Madam, please, wait a moment,' Reshma interjected. 'Do you know a woman named Sudha? The Anandhi we know is constantly in contact with her, and this Anandhi's father worked for Sudha.'

Upon hearing this, the principal instructed Ms Amritha to return to her class. She then turned to Reshma and Vetri. 'Please step outside for a while. I need to report this to the authorities. Don't worry, you'll be safe.'

'Madam, I'm certain that Sudha is involved in this. And if Anandhi's death was suspicious, shouldn't we investigate that too?' Reshma pressed.

'These are not matters we can handle on our own. Please wait outside,' the principal repeated firmly.

Vetri glanced at Reshma. After a brief moment of hesitation, they both left the office.

As they sat back down on the chairs outside, they saw Ms Amritha in a nearby building, motioning for them to come over. Though they were a little unsure, they walked towards her with a gentle smile.

'Listen, I don't know who you are or what you're after, but you need to leave as quickly as you can,' she whispered urgently. 'Sudha, the woman you mentioned, is the principal's younger sister. Anandhi's mother was a maid in Sudha's house, and her father was a worker there, too. This school, this village—it's not safe for you. Leave now, before Sudha's people come after you.'

Her words struck them like a bolt of lightning.

'What do we do?' Reshma asked her anxiously.

'Sudha is dangerous. You need to leave, as fast as you can,' Ms Amritha urged before quickly walking away.

Vetri grabbed Reshma's hand. 'Reshma, we need to get out of this damn place. Run!'

They sprinted. As they crossed the school grounds and reached the street, they heard Chinna, the peon, calling them from behind.

'If we take the main road, they'll find us easily. Let's take the side alleys,' Vetri suggested, guiding Reshma along a path in front of the school. They suddenly heard the roar of a jeep in the distance. Quickly, they ducked behind the gate of a nearby house.

The jeep stopped right in front of their hiding spot.

'What? They escaped? How is that possible?' a commanding female voice boomed from the jeep.

Vetri and Reshma cautiously peeked out and immediately recognized the woman sitting in the front seat of the jeep. She was the same woman who had frequently visited Paatti's house, pretending to be Anandhi's mother. Their hearts pounded with fear.

Chinna ran up to the jeep, panting. 'Sudha Akka, they ran that way,' he said, pointing down the road.

'Don't let them get away. Sami, turn the vehicle,' Sudha ordered.

The driver, Sami, began to reverse the jeep, through the gate where Vetri and Reshma were hiding. They hadn't anticipated this move. As the jeep turned, Sudha and the others in jeep spotted them behind the gate.

Two

Anandhi was heading to Amma Unavagam on Nungambakkam Street during her lunch break. She was alone since Ram, Vetri and Reshma were off for the day. Suddenly, her phone rang. The call was from a number used only during emergencies.

She answered immediately. 'Hello, Sudha Akka. What happened?'

'Listen, girl,' Sudha's voice was urgent. 'The boy and girl who live in the same house as you have figured out your identity. You need to leave Chennai as soon as possible.'

Anandhi's heart raced. 'Where are they now, Sudha Akka?' she asked, panicking.

'We haven't caught them yet. They slipped away right in front of me, but they're still in my area. I'll find them soon.'

'Akka, please let them go. I'll come in person.'

'Don't interfere. Do as I say. Someone will pick you up tonight. Be ready to leave.'

The call ended abruptly. Anandhi sank on to the steps of a closed shop near Amma Unavagam, feeling hopeless.

Three

Vetri and Reshma, barely escaping Sudha and her gang, sprinted through narrow alleys between houses, their hearts pounding.

'Reshma, run faster! If they catch us, we're done for,' Vetri urged, his voice strained.

People on the roadside stared at them, puzzled by their frantic pace. Sudha's gang wasn't far behind. As they dashed through the unfamiliar streets, they occasionally bumped into passersby but managed to keep their balance and momentum.

Sudha's jeep was waiting on the other side of the alley.

'Vetri, they might be waiting for us at the end of this path. They know this place better than we do,' Reshma said, stopping briefly to catch her breath.

Without a second thought, Vetri grabbed her hand and darted into a house on the right. The lady inside, engrossed in her TV show, jumped in surprise as they rushed through. They bolted into another house, then climbed over the compound wall behind it, landing in another alley. This alley led them back to the vegetable shop where they had first made inquiries. The old lady there eyed them with suspicion as they ran past her, gasping. Vetri held on to Reshma's hand, urging her forward.

'I can't, Vetri. My heart feels like it is about to burst,' Reshma panted.

'You should have expected all this,' Vetri said, pulling her along, refusing to let her stop.

Sudha's gang, realizing they had taken an alternate route, advanced in the jeep towards the next street. Reshma and Vetri heard the engine's roar drawing closer.

They were on the brink of being caught when, out of nowhere, the autorickshaw driver who had dropped them off appeared, stopping in front of them like a guardian angel.

'Well, I figured it would be a waste to head back empty, so I stuck around to see if you'd return sooner,' he said humbly.

Reshma and Vetri exchanged a look of surprise and relief before jumping into the autorickshaw.

'Brother, step on it! Go as fast as you can. I'll give you an extra hundred rupees,' Vetri urged. The driver immediately sped up, pushing his vehicle to its limits.

As they raced ahead, Vetri and Reshma kept looking back nervously.

'Why are you two sweating and out of breath?' the driver asked.

'Some stray dogs were chasing us,' Reshma replied, wiping her face anxiously.

'They're a real nuisance. During Diwali, I tie firecrackers to their tails,' the driver said casually.

Reshma shot him a horrified look.

The journey back took half the time it had taken to get there. They reached the railway station in just fifteen minutes.

Vetri handed the driver five hundred rupees. When the driver started to count change to return to them, Reshma stopped him. 'Keep it,' she said before rushing inside the station with Vetri.

A train to Coimbatore was just beginning to pull away from platform 1. That's when they heard an announcement about a train to Chennai arriving at platform 2 shortly.

Vetri grabbed Reshma's hand and jumped on to the moving train.

'Why are we on a train going in the opposite direction? Our train is about to arrive!' Reshma asked, frustrated.

Vetri pulled her inside and pointed towards the entrance of the station. They saw Sudha's gang arriving in their jeep, swarming the platform.

Nearly eight men, with intense expressions, ran up to the platform, scanning the surroundings. The grips of double-edged knives peeked from beneath their shirts. Vetri and Reshma quickly ducked out of sight.

'We'll get off at some station and catch a bus to Chennai,' Vetri said, still trying to catch his breath. Reshma remained silent.

The train carried them away from Vaniyambadi.

27

One

Underneath the Kathipara bridge, it was a night of celebration. Malli's twelve friends had organized a gathering to officially celebrate her admission into the dance academy. In reality, it was to help her heal from the wounds inflicted by her family.

Thilothama, the eldest and the best cook among them, took charge of preparing biryani for everyone, with a couple of others assisting her in the makeshift kitchen.

The rest of the group sat around Malli, engaging in casual conversation, cracking jokes and doing everything they could to lift her spirits.

'Is it ready yet?' one of them asked, rubbing her belly as she approached the kitchen.

'Oh, if you're that eager, why don't you cook it yourself?' Thilothama retorted playfully, shooing her away.

By the time the clock inched close to 10.30 p.m., the biryani was ready. The thirteen friends gathered to share the meal. Any trace of sorrow that had lingered on Malli's face was gone, at least for the moment.

After dinner, they urged Malli to dance. She agreed, paying her respects to the brand-new ghungroos given to her by the academy before fastening them to her ankles. Tucking the pallu of her saree into her waist, she began to dance, singing an old song as her friends watched.

Her friends cheered her on with loud applause. Malli was dancing again after such a long time; the rhythmic tinkling of the ghungroos brought her comfort. The thought that this sound would be part of her life from now on filled her with an even greater joy.

Seeing Malli's radiant smile, her friends felt a sense of relief.

The celebration was interrupted when a police patrol jeep pulled up nearby. Malli immediately stopped dancing and adjusted her saree.

'Malli, come with me,' ordered Subinspector (SI) Farooq of Guindy police station, who was sitting in the front seat, next to the driver.

Malli looked at her friends, who stared back at her and SI Farooq in stunned silence.

'Sir, can I come instead? She's not feeling well today,' Thilothama said, rising to her feet.

SI Farooq stepped out of the jeep, eyeing her coldly. 'If I call for Malli, she comes. I know how to make her feel good, and she knows it too. Get in the jeep.' He lit a cigarette, his voice rough and commanding.

Malli bent down to untie her ghungroos, but Farooq interrupted, 'Leave them on. I might need some entertainment if I get bored,' he sneered, a wicked grin playing on his face.

With a resigned expression, Malli walked towards the jeep. As she passed by the SI, he grabbed her butt roughly. In that moment, she felt a surge of anger, a desperate urge to scream or even attack him, but she swallowed her rage, feeling a familiar pain return in her chest.

All the thirunangais sat with their heads bowed, hearing only the tinkling of Malli's ghungroos as she stepped towards the jeep and the sound of the engine as it roared to life and drove away.

Two

Ram was asleep in his room when he received a call from Paatti.

'Ram dear, Vetri hasn't come back yet.'

He checked the time on his phone's display. It was midnight.

'Let me try calling him, Paatti,' he said, but as he was about to hang up, Paatti added, 'His phone is switched off. I called Reshma's mother also—she hasn't returned either.'

'Paatti, where is Anandhi?'

'She went looking for them. I'm scared something might have happened.'

Ram could hear the tremor in Paatti's voice and sensed she was close to tears. He sat up.

'Hey Paatti, don't worry. They're probably together, just out somewhere. If they run into any trouble, they'll handle it. We know them well. I'll come over right now. Please don't worry. Okay?'

He glanced at Kiran, who was sound asleep, and then quietly changed his clothes. Grabbing the keys to Bineesh's Bullet from the shelf, he slipped out through the balcony door. Before leaving, he remembered to send a message to Bineesh.

Three

SI Farooq and his driver, Kathirvel, arrived at their usual spot—a warehouse near Guindy—with Malli.

The SI ordered Malli to get out of the jeep and removed his belt.

'On your knees!' he demanded loudly.

Kathirvel opened a packet of peanuts and began eating, casually watching the scene unfold. Malli hesitated, standing in the same place, fully aware that failing to obey would result in a harsher punishment.

'Sir, I'm feeling unwell. Can you please let me go today?' she pleaded with her hands clasped and her eyes fixed on the ground.

SI Farooq's voice grew more menacing. 'A little while ago, you were dancing and jumping around! Don't think you can avoid this. Get on your knees!'

Kathirvel moved behind Malli and, with a rough shove, sent her sprawling face-first on to the ground. He laughed loudly, as if it was all a joke to him. SI Farooq grabbed Malli by the hair, lifted her up and forcefully kissed her.

'So, you had biryani for dinner, did you?' SI Farooq asked while spitting on the side. He roughly yanked at the end of her saree.

Kathirvel, still behind the jeep, added mockingly, 'Before you, it was Panchali who had the same "honour".'

Malli reeled in shock as SI Farooq tore away the saree from her body. He moved closer and slapped her hard across the face. She cried out in pain and collapsed to her knees. SI Farooq unzipped his pants and advanced towards her.

Four

By the time Ram arrived at Paatti's house, it was well past 12.30 a.m. Paatti was sitting anxiously on the verandah, her eyes fixed on the road. When she saw Ram, her worries melted into tears. Ram gently pulled her into a comforting hug.

'Paatti, please don't worry. You know what can happen if your blood pressure rises. When they both come back and ask for you, how do you think Anandhi and I will manage? Please try to stay calm,' he said, softly patting her forehead.

Just then, they saw Anandhi's Luna coming through the gate. Paatti quickly stood up.

'Any news, dear?' she asked, her voice full of hope.

Anandhi didn't have good news to share.

'Did you check the Besant Nagar area?' Paatti asked, her voice tinged with innocence.

Anandhi got off her Luna, walked over to Paatti and held her close.

'I went to Reshma's house. Her dad is really worried, but they understand how Vetri and Reshma are. They've decided to wait until morning.'

That was when Anandhi's phone rang. She stepped away from them, walked towards the gate and answered the call.

Five

Malli's screams echoed through the warehouse. She was sobbing uncontrollably, unable to even touch the burn on her left thigh, where SI Farooq had burned her with a lit cigarette. Her cheeks were swollen and red, bearing evidence of his brutal slaps. After SI Farooq left, Kathirvel approached, unzipping his pants.

'Turn around,' he ordered. Malli, sitting naked on the ground with her face buried in her palms, was still wearing only her ghungroos.

'I can't, sir. Please don't torture me any more. I'm a human being, just like you,' she pleaded, looking up with folded hands.

Kathirvel grabbed her hands tightly and struck them with all his might. Malli felt like the bones in her fingers had shattered. She cried out in pain, shaking her hands desperately.

Kathirvel laughed cruelly and stomped hard on her chest. The blow landed on the same spot where her brother had kicked her the day before. She had been dealing with intermittent chest pains and palpitations ever since. The force of Kathirvel's kick was too much for her already weak body to bear.

Six

Paatti sent Ram and Anandhi out again to search for Vetri and Reshma. Anandhi rode with Ram on the Bullet as they scoured the city, checking places like Marina beach to see if their vehicles were parked anywhere. Anandhi called Paatti periodically to ensure she was alright.

They searched relentlessly, visiting spots like Velachery and Porur lakes.

When they finally returned home, it was nearly 5 a.m. Paatti, still sitting on the verandah, was sleepy.

'Any news?' she asked anxiously.

'Paatti, please go and rest. Anandhi and I are heading to Reshma's house. I think we should convince their father to file a police complaint without any further delay,' Ram said gently.

Paatti nodded and went inside.

'I'm not coming with you, Ram. Paatti's alone here. I have Reshma's mother's number. I'll give it to you. Call her when you reach Mahatma Gandhi Road from Besant Nagar and she'll guide you,' Anandhi said, taking out her phone.

Ram nodded as she handed him the number and then climbed back on the bike.

Once Ram left, Anandhi inserted her secret SIM card into her phone and headed upstairs.

As Ram rode through Guindy, fatigue started to catch up with him. He spotted a tea stall, pulled over and ordered a tea.

'One more of those aruvanis has died,' a passerby said to the owner of the teashop.

'They always go with strangers. I think they'd live longer if they stop that practice,' the shop owner replied.

'But this aruvani was special. She had ghungroos on her ankles. Strange way to attract attention!' the man added, laughing.

Ram, who had been blowing on his hot tea, froze and looked at the man.

'Where did you see the body?' he asked, setting the tea down.

'It's in the garbage bin near the warehouse,' the man said offhandedly.

Ram sprinted to his bike, started it and sped off, leaving his tea unpaid for. He did not even hear the shop owner calling after him.

He headed straight to the area beneath the Kathipara bridge. It was still dark, and the thirunangais were asleep. He parked the bike and sprinted to Malli's makeshift room, which was set off by sarees. The sight of the empty space ignited a wave of panic in him. Desperately, he shook Malli's friends awake. They were bewildered, trying to make sense of his frantic behaviour.

'There's a body with ghungroos on the ankles in the garbage bin. Is it Malli?' Ram asked each of them, his voice trembling.

Thilothama was the first to scream. She bolted towards the garbage bin. The others, along with Ram, followed closely behind.

When Thilothama saw the legs adorned with ghungroos, she began beating her chest and fell on her knees, wailing. By then, the others and Ram had also reached the spot. One of them turned the body over.

Despite the dim light, Ram recognized Malli's face instantly. A crushing sense of helplessness overwhelmed him. He stumbled away from the group gathered around the garbage bin and sat down on the road. His breathing became heavier, until finally, it escaped as a heart-wrenching cry.

That morning, the city of Chennai awoke to the anguished wails of Ram and the thirunangais beside the garbage bin.

A gentle, unexpected rain began to fall, soaking the earth on that sorrowful day.

28

One

Ram made a call home at that unusual hour. He waited anxiously to hear his mother's voice. When she finally answered, he broke down.

'Ramu, mone. Please don't cry. What happened? Tell me.'

'Amma … Chennai is a terrible place. It's where people get lost or killed. Vetri and Reshma are missing. Malli was murdered and left on the street. The police took her away … she wanted to study at the academy so badly, to wear those ghungroos on her ankles …' His voice cracked and his body was wracked by sobs.

Ram always confided in his mother, so she didn't need him to finish his sentences to understand his pain. But she needed to grasp the full picture. Gently, she asked for details until she had a clear understanding of the situation. Ram continued crying.

'Mone, please don't cry. If you can't stay there, you can come back home. Your father won't be angry, I promise. But before you leave, you have responsibilities to fulfil. You need to find Vetri and Reshma. And you have a duty to Malli—there's no one else to speak for her or to see to her cremation. Do what's necessary, and then come back home.'

After the call, Ram wiped his tears and stood up from Malli's makeshift room of sarees. All twelve of her friends sat in their own makeshift rooms, their faces tear-stained.

The slight drizzle of the early morning had turned into a downpour by the time the police took Malli's body away. Thunder roared, shaking the earth and everyone on it.

Raindrops fell slantingly into the makeshift rooms. Ram shielded his mobile phone with a small piece of plastic he had found nearby. Then he walked to Guindy railway station in the downpour. Malli's friends, overwhelmed with grief, watched him leave.

He crossed over to platform 2 via the foot overbridge and approached the bench where he used to sit with Malli. The bench was drenched. He gazed at the spot where her name was written beside his.

'Let me have a place beside your name, at least on this cement bench.' He remembered her words.

'Not just on this cement bench, Malli. You're in ...' His voice cracked as he pointed to his heart. Trains came and went. Passengers and passersby glanced at Ram as if he were mad. He stayed a while longer, then wiped his face roughly and walked away.

Thilothama, who was standing by his bike near Kathipara bridge, approached Ram, drenched.

'They won't release her body from the mortuary to people like me. Ram, can you please try?'

'Is there anything we can do for her, akka?' he asked, his voice trembling.

'They've taken the lives of two others before. One was murdered and dumped, just like Malli. The other fought for life in a hospital for days before passing away. Yet, both incidents were recorded as accidental deaths by the police,' Thilothama said.

'But the postmortem report should reveal the torture they endured, right?'

'Nothing will happen, dear. When this happened before, we filed a complaint with the district collector through the thirunangai community. But after investigations, the postmortem report still recorded that both had died in road accidents. The police and doctors are in cahoots. The only thing we can do is give them a decent and respectful cremation. We have no idea where they buried the others who died. Even if we approach them, they won't give us the body since we don't have any identity cards. That's why I need your help.'

'Come, let's go to the mortuary,' Ram said, pulling out his bike's key.

Thilothama turned to look at her friends. Then, as he started the Bullet, she climbed on to the back seat. By the time they reached the mortuary at Rajiv Gandhi Government General Hospital, it was 11.30 a.m. The rain hadn't let up.

The hospital staff on duty at the mortuary informed them that Malli's body, after the postmortem, had already been taken for burial by the police a while ago. They had no information about the names of the cops or the burial ground.

An elderly staff member handed them a plastic cover. Inside were the ghungroos removed from Malli's ankles during the postmortem.

'If you want, take it. If not, you can put it in the garbage bin.'

The ghungroos had been cut from her ankles with scissors. One side still bore the strong knot Malli had made.

'What dreams you had, Malli! You wanted to learn dance, to perform in big shows. You dreamed of building a home in Chennai, a safe haven for homeless aruvanis. And now what? You end up as an anonymous body, your ankles and dreams burned away.' Thilothama sobbed, looking at the ghungroos before handing them over to Ram.

'She really liked you. You keep these,' she said and placed them gently in his hand. With heavy hearts and under the pouring rain, they both walked towards the bike parked in front of the mortuary.

Two

'Ram, Reshma's father filed a complaint at the police station this morning. They just called back to say that they found Reshma and Vetri's two-wheelers in the parking lot at Chennai Central railway station. They checked the CCTV footage and saw that they purchased tickets to a place called Vaniyambadi. But the CCTVs at Vaniyambadi aren't working, so they can't confirm if they actually got there, or where they went afterwards. Do you know of any friends or acquaintances in Vaniyambadi? I called to ask about that.'

Hearing Reshma's mother's question, Ram's eyebrows furrowed. The name sounded familiar, but he couldn't quite place it. Since he wasn't sure, he said he would call back and then disconnected the call.

He went to his apartment in Iyyappanthangal to freshen up before heading to Paatti's house. 'Oh, you're completely drenched. Any news? Are they back?' Bineesh asked as soon as he opened the door.

Ram dried his hair with a towel and looked at Bineesh, who was waiting expectantly for him to speak.

'Malli passed away, Bineesh Etta,' he said in utter despair.

'I saw it on the news. When they mentioned Malli from Guindy, I guessed it was her. It was an accident, wasn't it?' Bineesh asked.

Ram shook his head, denying it. 'The police took her and killed her. They can write any reason they want for those who have no one to claim them. Who will go and question them? Even if someone tries, it all ends in vain,' he muttered.

'How can all this happen in one single day?'

Ram held up his hands in despair.

When Ram came out after his bath, Kiran had also arrived. With many areas in Chennai waterlogged after the heavy rains, his college had declared a half-day holiday.

'Bineesh Etta, where is this Vaniyambadi?' Ram asked the question that had been nagging him.

'It's a bit away from Chennai. Well, it's the place where that girl—Anandhi—is from.'

Hearing that, a million questions darted through Ram's mind.

'Chetta, Reshma's mother called me a while ago. The police found her and Vetri's two-wheelers in the parking lot at Chennai Central railway station. They purchased tickets to Vaniyambadi, and after that, there's no news about them.'

Bineesh and Kiran were equally puzzled.

'I suspect she might have some role to play in their disappearance,' Bineesh said, looking at Ram.

Just then, Ram received a call from Anandhi. He told them it was her before answering.

'Hello, Anandhi,' he answered.

'Ram, where are you?' Anandhi asked.

'I'm in my apartment. What happened? Any problem?'

'No, nothing. I just called after I heard about Malli.'

'Hmm …' he responded with a heavy heart.

'Ram, I need to talk to you in person. I'm in college now. Can you please meet me at Besant Nagar beach this evening?'

'Oh, then who will be with Paatti?'

'Don't worry. The lady who used to come and help is with her now. I ensured she would stay with Paatti before I left this morning. Paatti didn't sleep a wink last night, so she's fast asleep now. And you haven't slept either. I know what you're going through, Ram. So, get some rest. We'll go to Paatti's together in the evening.'

After hanging up, Ram told Bineesh and Kiran that Anandhi had asked him to meet her at the beach that evening.

'You remember I once said there's something simmering deep within her, and that soon it would be set ablaze? I think today's the day,' Bineesh said, looking into Ram's tired eyes.

Ram felt a deep sadness. His exhaustion was evident.

'You should get some sleep,' Bineesh urged.

Ram finally fell into a deep sleep, only to be awakened a few hours later, at 5.30 p.m., by his phone ringing persistently. It was Anandhi.

'Hello, Ram, I'm leaving now,' she said as soon as he picked up.

'Okay, Anandhi. I'll be there soon.'

The rain had stopped by then. As he crossed the Kathipara bridge, he glanced towards the place where Malli's friends lived. He saw Thilothama sitting on one side, cooking. The other eleven friends were there, too, grief-stricken.

It was slowly getting dark. Because of the day-long rain, only a few people were at the beach. Anandhi was waiting for Ram in the parking area.

'Shall we walk in that direction?' she asked, pointing towards the seashore. He nodded.

A series of red lights from fishing boats could be seen in the distance.

'Paatti?' Ram asked as they walked.

'I went to check on her before coming here. She's fine.'

'Did Reshma's mother call you?'

'No.'

'You didn't call her either?'

'No, Ram. I had a busy day at work, so I couldn't call,' she said, her gaze wandering.

'Okay. Anandhi, you're from Vaniyambadi, right?'

Hearing his sudden question, Anandhi paused for a moment.

'Did you know that Vetri and Reshma were last seen travelling towards your hometown?' he asked, his tone suggesting that something was up.

She nodded. By then, they had reached the seashore. No one was around.

'What do you want to tell me?' Ram stood facing her, his arms folded across his chest.

Anandhi fidgeted with her fingers. 'Reshma's mother did call me, Ram. I didn't tell her that Vaniyambadi is my hometown. She might have tried calling Paatti, too. I put her phone on airplane mode to avoid all calls,' she said.

Ram wasn't surprised. 'I don't care about all that. All I want to know is where are Reshma and Vetri?' he demanded.

Anandhi noticed the change in Ram's tone.

Without replying, she quickly looked around and made a phone call.

'The weather is cold,' she said before disconnecting.

Ram felt a surge of irritation.

'Who are you? Are you trying to fool me? You've made calls like that before, in the park, remember?' he snapped, stamping hard on the damp sand, as if trying to release his frustration.

'Ram, I'm here now to tell you something—the three of you.'

'Three? Are you out of your mind?' he asked, clenching his teeth.

She pointed towards the sea in response. Ram saw a boat with a red light approaching the shore. As it drew closer, the engine was turned off. Four or five people got off, pushing it towards the beach.

Initially, Ram couldn't make out any faces in the dim light, but as the boat reached the shallow water where the waves broke, two more people jumped off. Even in the darkness, Ram recognized them.

'Vetri and Reshma,' he said in surprise, continuing to stare in the direction of the sea.

29

One

Vetri and Reshma got down from the boat and walked towards the shore, swaying with the waves. The people who had brought them quickly got back on the boat and sped away into the sea.

Ram stared at Anandhi, shocked at the unusual events unfolding before him. Even when Reshma and Vetri reached him, he couldn't fully grasp what was happening. Both of them hugged him in relief.

'I know you three are confused,' Anandhi said, looking at them huddled together.

'Who are you?' Reshma asked, pulling away from Ram.

'You're that Sudha's daughter, aren't you? What's your intention living in Chennai?' Vetri also questioned, clearly suspicious.

'Why did you save us from them?' Reshma asked, her voice trembling.

'What the hell is going on here? I'm already pissed off with everything that has happened. Please, don't make me go crazy,' Ram said, folding his hands.

'Ram, she's not who we thought she was. We went to her native place. Even her name is fake. There are big gangster groups behind her. We managed to escape by train, but they caught us at the next station. They even took our phones. We thought we would be killed, but then their leader, that lady named Sudha, came and told us that since Anandhi had begged and pleaded, they were sparing our lives. They blindfolded us, put us on this boat and brought us here. She's a big shot. We should be careful with her,' Reshma said, turning to Ram.

Anandhi unzipped the side pocket of her bag and took out two mobile phones. 'These are your phones. If you turn them on, the police will trace your location. Or you can call them if you wish to. I'm not going to run away,' she said calmly.

Vetri snatched the phones from her hand and handed Reshma's phone back to her.

'But before you hand me over to the police, you should have the patience to hear what I have to say. You owe me that much,' Anandhi said, her eyes scanning each of them.

Ram stood there anxiously, while Reshma's thumb was an inch away from switching on the phone. Seeing Anandhi's imploring eyes, Reshma hesitated, put the phone into Vetri's pocket and sat down on the sand. Anandhi looked expectantly at Ram and Vetri.

'Just spill it already, whatever you have to say. And whatever it is, I'm not going to trust you ever again,' Vetri said angrily as he sat down, followed by Ram.

They waited, their eyes fixed on Anandhi. She took a deep breath and scanned the surroundings one last time before beginning.

'Yes, you're right. My name isn't Anandhi. And I'm not from this country.'

Reshma's hands flew to her mouth in disbelief, and Ram nearly did the same. Vetri looked around to ensure no one was eavesdropping.

Anandhi analysed their expressions before continuing.

'Try to believe what I'm about to say,' she began. 'You might not have experienced even a fraction of what I've been through, so it might be hard to understand. But since we've come this far, I'll share it all.'

Anandhi scanned the surroundings once more and then said, 'My story began in Jaffna, Sri Lanka. My circumstances were shaped even before I was born. The war in Sri Lanka started in 1983. I was born twelve years later, when it was at its peak. As a child, I was terrified of everyone, even my own parents. I witnessed bomb shells exploding right before my eyes, killing the people sitting next to me. I never saw a trace of happiness on anyone's face. Bombs could drop at any moment, and death was always looming over us. Some people didn't die right away. They suffered terribly, with shrapnel lodged in their bodies, enduring excruciating pain before finally dying in agony. I've seen so many deaths that I've become numb to bloodshed and suffering.'

All three listened intently as Anandhi continued.

'Though I was born in a remote village in Jaffna, all I remember is a life of constant fleeing. My father explained everything to me once I was old enough to understand. It's a cruel irony to divide a country's citizens based on the language they speak, isn't it? And what happens when the ruling government supports such divisions? My neighbour, a girl my age, enjoys all the privileges of rights, freedom and government-sponsored higher education simply because she's from a Sinhalese family and speaks Sinhala. Meanwhile, people like me, born into Tamil families, are denied the right to study or even earn a living. The government mocked us, calling us "Tamil dogs".

'Some among us decided to fight back against this injustice. That was the beginning. The government used the Sri Lankan army to suppress those who dared to speak out and killed them. Those left behind couldn't stay silent—they attacked the army camps, avenging the deaths of their loved ones. Since all the soldiers were Sinhalese, the government framed it as a conflict between two groups. When majority of a country's population is Sinhalese, it becomes easier to suppress the Tamil minority, doesn't it? And so, what started as a government-driven division escalated into a full-blown war between the Sinhalese and Tamilians.

'Initially, it was a struggle for Tamil rights, but it soon became a fight for survival. Actually, it was not just a conflict. Sinhalese forces began attacking anyone who spoke Tamil. They burned down schools where Tamil children studied, locked women and children in buses and set them on fire, and even dipped small children in boiling tar. Women were gangraped in front of their families. These atrocities were supported by the Sinhalese army in Tamil-dominated areas. Even those who surrendered, claiming that they were not against the government, were shot dead. Before dropping bombs on the Tamil population, they cut off necessities like food, water and medicine. We tried peaceful protests, like satyagraha and fasting, but nothing worked. With no other option left, the leader of the LTTE (Liberation Tigers of Tamil Eelam), Velupillai Prabhakaran, and his followers decided to fight back with weapons.'

Ram didn't know much about Sri Lanka or the war there. Everything Anandhi shared was new to him. He only knew from newspapers that the LTTE was considered a terrorist group.

'Are you an LTTE activist?' Vetri asked anxiously.

Anandhi smiled gently and said, 'I wonder how long it will take for people to distinguish between a Sri Lankan Tamilian and a member of the LTTE.'

Reshma then asked, 'What changed in your lives with the arrival of Prabhakaran?'

Anandhi's smile remained as she replied, 'With his arrival, those who once mocked us as "Tamil dogs" began to consider us "Tamil Tigers". Even a newborn Tamil child was seen as a "Tamil Tiger". The Sri Lankan government labelled us all as "terrorists" in the eyes of the world, and the army continued to kill thousands of innocent Tamils on that pretext. This was more than enough for the Tamil people, who had long endured neglect, ridicule and racism, to rally behind our leader, Velupillai Prabhakaran. Many joined the Eelam War of their own free will. Tamil families began migrating from Sinhalese-dominated areas to the northeastern regions like Mannar, Mullaitivu, Vavuniya and Kilinochchi.

'In Mullaitivu, those who joined the LTTE received weapons training from the Tigers. During this time, weapons and supplies were secretly transported from India, through a covert network, especially in Tamil Nadu. Under the control of the Tamil Tigers, women and children in the northeast could finally sleep peacefully. People began to settle in areas beyond the reach of the Sri Lankan army. Kilinochchi, with its abundant water, allowed us to farm and sustain ourselves. It was there that my mother gave birth to my younger brother, Raja, when I was eight years old. For the first time, I felt a bit of happiness. I took care of him more than my mother did. My mother would tease me, asking who the real mother was—she or me? And so, a few years passed under the protection of the Tigers.

'I was fourteen, and Raja was six. Near our huts, there was a lake with the shores covered in long grass. Every December, blue flowers would bloom there, swaying beautifully in the wind. Ever since Raja learned to walk, we would go to the lakeside every December to watch those beautiful flowers. While some older kids swam in the lake, we would sit on the shore, as neither of us knew how to swim.

'One day, our father took us to the lake. It's one of my fondest memories of Kilinochchi. That day, he taught both of us how to swim. Afterwards, we bathed and ran and played among the grass dotted with blue flowers. It was then that we heard a loud explosion at a distance. Our father quickly took us back to our hut. We later learned that a Tiger, who was a suicide bomber, had attacked a passing Sri Lankan army vehicle. This incident enraged the army. From that day on, gunfire and explosions became routine in Kilinochchi.

'Then came January 2009, when the war escalated even more. The Sri Lankan army and government were desperate to capture Velupillai Prabhakaran to save face in front of the world. They did everything they could to portray the LTTE as a terrorist group. They never let the world know what was happening to people like us, living in areas protected by the LTTE. Instead, they spread lies that we were all terrorists. In our area, nearly three hundred people lived close together in huts. One night, while I was sleeping with my parents and little brother, the area was hit by bombs.

'Bombs and shells rained down from the sky, unleashed by the Sri Lankan army. People were torn apart, their body parts scattered. Terrified women and children ran in every direction. In the chaos, we lost Raja. My father, with his leg severely injured, somehow managed to lead my mother and me to the lakeside. He planned to keep us safe there while he searched for Raja. But what awaited us was truly horrific.

'A few local Sinhalese men used to assist the army with daily chores. During the war, their main intention was to find and molest women fleeing from affected areas. We passed right in front of them as they were assaulting a few women who had escaped during the army attack. Outnumbering the women they had captured, they took turns to satisfy their lust. And then they noticed us. When my father tried to escape with us, they beat him to a pulp. Then, they dragged my mother and me through the grass and blue flowers.

'I tried to resist and escape many times, but hunger had left me too weak to protest. My father had to witness the worst. Right in front of his eyes, his wife and young daughter were brutally raped. He couldn't stand it. He grabbed a knife from one of them and slashed his own throat, dying on the spot. I was abused by the man who appeared to be their leader, while my mother was subjected to abuse by several of them who took turns. Eventually, they pushed a rifle into my mother's vagina and killed her, laughing hysterically all the while.'

Ram couldn't bear to look at Anandhi's face; he didn't dare to. Reshma's eyes filled with tears. Vetri stood up, walked up to Anandhi and knelt in front of her on the sand, his eyes moist.

'Sister, please forgive me ...' Vetri hugged her.

The tears streaming from Anandhi's eyes soaked his shirt.

30

One

'I'm not done yet, Vetri,' Anandhi said, wiping her eyes firmly.

The beach was silent except for the sound of the crashing waves.

Anandhi continued. 'After that incident, when I regained consciousness, I found myself under the protection of the Tamil Tigers. They told me they had beheaded those who had abused my mother and me. I was the only one they had found alive near the lakeside covered in blue flowers. I was physically and mentally shattered. They cared for me as best as they could, but my health continued to decline at the modest facilities of their camp.

'Though I could barely stand, my thoughts were consumed by Raja. Despite my excruciating pain, I kept insisting that he be found. My only comfort was knowing that his body wasn't among those recovered from the scene. I was determined to find him, no matter what. But as my condition worsened, it became clear that I needed critical care. Eventually, they decided to send me to India by sea. I resisted at first but eventually agreed, weakened by my failing health.

'The very next night, they placed me on a cot, covered me with a cloth and piled dried leaves and creepers over me to conceal me from the eyes of the Sri Lankan helicopters as we travelled through the forests of Mullaitivu. They carried me on their shoulders carefully, without much wobbling, all the way to the seashore. There, at a deserted spot, a fishing boat was waiting for me. Just as I was about to leave on that boat, quite unexpectedly, Veluppillai Prabhakaran came to see me. He gently and fondly patted my forehead, a gesture only my father had done before. In that moment, I broke down, crying inconsolably, calling out for my father. Even in the darkness, I could see the glimmer of tears in his eyes.

'I begged him to find my brother. He told me to go to India and promised that, when I returned, he would reunite me with my brother somehow. Finally, the boat began to move away from the Sri Lankan shore. It was my first time travelling across the deep sea. I became seasick, vomiting repeatedly. The motion of the boat caused me to start bleeding again, and I felt the wetness on my inner thighs. Exhausted, I lay on the boat's deck and looked up at the sky. The stars were the clearest I had ever seen.

'My father used to tell us a story, pointing to the brightest twin stars in the sky. According to him, God had created a shortcut for parents who reached heaven to see their children. He made two holes in the walls of heaven, and it is believed that if a father and mother look through them together, they can see their children. My father told me that those twin stars were the eyes of parents. As a child, it didn't make much sense to me, but during that boat journey, I understood what he meant. I gazed up at those twin stars and poured out all my worries and pain. My mind was consumed by memories of my father, mother and Raja.

'By the time the boat reached the shores of Rameswaram, it was dawn. A woman named Sudha from Tamil Nadu, who was secretly helping the Tigers, was waiting there, signalling with a torch. She called out for me to get down quickly before anyone noticed and shone the torch on my face. The unbearable pain in my lower abdomen made it impossible for me to even lift myself up. Somehow, I managed to remove the cloth that covered me and showed her my blood-soaked clothes. She saw how emaciated I was, with my bones protruding from my chest.

'She climbed into the boat. "Forgive me, girl. They only told me that a sick girl was coming. I didn't know anything else," she said and effortlessly lifted me in her arms. From there, they took me by car to an old hospital called Akka Thankachi Madom in Rameswaram. Sudha Akka and a middle-aged Malayali doctor named Ramachandran, who had agreed to treat me in secret, asked me for details about what had happened. Somehow, I managed to make them understand what I had gone through. When the doctor realized it was a rape case, he immediately provided emergency treatment. At one point, my condition worsened. That entire night, Sudha Akka and the doctor stayed by my side, caring for me. Gradually, I began to recover. They ensured I received food and medicine at the right times. However, every night, I woke up from nightmares of my parents and me being tortured by the Sinhalese men.

'I was reluctant to even go out of my room. But Sudha Akka and Dr Ramachandran insisted and eventually took me out one evening to walk around the hospital premises. The compound was lush and green. In fact, Akka Thankachi Madom was primarily an elderly care home; the hospital was just an annexe for their treatment. There was a large pond between the hospital building and the dormitory, with the same long grass and blue flowers growing along its banks. At first, I was frightened by the sight of those flowers, but over time, I began to sit near the pond every evening with Sudha Akka. She told the care home residents that I was her daughter, that I was being treated for anaemia.

'I avoided talking to the residents, not wanting to pile lies upon lies, but I did show compassion to some of the mothers who seemed depressed. It took almost two months for me to recover, both physically and mentally. By the time I left, I had gone from a mere twenty-eight kilos to forty, thanks to Sudha Akka's love and care. She also prepared me to face any challenges that might come my way. Dr Ramachandran, who was also a Kalari expert, taught me some self-defence moves that could help me defeat a healthy man within seconds. This training greatly improved my self-confidence.

'One day, Sudha Akka took me to the Ramanathaswamy Temple in Rameswaram. The temple has twenty-two wells, each with its own holy water. Akka drew water from each of those wells and bathed me. As she did that, she said, "As long as a girl is like a flower, there will be those who seek to destroy her. But when she becomes a burning ember, no one will dare to touch her. From now on, you are not a flower—you are a burning ember."

'I wasn't the type to believe in resurrection through holy baths, but since I was longing for a fresh start, I felt that I needed it. The very next evening, as I sat by the pond, I received the most exciting news from Sri Lanka—the Tigers had found Raja in a village called Vavuniya, near Kilinochchi. The moment I heard the news, I screamed with happiness and started running around the pond. The people at the care home probably thought I was mad. But from that day on, all I wanted was to return to Sri Lanka.

'The days that followed were heavy with the weight of waiting. A few days later, Dr Ramachandran informed Sudha Akka that I was completely healthy. Hearing this, Sudha Akka, who had been waiting for this news, arranged for my return. I said goodbye to all the residents of Akka Thankachi Madom. I didn't know how to properly thank Dr Ramachandran, but as I struggled to find the words, he firmly held my hand and offered me some advice: "If anyone touches you without your permission …" He then made a gesture, running his index finger across his neck, and winked.

Two

'By midnight on 17 May 2009, Sudha Akka had secretly brought me to the shore of Rameswaram. She even handed me a large packet filled with toys and chocolates for Raja. She looked me up and down, teasing me saying I looked like a beauty queen. Then, she held me close and kissed my forehead. The girl who had arrived at that very shore on the brink of death was now standing healthy and strong, all thanks to her. She could have easily ignored me, instead, she embraced me as if I were her own daughter. I expressed my gratitude to her as best as I could. We stood there, waiting for the boat to arrive.

'But fate had other plans. Minutes before the boat was due to arrive, we were hit with devastating news. The Sri Lankan army had murdered Velupillai Prabhakaran and his people in the ongoing war. They had also bombed and destroyed all the areas protected by the Tigers, killing more than fifty thousand people. We also learned that the government had secretly ordered the execution of all remaining LTTE members and those under their protection, regardless of age.

'Sudha Akka, knowing this, stopped me from going. I stood there on the shore, looking at the sea, the boat and the packet of toys in my hands. Raja's face filled my mind. In a gap of just one day, we stood separated—stranded on opposite sides of the same sea, in two different countries.

'The Sri Lankan government was yet to officially announce Prabhakaran's death. Once the news broke, the Indian coastal areas would be under the Indian Army's surveillance. Sudha Akka knew this all well, so she took me to Tirupur. Two days later, the news of Prabhakaran's murder was finally declared.

'Understanding the torment I was going through, Sudha Akka began secretly gathering information on all those who had migrated to India from Sri Lanka by sea during the war. Despite her efforts, she couldn't find any trace of a six-year-old named Raja. The government never released the names of those who were killed in the war. Even the official death toll was grossly understated, revealing only one-fourth of the true number.

'During the war, Sudha Akka helped many Tamil refugees who fled from Sri Lanka to Tirupur. They were secretly sheltered in an old, locked-up factory in Tirupur. Soon, fake ID proofs were created for them and jobs were found in various garment factories and mills in Tirupur. As they began earning salaries, Sudha Akka instructed them to gradually move out and rent small houses. Sudha Akka kept me with her in Tirupur, though she frequently travelled to her native place, Vaniyambadi.

'Many of the people who had crossed the sea from Sri Lanka during the war were acquaintances of mine. I constantly asked around for news of Raja. One of them, an LTTE member, told me that ever since they brought him back from Vavuniya, Raja would sit staring at the sky every night, fixated on a particular star. But after the last attack, no one knew what had happened to him. Gradually, I came to terms with the harsh reality. To keep myself from overthinking, I started working at a garment mill with the others. In the evenings, I studied the books that Sudha Akka brought for me.

'Sudha Akka used to bribe the policemen of Tirupur every month to ignore those of us who spoke Sri Lankan Tamil. She had strong connections with politicians and other influential people, which helped make our lives in Tirupur safe and secure. Days, months and years passed. Our lives as Sri Lankan Tamils became confined to the Tirupur area. Even though our Sri Lankan Tamil slang changed drastically, we didn't want to move out into the world. Our only thought was to somehow live out the rest of our lives. Eventually,

Sudha Akka insisted I stop working at the garment mill and take a computer course at a nearby institute. That decision marked a significant turning point in my snail-paced, aimless life.'

Suddenly, Ram's phone rang. It was Reshma's mother. Vetri told him to answer it.

Ram picked up the call just before it ended and put it on speaker. 'Hello, aunty.'

'Ram, I need to ask you something.'

'What's the matter, aunty?'

'It's about that girl—Anandhi. Did you know her house was in Vaniyambadi?'

'No, aunty, I didn't. What happened?' he asked, trying to keep calm.

'Our local police station got a call from the Guindy police station a while ago. They went to Vetri's house and spoke to the old lady. She told them Anandhi's house is in Vaniyambadi. I even called Anandhi this morning and asked about that place, but the liar hid it from me. Now her phone's switched off since evening. I've informed the police of my suspicions. They assured me they'll investigate further. Have you seen her, or tried calling her today?' she asked, anger evident in her voice.

'No, aunty, no one has called me today. Let me check, and I'll call you back.'

He was about to hang up when she continued.

'Whether you call me back or not, I don't care. But listen, Ram, if this is some conspiracy involving you all, I'll show you my true colours. I have a wedding in my family tomorrow, and I'm not able to focus on it because of this damn issue.'

Her words filled Ram with both fear and anger. He muttered a quick goodbye, disconnected the call and looked at Vetri, Anandhi and Reshma.

'Vetri, you need to take Reshma to her house as soon as possible. We need to settle these issues before the police start asking questions about me,' Anandhi said, quickly swapping her secret SIM card for her regular one.

As Vetri and Reshma stood up, Ram handed Vetri the keys to his Bullet. They hurried towards the road, understanding the urgency of the situation. Ram and Anandhi watched them until they disappeared from sight.

Three

SI Farooq from Guindy police station dialled Anandhi's number again. When he heard the call go through, his face lit up.

31

One

The rain resumed after a brief break. Despite the proximity of Reshma's house to the Besant Nagar beach, Vetri rode as fast as he could. When they arrived, they saw a sleek car parked outside, soaked in the rain.

'That must be my uncle,' Reshma said, pointing to the car.

Vetri rode the bike into the compound. On the porch stood Reshma's father, her mother, her mother's elder brother, his wife and their son, who was about Vetri's age. Vetri turned off the engine and parked. Reshma got off the back seat, anxiety evident on her face.

Her mother came out into the rain, walked up to Vetri and slapped him hard. Grabbing his collar, she pushed him off the bike.

'You bastard! You did all this to torment me on your mother's, that prostitute's, orders? Don't you dare see my daughter again!' she roared and struck him repeatedly in her rage.

Vetri didn't resist. No one intervened except Reshma. Some blows landed on her, too, but finally she caught her mother's hand.

'Enough! How can you beat him without knowing what really happened?' she burst out.

Her mother laughed bitterly, mocking her.

'Oh, how touching! A loving sister! Do you really think you share the same father? His mother was a prostitute. Even she isn't sure who his father is!' Reshma's mother screamed, her voice filled with venom.

Despite this vicious insult, which even questioned his parentage, their father remained silent. Vetri looked at him.

'And how should we address you? You, who wormed your way into a respectable family and stole the father of that house? I know your story too, Amma. Don't push me, or I'll speak up,' Reshma, blurted out, having long waited for this moment.

'Did you hear what this wretched girl said about me? I'm sure his mother, that bitch, taught her this nonsense,' her mother cried, faking tears as she looked at her brother, who now stormed out, grinding his teeth. As he approached, he pulled out the long belt tied around his dhoti.

'What did you just say, you filthy bitch?' he yelled, charging at Reshma.

Vetri leaped and stood in front of her, blocking him.

'You may be her uncle, but she's my sister. If anyone dares to touch her or hurt her, I'll break their hands,' Vetri warned, his voice firm. Reshma's uncle was stunned by Vetri's defiance.

'Reshma, these people have lost their minds. You don't need to stay here. The law allows a woman to leave with her lover, or even her brother. Come away with me,' Vetri urged.

Vetri firmly grasped Reshma's hand and walked towards the bike.

'Reshma.'

She turned around, surprised to hear her father's voice, which was rare.

'Speak up like that more often, Appa, or we might start thinking you've forgotten how to,' she said, her voice tinged with frustration.

Vetri started the bike, casting a challenging glance at Reshma's mother. With everyone watching, he rode off with Reshma into the pouring rain.

Two

Ram and Anandhi sought shelter under the awning of a closed shop as the downpour intensified. It was around 10 p.m.

Ram glanced at Anandhi while squeezing the water out of his shirt. Anandhi was on the phone, informing the lady with Paatti that Vetri and Reshma had made it back safely. She whispered something into the phone before hanging up. Just as she was about to slip it into the side zipper of her bag, it started ringing again. It was SI Farooq. Not recognizing the number, she silenced the call and put the phone away.

'Was that Vetri or Reshma?' Ram asked.

'No, it was someone else,' she replied, avoiding his gaze.

At that moment, Ram's phone rang. It was Reshma. He answered quickly.

'Reshma, what's up?'

'Well, Vetri delivered some dramatic lines and walked out with me. We're heading to Besant Nagar now. I'm starving. Can you meet us at Little Italy near the beach?'

'Sure. Call me when you get there.'

'Is Anandhi okay, Ram?' Reshma asked, her voice lowered.

'Not sure. We'll be there by the time you order,' he replied.

Anandhi stood watching the raindrops splatter on the road. Ram felt that, under the streetlight, the rain looked like thick threads rushing down to the earth. Ram moved closer to her. She remained still, not acknowledging him. He slowly extended the small finger of his left hand, letting it brush against the small finger of her right hand. His heart raced as he made contact without her permission. At that moment, Anandhi turned away from the road and looked directly into his eyes.

'Would you mind lifting the ends of my moustache with your little finger just one more time?' Ram said.

Anandhi was taken aback by his request. Memories of that night in the Thanjavur lodge, when she had playfully lifted his moustache with her little finger, came rushing back.

'Don't you like me?' he asked, noticing her silence.

She shook her head, avoiding his eyes.

'You don't?'

'No, Ram.'

She turned away again, trying to distance herself. Ram moved forward and stood in front of her, blocking her view.

'Are you sure you don't like me at all?' he asked, his voice laced with hurt, as if his dreams had crumbled.

'I can't, Ram. Please understand,' she said.

She kept looking down, avoiding eye contact. He moved closer, his voice soft but insistent. 'Just tell me if you like me or not.'

A warm tear from Anandhi's eye landed on Ram's foot. It felt like it burned him from head to toe. The usually bold Anandhi, who had faced so many challenges without flinching, was crying in front of him. He was shaken. He pulled her close. When his lips and beard touched her neck, she quickly moved away.

'I can't do this, Ram,' she repeated, her voice trembling.

'Why not, Anandhi? I know you like me.'

'First, understand that my real name isn't Anandhi. My name is—'

He quickly interrupted her before she could finish. 'Anandhi, only that name suits you. I don't want to know any other name,' he said, almost pleading.

Anandhi gazed at him in silence. The only sound around them was of the raindrops.

Reshma called Ram again to let him know they had arrived at Little Italy. Ram and Anandhi headed to the restaurant together.

Three

It had just begun to rain at the Guindy police station.

Although the Besant Nagar station had informed them that Vetri and Reshma were back safely, SI Farooq was still fixated on a piece of paper that had some notes about Anandhi. He also had her certificate, which he had got from Paatti. Anandhi, an employed person living as a paying guest, had failed to provide copies of her Aadhaar card or voter ID as proof of identity, offering only a simple certificate instead. This puzzled him. Despite numerous attempts, she hadn't answered any of his calls, fuelling his suspicions.

He read aloud the name of Anandhi's workplace again. 'Chennai Academy, Nungambakkam.'

'Kathirvel!' he called out.

Driver Kathirvel hurried in after flicking his cigarette away.

'Check the contact number for the principal at Chennai Academy, Nungambakkam. Who knows, maybe we will get a chance to go to the warehouse tonight itself,' SI Farooq said.

A smile spread across Kathirvel's face as the rain, accompanied by thunder, intensified outside.

Four

As it was a rainy night and nearing closing time, Little Italy near the Besant Nagar beach was less crowded. Ram and Anandhi were seated at a corner table near the entrance, waiting for Vetri and Reshma to finish their meal. Anandhi had ordered only a juice, stating she wasn't hungry. Ram wasn't eating either.

While they were waiting, Anandhi received a call from Principal Srinivas. She was alarmed by the call at that late hour, past 10 p.m.

'Hello, sir.'

'Anandhi, where are you?'

'I'm at a restaurant, having dinner.'

'Is everything okay? Has something happened?'

Anandhi was taken aback by the question.

'No, sir, everything is fine. What's the matter?'

'I just got a call from the Guindy police station. They were asking about how long you've been working here, your character and details about your salary payments. I told them we typically pay all staff by bank transfer, but we pay you in cash. They also inquired whether you have a bank account and if you joined the job with just a certificate instead of valid address proofs. I spoke well of you, mentioning that you've handed in your resignation and are serving your notice period. However, they didn't explain the issue despite me asking repeatedly. They asked me to call you and, if you answer, to instruct you to urgently call back the number ending in 844, from which you might have missed calls.'

Her heart raced, and she felt a cold chill take over her body.

'I'll call them right away, sir,' she said.

'But, Anandhi, what's the problem? Why did they contact me?'

'It's just a minor misunderstanding, sir. We can discuss it in detail when we meet at college. I'm sorry for any inconvenience.'

'Alright. If you need anything, feel free to reach out. Goodnight,' Principal Srinivas said and ended the call.

'What's going on?' Reshma asked, pausing between bites.

Anandhi didn't answer immediately. She signalled to the boy at the counter to bring some cold water and then looked at the three of them.

'As I suspected, things are slipping out of my control. It looks like the police have caught on to me. The principal got a call from the station, with detailed questions. When I called Paatti, she told me the police took my ID proof. But now, I think they've realized it might be fake. They'll figure it out soon enough. Still, I'll try one last thing.'

Anandhi opened her call list and dialled the number ending in 844. She drank a full glass of cold water as it rang. The call was answered by SI Farooq.

'Hello,' Anandhi said.

'Yes, tell me,' SI Farooq responded.

'Sir, you've been trying to reach me. My name is Anandhi.'

'Oh! Anandhi Madam. You seem to have trouble answering calls, don't you?' he said, mockingly.

'It's not like that. I didn't pick up because it was an unfamiliar number.'

'Oh, really? Well then, let's get acquainted. I'm Farooq Ahmed, SI at the Guindy police station. Age thirty-five, from Saligramam. Now, please introduce yourself.'

Anandhi could sense the sarcasm.

'Yes, madam, go ahead and introduce yourself,' he repeated, almost taunting her.

'My name is Anandhi Ramaswamy. I've been working as a receptionist at Chennai Academy for the past year and a half. I'm from Vaniyambadi.'

'And your age?'

'Twenty-three.'

'Well, Anandhi Madam, you don't have a bank account, do you? Why is that?'

'I don't have a habit of saving, that's why.'

'Oh, so you are a spendthrift, huh?'

'No, sir, that's not true.'

'So, the details you just gave me are final, aren't they?'

'Yes, sir. What's this about?'

'Nothing major. It's just about a small missing person's case.'

'But they've come back, haven't they? What's the problem then?'

'There aren't any problems so far. I got an update from the Besant Nagar police that they're back. But still, when something seems off, it's good to clear it up, isn't it? A statistic from the department says there are around one hundred thousand people living in Chennai with fake ID proofs. We can't check everyone we meet on the street, can we? So, when cases like yours come up, we do a thorough check. We know you're not on that list, madam. But just for clarity, bring your Aadhaar card and voter ID. And since you have a vehicle, get your driving licence, too, to the Guindy police station.'

'Now? I can't come to the station now, sir.'

'Oh, really? Fine, we can come to where you live. We'll be there in ten minutes.'

Anandhi felt a surge of panic. 'No, sir. I'll come to the station.'

'Well then, something's not quite right, is it, Anandhi Madam?' he laughed.

'There's nothing wrong. I'm not at home right now. I'll come as soon as I get home, no matter how late it is,' she said, her frustration evident.

'Oh, how generous of you. So, until then, we should all wait here like dogs, huh? I don't care where you are or what you're doing. I'm giving you exactly one hour. You need to be here within that time. If not, you'll see a different side of me. Got it?'

SI Farooq hung up.

Anandhi sat there, staring at the remaining water in her glass, still holding the phone to her ear. Suddenly, her phone rang again.

Ram, Vetri and Reshma realized the call had been disconnected only when they heard the phone ring again. Startled, Anandhi moved it away from her ear. It was SI Farooq again. She answered the call and brought it closer.

'Well, Anandhi Madam, I forgot to mention one important thing. It's an offer. If you have all the proofs I mentioned earlier, come straight to the police station. But if you don't have them, don't worry. I'll give you another location. Just come there and we'll settle everything. And remember, this offer isn't available to everyone, okay? After all, madam is the receptionist of a college here, right? We might show some leniency. One hour. Sharp.'

SI Farooq ended the call with a sinister laugh.

32

One

Anandhi stood at the parking lot in front of Little Italy, gazing out at the rain-soaked road. The downpour continued unabated, with occasional flashes of lightning illuminating the night sky.

After ending the call, she had walked out of the restaurant with a look of determination. Ram, Vetri and Reshma repeatedly asked her what happened, but she remained silent. However, judging by the conversation, they understood the call was from the Guindy police station.

The three of them stood at the parking lot, concerned about Anandhi. After a moment, she turned to face them, her expression filled with disappointment.

'I saw this coming the day I left Tirupur for Chennai a year and a half ago. That's why I kept my distance from everyone I met in this city. But despite my resolve, first Paatti and then the three of you entered my life. Many a times, I seriously considered moving away to maintain that distance, but each time, I found myself growing closer to you all. Eventually, I began to fear that one day I might have to leave suddenly, without even saying goodbye. That fear made me want to share my story with you many times. But I was terrified that you might not accept it, and would jeopardize my goals. That fear held me back.

'So, I made another decision. I didn't want to leave you all with unanswered questions if I ever had to leave the city abruptly. So, I wrote down my life story, including what I shared with you earlier, in a diary and hid it inside Paatti's Padmini car. I believed that was the safest place in the house. When I called Paatti earlier, I told her where to find it. Now, like you, Paatti knows everything about my past. Once you get home, please read the diary to know about the rest of my story. Afterwards, destroy it. If not, it could disturb the peaceful lives of many people.

'You all brought joy and love into my monotonous life. I'll never forget you, all or Paatti, or the bond we shared, as long as I live. I wanted to tell you all this now, just in case I don't get another chance to do so. Well then, I'm going to meet the SI.'

Hearing Anandhi's words, the three of them were stunned. Ignoring their shock, Anandhi pulled out her phone and dialled SI Farooq's number. He picked up on the first ring.

'Hello, Anandhi Madam. What's up?' he asked, his words dripping with mockery.

'Sir, I accept your offer. Where should I come?'

'Wow, superb! Smart choice, I like it.'

'Where should I come?' Anandhi repeated, her tone steady.

'Ah, you seem to be in more of a hurry than I am. I like that, too. There's an old warehouse on the right side of the road where the Kathipara bridge ends. No one will disturb us there—just the two of us. If you don't know the place, I can come and pick you up.'

'It's okay, sir. I know the place. It's eleven now. I'll be there in half an hour. You can be there accordingly,' she said.

'Good girl. And if possible, come in a saree. I'm not a fan of these modern outfits, okay? And—'

Before he could finish, she disconnected the call.

'What are you up to?' Ram asked angrily.

'If I don't do this now, it will affect the lives of many others, including Paatti and the three of you,' she said with determination.

'Anandhi, if you call Sudha Akka, you can escape safely, right?' Reshma suggested, grabbing Anandhi's wrist, trying to offer a solution.

'It's possible. But, Reshma, as I just told you, it won't be easy for me to vanish from the police suddenly. Besides, whatever happens to me now or in the future, Sudha Akka and her team shouldn't know. If they find out, everything I've struggled for will be for nothing.'

The three of them were taken aback yet again.

'What are you going to do without their knowledge?' Vetri asked anxiously.

'Vetri, you'll find all the answers in that diary. Please don't ask me anything more,' she said, looking him in the eye.

'Anandhi, I know you well. I'm sure you're not going to comply with that policeman's demands. You must have a plan. But you should know that the police station isn't safe. These same policemen took Malli away and tortured her. She didn't survive,' Ram warned.

'It's okay, Ram. I'm already late. You should head to Paatti's house.' Anandhi reached into Ram's shirt pocket and took the key.

'Anandhi, please,' Ram pleaded, gripping her hand tightly. She paused and looked deeply into his eyes for a brief moment. She could see the silent plea: 'Don't leave me, please' in his gaze. She smiled softly at him, then gently freed her hand and walked towards her Luna.

Anandhi started the two-wheeler and sped away into the downpour. Ram, Vetri and Reshma stood there, watching her go with their hearts pounding.

Two

The power went out because of the rain and thunder, but Paatti continued reading Anandhi's diary in the light of a candle. She only paused when her eyes filled with tears, feeling Anandhi's struggles unfold right before her. She thought that if Anandhi had shared the story in person, she would have stopped her midway, unable to bear the rest. Wiping her eyes firmly, she adjusted her glasses and continued reading:

> Under Sudha Akka's insistence, I stopped working at the garment mill in Tirupur and joined an institute nearby to pursue a computer course. That period marked a significant turning point in my otherwise slow and aimless life.
>
> One day, after class, I was casually browsing through the internet when I came across an article. It detailed the experiences of a photographer covering the Sri Lankan war. The article was accompanied by several photographs he had taken, each one a haunting reminder of my memories of war-torn Sri Lanka. As I clicked through the images, the faces of tormented victims filled my screen. But there was one photograph that stopped me in my tracks. My heart began to pound. The caption read: 'People escaping in a boat during the war.' Among the panic-stricken faces of the women and children in the boat, I saw Raja. I stared at the screen, sobbing uncontrollably. I still don't know if my tears were those of sorrow or joy. My little brother, whom I had long thought dead in the war, was alive! It was the greatest news I could have ever received, but I kept it to myself.
>
> The article was written by a photographer named Amrith Das. According to the article, he too had escaped the war zone in a boat. The photo of Raja in the boat was taken by him from

another boat, so I assumed they all fled together. Desperate to contact him, I reached out to the online media outlet, providing the details of the article. They didn't have his phone number, but they gave me his email address. I created a fake email account and sent him a message. In it, I wrote about Raja and myself in detail, even pointing out Raja in the photo he had taken.

The days that followed were filled with anxious anticipation. I checked my email obsessively every time I reached the computer class. I hopped from temple to temple, praying for a reply from Amrith Das. But as the days turned into weeks, my hopes began to fade. I eventually brought it up with Sudha Akka, who immediately dismissed my concerns and scolded me for scratching at old wounds. She was angry, said that I was wasting my life thinking about a brother who would never return. That hope, too, was crushed. I told her that there was a child in the photograph who looked like Raja. However, she informed me that she had complete records of all those who came to India during the war, and that Raja's name was not among them.

Days passed. I continued checking my email inbox every day. Then, twenty-four days later, there was a reply from Amrith Das. He confirmed that there was indeed a boy named Raja with them on the boat. The boat didn't head to India; instead, it went to Australia, sailing for days. They reached Christmas Island, which is part of Australia, and surrendered to the authorities. Afterwards, they were moved to various refugee shelters. Amrith had lost contact with Raja since then. He recalled how Raja, unlike the other children who slept at night, would stay awake, silently crying while staring at the stars. According to Australian law, refugees are held in detention for three months before being released. But where would a six-year-old boy go after that? The thought haunted me.

As the days went by, I resolved not to be disheartened but to think of ways to find Raja. But who in Australia could search for him? With no other option, I pleaded with Amrith Das for help. Despite struggling to make ends meet in Australia, he understood my torment and made inquiries at the refugee shelters. Unfortunately, Raja was nowhere to be found. Amrith suggested an alternative: many people secretly travelled by boat from India to other countries, including Australia. But such journeys were perilous and uncertain. The boatmen demanded different amounts for travel to different destinations. Amrith informed me that if I was determined to go to Australia, he would try to connect me with those who could help. He also promised that if I managed to reach the country, he would assist me in finding Raja. See, Raja is the only family I have left. Knowing he is alive, how could I not search for him? I told Amrith to keep me informed about any boats leaving for Australia from India.

I knew how Sudha Akka might react if I told her about the new information I had about Raja, so I kept it a secret. Even if I shared it with her, she wouldn't allow me to take such a risky step. I was certain of that. To test the waters, I once casually asked akka if she had any connections in Australia. When she said no, I felt more confident that my decision to not share anything with her was right. I continued to wait for Amrith Das's email. One day, it arrived. It said boats departed twice a year from Munambam in Kerala. However, to secure a spot on the next year's boat, I had to pay the amount upfront and book in advance. The travel expense totalled three hundred thousand rupees. I also needed to set aside money for expenses after reaching Australia and to compensate Amrith Das. I needed to raise at least five hundred thousand rupees in total. Amrith offered to pay an advance of one hundred thousand rupees to the boatmen, with the understanding that I would repay him after reaching Australia. He urged me to make a decision quickly.

Though I didn't know Amrith Das personally, I decided to trust him. From that point on, my thoughts revolved around how to raise that amount in such a short time. Even if I worked day and night at the garment factories in Tirupur, it would take me a decade to save that much. That's when I thought about moving to Chennai. I had heard that Chennai was the perfect place for the ambitious to make money. When I told Sudha Akka about my plan, she resisted. I explained that I needed a change from the stifling atmosphere of Tirupur. She warned me about the dangers of getting caught by the police in Chennai. Disappointment took over me, pulling me back into a state of depression like before. I started losing my enthusiasm and will to live. Sensing my despair, Sudha Akka handed me a certificate. It belonged to the daughter of one of her teammates, but the photo on it was mine. Akka explained that the certificate's original owner had died in a bus accident, and that I could use her identity in Chennai. The certificate would be enough to secure accommodation and a job in Chennai. They also gave me a fake Aadhaar Card in the name of Anandhi for emergency checks. They strictly advised me not to use it for activities like getting a SIM card. That's how I became Anandhi.

Before leaving Tirupur, they gave me a SIM card for general use and another secret one to contact Sudha Akka. They instructed me to use an old keypad mobile to avoid GPS tracking. I followed all their instructions diligently. I used the secret SIM to communicate with both Sudha Akka and Amrith Das. Within the first week of arriving in Chennai, I secured a job at the college. I also explored all possible ways to earn money. However, it took nearly six months of trying different jobs and building a network before money started coming in. During this time, I acquired an old Luna registered under a deceased person's name, knowing that the police often overlook such vehicles during checks. Slowly, the money began to pile up, giving me the confidence to inform Amrith Das to pay the advance for the boat leaving the next year.

I had exactly one year ahead of me. Raising five hundred thousand rupees in that short span was a herculean task, but the thought of Raja fuelled me to overcome every obstacle. As time passed, a friend of Amrith Das in Chennai met me secretly several times to collect money. When he couldn't come, I left the money at a shop near our college, following Amrith's instructions. He handled everything from Australia. So far, I've handed over four hundred thousand rupees. The boat will leave from Kerala on the fourteenth of next month. I have just one month left. If I manage to raise the remaining one hundred thousand rupees, I can leave India.

By the time you read this diary, I may not be with you. I know you've been troubled by questions about me and why I've been working so hard to make money. I hope this explains why I've been so secretive and driven. I never intended to deceive any of you. If my actions have hurt anyone, please forgive me and understand it was all part of my effort to find my brother. If fate allows, we will meet again, Paatti, Vetri, Reshma and my dear Ram.

With love,

Yours,
Anandhi (May the name remain the same)
14-12-2018

33

One

After Anandhi left Little Italy, Ram, Vetri and Reshma followed her on the Bullet. The rain was still coming down hard. When Paatti called, Vetri had to try hard to answer without getting the screen wet.

'You have to stop her, Vetri. If she falls into the hands of the police, she might never see the world again,' Paatti said anxiously.

'We're following her, Paatti, but we don't understand what she's up to. That SI told her to come to an old warehouse in Guindy,' Vetri replied.

'She's walking into even bigger trouble. Stop her at any cost,' Paatti urged before disconnecting.

By then, they were halfway there to Guindy. Despite the downpour, they could see Anandhi in the distance. Ram kept just enough distance between them so that he could close in within seconds if needed, but they lost sight of her near the Velachery signal, where the main road split towards Guindy. Anandhi sped away while the traffic signal turned from yellow to red. Ram, trapped in traffic, kept the engine revving, anxiously watching the timer as it ticked down from one hundred and twenty. Anandhi, meanwhile, had raced ahead.

She didn't see SI Farooq as a significant threat, confident that she could use her Kalari moves to defeat a strong opponent within seconds. In fact, she planned to incapacitate him enough that he would never again misuse his power to harass another woman. She felt no guilt about it.

Despite the heavy rain and clouds, she looked up at the sky. 'Appa … Amma …' she called out, just as she always did before making a major decision. Then she accelerated towards the warehouse.

Two

All the thirunangais had huddled together under the Kathipara bridge, unable to sleep. The rain and strong winds had driven water into their makeshift rooms made of sarees. The waste from the nearby drainage had spilled over in a corner, releasing a foul stench. SI Farooq and Kathirvel looked at them and moved on.

The thirunangais noticed the red taillights of the police jeep stop near the warehouse. They guessed that the officers had found another victim for the night. Thilothama, drenched, immediately stood up and walked towards the pile of drainage slurry. With fierce determination, she scooped up handfuls of the slurry and smeared it all over her body and clothes, covering herself entirely in the black waste.

'We need to pay our respects to Malli's departed soul, don't we?' she said.

The other thirunangais understood her intention. They gathered around the pile of slurry and began smearing themselves with the filth, their actions fuelled by a shared resolve.

Three

Paatti slid into the driver's seat of the Padmini for the first time in five years. She turned the key in to the ignition. The car roared to life, as if it had been eagerly awaiting her touch. She switched on the headlights and wipers, looking to her left. It was the first time she was driving the car without her husband by her side. Ignoring the vow she had taken, she shifted into first gear and drove forward with resolve.

Four

Anandhi rode through the gate of the Guindy warehouse and made her way along a path lined with overgrown grass. At the end of it, she spotted a jeep with a faint light glowing inside.

The tall grass on either side of the path was flanked by the dark, looming building of the warehouse. As Anandhi approached the jeep, she saw SI Farooq standing on the verandah opposite the jeep, smoking, while the rain continued to beat down. She left the engine of her Luna running and stood in the rain, trying to memorize every detail about him. SI Farooq motioned for her to turn off the headlights. Anandhi observed him closely one more time as he shielded his face from the light, and then she switched off engine, leaving only the faint glow from the jeep.

She dismounted and walked towards SI Farooq. To her surprise, she saw Kathirvel sitting in the driver's seat of the jeep, snacking on groundnuts. That was unexpected. She had anticipated SI Farooq to be alone. Undeterred, she proceeded to the verandah.

As she approached, SI Farooq pulled out a paper from his uniform's pocket and held it up. The dim light from the jeep illuminated it. It was a copy of Anandhi's certificate.

'You're not just some local girl, like this photo suggests. You're outstandingly sexy,' he leered, his eyes wandering over her body. His eyes lingered on Anandhi's wet chest, and he gulped down his saliva, clearly enjoying the view.

'Babe, I told you to come in a saree. Well, it's okay. Tomorrow onwards, wear a saree, alright?' His voice oozed with lust as he flashed a predatory smile at her and slipped the certificate back into his pocket.

Anandhi's expression remained unchanged; her smile remained unwavering. She extended her hand as if to take the certificate from him.

'Let's see how you perform first. Then we'll decide whether this evidence gets destroyed or not,' he said, grabbing her hand.

From the driver's seat, Kathirvel ogled at Anandhi, scanning her from head to toe. Always one to wait for his turn, he was pleased with the catch they had for that night.

Five

Ram and his friends parked near a garbage bin, ensuring they remained out of sight. They quickly ran towards the gate of the warehouse, taking cover behind it. Peering inside, they could make out the shape of a jeep through the downpour.

Ram didn't hesitate. He slipped inside first, with Vetri and Reshma following close behind.

'What's your plan?' Vetri asked as he caught up with Ram.

'First, we need to figure out what Anandhi's plan is. Until then, we stay hidden. If her plan goes south, we'll step in. Whatever happens, we'll face it together.'

Ram pointed towards the verandah of a building to their left. They quickly moved in that direction, pushing aside the tall grass as they advanced.

Meanwhile, SI Farooq, trying to assert his dominance, removed his uniform shirt, flexing his muscles in an attempt to lure Anandhi. She observed him carefully, her thoughts racing. She knew she could take SI Farooq down if she struck his vital points, but Kathirvel was a concern. He could retaliate and catch her off-guard. He might even call for backup through the wireless set, lock the jeep and flee, or even use a gun if there was one in the vehicle.

As she calculated her options, SI Farooq removed his belt, unbuttoned his pants and pulled down the zip, his intentions unmistakably vile.

Anandhi quickly assessed the distance between herself and SI Farooq, calculating how many steps it would take to close the gap and strike the back of his head. Meanwhile, Ram, Vetri and Reshma had quietly reached the back of the jeep. From their position, they saw the half-naked Farooq illuminated in the dim light from the vehicle, but they were still clueless about Anandhi's plan.

Just as SI Farooq pulled his pants down, a strange and pungent smell hit his nose, and he heard footsteps approaching. Panicked, he hurriedly tried to cover his exposed erection with his uniform shirt and struggled to button his pants. Anandhi, poised to attack, hesitated. She, too, had noticed the foul odour.

At the same time, Ram and his friends also caught a whiff of the stench. They turned around and saw several shadows moving swiftly down the path lined with tall grass. The three of them crouched low behind the jeep, only to straighten up in shock and dismay. Ram's eyes widened as he recognized the figures approaching. They were the thirunangais.

The shadows rushed towards the verandah, approaching SI Farooq and Anandhi. SI Farooq's panic escalated as the dark human shapes closed in on him. Kathirvel quickly jumped out of the jeep, but before he could react, nearly five of the figures had surrounded SI Farooq.

Anandhi, confused by the sudden turn of events, struggled to comprehend what was happening. The shadowy figures then leaped on to Kathirvel as he tried to come to his senior's aid. At that moment, Ram sprinted towards the verandah, grabbed Anandhi by her hand and swiftly pulled her behind the jeep.

Anandhi was startled to see Ram, Vetri and Reshma there. The three of them embraced Anandhi tightly, their hearts pounding with a mix of relief and confusion as they tried to make sense of the chaotic scene unfolding around them.

Six

Under the torrential downpour, the vintage Padmini raced through alternate routes towards Guindy. The wipers swept back and forth tirelessly, clearing the windshield and guiding the way ahead. Though Paatti struggled at first, the seasoned driver within her soon resurfaced, taking full control. She pressed the accelerator harder, feeling the car respond.

'Padma, come on!' she called out excitedly from inside, urging the car forward with renewed energy.

Seven

A massive thunderclap reverberated. In no time, the twelve enraged thirunangais had overpowered SI Farooq and Kathirvel. While some of them helped the two men struggle to their feet, Thilothama retrieved two rocks she had brought along, gripping them firmly.

She knelt before SI Farooq, who was held down tightly by her companions, and unbuttoned his pants, yanking them down along with his underwear. Farooq made one final, desperate attempt to break free, but his strength was no match for the combined power of the thirunangais.

Thilothama positioned the rocks on either side of his exposed penis and, with all her might, smashed them together, crushing it.

SI Farooq's agonized screams echoed off the warehouse walls, mingling with the drumming of the relentless rain.

Reshma and Vetri covered their mouths in shock and disbelief. Anandhi remained expressionless, her face unflinching.

Ram felt a deep, long-festering wound within him beginning to heal, all thanks to the thirunangais.

A moment later, Kathirvel's screams pierced the air as well.

'Vetri, take them and go to Paatti. I'll come on Anandhi's Luna,' Ram instructed, his voice steady.

'A copy of my certificate is in his pocket,' Anandhi informed him.

'I'll handle everything. Get out of here as quickly as you can. It's dangerous for you to stay any longer,' Ram urged, pointing towards the exit. Vetri grabbed Reshma and Anandhi, and they sprinted towards the gate.

Ram walked briskly towards the thirunangais. Some of them were still furiously stomping on and thrashing SI Farooq and Kathirvel, unable to contain their anger.

When they saw Ram, their expressions softened. They cast him a loving glance before running out into the rain together.

Eight

Vetri, Anandhi and Reshma had barely sprinted out of the gate when they stopped abruptly. Paatti's Padmini was parked in front of them.

'Kiddos, get in fast,' Paatti urged, managing to open the door on the left side.

'You both get in. I'll wait for Ram,' Vetri said, opening the back door for Anandhi and Reshma. After they got in, Vetri remained by the warehouse's gate, peering inside to check on Ram.

Ram was rummaging through SI Farooq's pockets, searching for Anandhi's certificate. He finally found it. He had remembered to keep one hand over his face, as a precaution. With a final glance at SI Farooq and Kathirvel, who were writhing in pain on the ground, Ram quickly made his way to Anandhi's Luna parked near the police jeep. He kick-started it and raced towards the gate.

34

One

When Ram and Vetri arrived at Paatti's house, it was well past 1 a.m. The Padmini was back in the car shed, just like before. Ram felt as if the last few hours had been part of a strange and surreal dream. After parking the Bullet and Luna next to the Padmini, they quietly entered the house.

Inside Paatti's bedroom, Anandhi sat drenched on a chair, while Reshma sat on the floor, leaning against the wall. As soon as Paatti saw Ram and Vetri walk in, she stood up.

'What happened, dears? Are those policemen still alive?' Paatti asked anxiously.

Ram nodded.

'Oh God! I hope someone finds them before they take their last breath. If not, we'll all be in trouble,' Paatti said, her worry evident.

'But we didn't do anything to them. Some gang with a grudge did it,' Vetri tried to defend.

Ram chose not to disclose the identity of the group clad in black they had encountered at the warehouse.

'But when that happened, everyone, including you and me, was in the area, Vetri,' Paatti fretted.

'Well, Paatti, why were you there?' Reshma asked, getting up.

'Do you expect me to sit happily at home when my kids are in danger?' Paatti's voice was firm, leaving Reshma with nothing to say in response.

'Don't worry Paatti,' Ram said gently. 'I don't think there are any CCTVs in that area. If there were, they wouldn't have called Anandhi there. Plus, they dumped Malli's body in a garbage bin nearby. It's clear there's nothing there that could incriminate them. Whatever happens, we'll have to wait until tomorrow morning to know more.'

Anandhi sat silently, taking in their conversation without uttering a word. Paatti took a towel and Anandhi's diary from the cupboard, then walked over to Reshma. She dried Reshma's hair and handed her the diary. Reshma quickly moved to the table with it. Vetri took the towel from Paatti when she was done with Reshma and dried his hair, joining her afterwards.

Finally, Paatti dried Ram's hair before going to Anandhi and doing the same for her. Once Paatti stepped away, Ram looked at Anandhi.

He felt like she was an author awaiting a review from her readers.

Ram pulled out the wet copy of her certificate from his pocket and handed it to her. She pressed it tightly in her palm and looked into Ram's eyes. Then she gestured towards Vetri and Reshma.

'That's written in Tamil, isn't it, dear? How will Ram read it?' Paatti asked, her voice softening. 'Son, come with me to the kitchen. It seems none of you have eaten anything.'

Paatti headed towards the kitchen. Ram softly patted Anandhi on the forehead before following her. As soon as he was out of sight, Anandhi gently placed her feet on top of Ram's wet footprints.

As Paatti placed sweets on to plates, she explained the contents of Anandhi's diary to Ram, who listened attentively. The rain outside had begun to weaken, its intensity now reduced to a low patter.

Meanwhile, Reshma, having finished reading the diary, walked over to the calendar hanging near the window. She traced her fingers across the dates and confirmed the day.

'January 8,' she murmured to herself before quickly turning to Anandhi. 'So, you'll be in Chennai for just four more days?' Reshma asked, concerned.

Anandhi smiled. 'My plan was to leave the city in two days. If that had happened, I would have told you about this diary only after reaching Kerala. But you've managed to change all those plans,' Anandhi said, looking at Reshma with a gentle gaze.

Reshma's expression hardened slightly. 'I admit I made a mistake that could have caused you harm. But are you really foolish enough to trust some random person and get on a boat to Australia? Do you even realize how far Australia is from India?'

Reshma pulled out her phone from the pocket of her slightly wet jeans. Despite the dampness, it powered on as soon as she placed her index finger on the back. She quickly typed 'India to Australia' into the Google search bar. The result appeared: 7,404 kilometres. She turned the screen towards Anandhi, frustration and concern clear on her face.

By the time Vetri finished reading the diary and joined them, his face mirrored the array of doubts that Reshma had just voiced.

'Look at this,' Reshma said, holding up her phone. 'Seven thousand four hundred and four kilometres. The distance from Kanyakumari to Kashmir is just around three thousand kilometres—this is almost double, and across a deep ocean. And you're talking about a boat sent by someone, sneaking past the coast guard? Even if such a boat existed, how would it cover that distance?'

Her voice betrayed her anger as she pressed for answers.

Just then, Paatti and Ram entered the room from the kitchen. Paatti handed a plate of sweets to Reshma. Usually, she would grab the snacks, but that day she simply placed the plate on the bed and turned back to Anandhi, her face still carrying the weight of the unanswered questions. Sensing Reshma's concern, Anandhi gently guided her to sit in the chair beside her.

'Reshma, a lot of things happen in this world, which we know nothing about,' Anandhi began. 'This is just one of those things. It's not the first time they've helped people cross the sea. They even have medicines for passengers in case anyone falls ill. They also carry food that has a long shelf life, which is what we'll eat during the journey. If we manage to dodge the coast guard, we'll reach the open ocean without having to worry about entering any other country's territorial waters. Once we're out there, no other country can claim us. From there, we head straight to Australia. In about forty to forty-five days, we should reach Christmas Island. Once we arrive, we'll turn ourselves in as a group to the police. We may have to stay in a refugee detention centre, but after that, Amrith Das will take care of everything. I had to pay him another hundred thousand rupees, which I did in two instalments over the past few days. Now, I can travel peacefully,' Anandhi explained patiently.

'But it's the deep sea, Anandhi. What if something happens?' Reshma couldn't hide her concern.

'Then so be it. It's far better than leading an uneventful life, isn't it?' Anandhi smiled wide, trying to lighten the mood.

Vetri wasn't convinced. 'Anandhi, why don't you wait for one of us to give it a try? We can try to get an Australian visa and go there legally. Or at least get a tourist visa. We can go and search for Raja,' he suggested.

'Vetri, I know you're saying this out of love for me. But it's been almost ten years since Raja went missing. By now, he must be over sixteen. He could have changed drastically. Have any of you seen him before? How are you going to find him out there? But I can. No matter how much he's grown or how big the crowd is, I can identify him. If I could have entrusted this task to someone, it would have been easier just to hand all that money to Amrith Das. After all, he was with Raja on the boat for days. But some responsibilities are ours alone to fulfil. So, I have to be the one to search for him, Vetri,' she explained with quiet determination.

'But ...' Reshma started to say something, but Ram stopped her.

'If she sincerely wishes to go, then let her. We may not fully understand her pain since we're surrounded by relatives and friends, but think about it for a moment. The only family she has left is her little brother, Raja. If I was in her shoes, I'd find a way to arrange the money and get to Australia, too. While we were living our lives happily in front of her, she never joined us. Instead, she saved every penny. That shows how eagerly she wants to see him, to hold him close again. So, no matter what, we have no right to stand in Anandhi's way.'

When Ram said this, Paatti, Reshma and Vetri couldn't help but agree.

'We're all drenched. Let's not catch a cold. I'll get a change of clothes for Reshma.'

When Anandhi stepped out of the room, the rain had finally stopped.

'What's your final decision about Anandhi?' Reshma asked, showing no intention of leaving.

'Let her go, Reshma. It's her goal that brought her into our lives. How can we stop her from pursuing those?' Paatti echoed Ram's sentiment. Reshma couldn't disagree.

A short while later, Anandhi returned, having changed into dry clothes and with a dress for Reshma. It was a pink churidar, one of the best in her collection.

'This is my favourite dress. You take it. I can't carry so much in any case,' she said, handing the dress to Reshma.

'You've been through so much, all because of me. I'm so sorry,' Reshma said, her eyes welling up.

'Oh, don't worry about it. I expected even worse, so this is nothing. And despite the trouble, you came to the warehouse to save me, didn't you? That's my kummanamoonji!' Anandhi said with a smile, playfully tapping Reshma on the head.

'Anandhi, listen. I'm not ready to part ways with you, Paatti, Vetri and Ram just yet. I don't know if it's possible, but let me ask you this: once you find Raja, can you come back? We can continue our lives, explore Besant Nagar, visit the temple festival at Paatti's Alligramam and enjoy ourselves,' Reshma said, almost like a little girl.

'First, let me find Raja, Reshma. We can talk about everything else afterwards. Now go and change. And you two, get out of here!' Anandhi said, trying to sound serious as she pointed to Vetri and Ram.

'Get lost, you crazy nut!' Vetri shouted back playfully as he and Ram headed for the other room.

Two

The constables, who had been on night patrol at the Guindy police station, returned, noticing that SI Farooq's wireless set had not responded for a long while. Despite multiple attempts to reach him and Kathirvel on their mobile phones, they had received no answer. Knowing about their regular night activities and interests, the officers decided to investigate the warehouse.

Three

At sunrise, all of Chennai gleamed, freshly washed by the rain. As always, small teashops were the first to open, followed by other shops, while vehicles filled the roads and people hurried along the crowded footpaths.

But something was different. Paatti's courtyard, usually adorned with a kolam, was bare. Anandhi's Luna remained parked in the shed. Inside, Paatti and the others sat on the sofa and nearby chairs, sleepy but fixated on the TV. Finally, the news they had been waiting for arrived, making their hearts race.

'Guindy police station's SI Farooq Ahmed and driver Kathirvel Ramalingam have been found attacked. The incident took place early this morning. Their colleagues launched a search when the duo failed to return after night patrol and found them at an abandoned warehouse in Guindy. They have been severely beaten. There have been reports that this warehouse, which has been closed for years, has been the site of illegal activities allegedly supported by the police. City Commissioner Chandrasekhar has informed the press that the involvement of these two policemen in such activities will be investigated. We have received information that as soon as SI Farooq Ahmed and driver Kathirvel Ramalingam, who have been admitted to the emergency department at Sri Ramachandra Hospital in Porur, recover, their statements will be taken,' the newsreader said and then moved on to other stories. Vetri muted the television.

'If the media suspects something, they'll dig deeper, and this could become a major scandal. It could bring disgrace to the entire police department. That's probably why they chose to withhold much of the information from the media,' Paatti said.

Just then, a car horn blared outside the gate. It was Balaji Annan's Omni van.

'Hey Balaji, I am coming,' Paatti called out, looking outside before heading to the kitchen to fetch the boxes of sweets. Anandhi and Reshma followed to help her. When Ram and Vetri stepped on to the verandah, Balaji raised his hand in greeting. They both smiled back. Paatti, Anandhi and Reshma carried the small cartons outside.

'Oh no! Only this much?' he asked, eyeing the boxes.

'I could only manage this much. Take it and go,' Paatti replied, heading towards the gate.

'Paatti, you're getting lazy these days, huh?' he teased as he loaded the boxes into his van.

'Annaa, I'm heading home. I don't think I'll be back anytime soon. Keep an eye on Paatti for me, okay?' Anandhi said.

'Oh, really? Paatti, in that case, should I send someone new to see the room? A girl who visits my shop was asking about a place to rent.'

'We'll talk about that later, Balaji. You get going now.'

Paatti sent him off and walked back to the house. She noticed some dirt on one side of the Padmini. While Anandhi and Reshma went to the verandah to join Ram and Vetri, Paatti headed over to clean the car.

Within minutes, she was busily wiping the car. 'Why did you leave that diary in the car?' she asked Anandhi, busy with a cotton cloth.

'I never liked that promise you made on an impulse. I've sensed that you regretted making that vow about the Padmini. As far as I can tell, you care about this car as much as you cared about Thaathaa. Once you get back into it, I'm sure it will keep you good company, even when I'm gone. You won't have to wait for others, or their free time, if you want to go out,' Anandhi continued, gazing at the car. 'How long can it just sit in the shed? She was happily roaming around when Thaathaa was alive.'

'How are you planning to get to Kerala?' Paatti asked Anandhi, changing the topic.

'By train.'

'Why don't we take the Padmini?'

Reshma, Anandhi, Vetri and Ram exchanged surprised looks.

'Paatti, are you serious?' Vetri asked, unable to believe it.

'It's six hundred and seven kilometres,' Reshma quickly said after checking Google.

'Distance is nothing for Padma. When else will we get the chance to take a trip together? By the time she gets back from Australia, who knows if I'll still be around. Shall we go for a long drive, dears?' Paatti asked, leaning against the Padmini with her arms crossed.

35

One

Ram visited the apartment only once all this while, spending most of his time at Paatti's house. Paatti had prepared many special dishes, just for them.

As they were about to sit down for lunch, the doorbell rang. When Vetri went to the door, he found their father standing there. He called out for Reshma, and she joined him at the door. The others gathered, too, unsure of what was happening.

'Appa, if you've come to take me back, I'm not going with you now. I'll return in two days, but remember that I'm coming back only for you, not for Amma,' she said, avoiding his gaze.

Paatti realized it was Vetri and Reshma's father. She invited him to sit in a chair on the verandah. After settling down, he called Reshma to his side.

'Paappaa, I haven't come to take you home. I came to tell you not to come back. After you left, your mother and her brother have been spreading all sorts of terrible lies about you to the relatives. Since you were a child, I've never heard her say anything kind. She's the very definition of what a mother shouldn't be. As for me, I deserve this. Maybe it's God's punishment for how I treated Vetri's mother over trivial matters.

'Now that you have a good opportunity in the movies, what you really need is peace of mind. It's better for you to stay with your brother. I know he loves you more than anyone else in this world.

I won't worry if you're in his care. Don't come back to that hell, paappaa. Whenever I miss you, I'll come here to see you.'

His eyes teared up. Reshma hugged him and gently kissed his forehead. Vetri approached and placed a firm hand on his father's shoulder. Their father insisted on giving Reshma some money before leaving, despite her reluctance. As he prepared to go, Paatti urged him to stay for lunch. Unable to refuse the warmth and care shown to him, he joined them for a meal, enjoying Paatti's special dishes. When he left, Vetri held Reshma's hand firmly.

That evening, they went to the Besant Nagar beach. Like Anandhi, they chose not to play their usual game of kadalamma kalli. Instead, they all stood hand in hand, stepping into the waves until the water reached their knees. Each wave brushed against their legs before retreating to the shore.

Reshma occasionally moved away from the group to talk on the phone. After noticing this several times, Vetri grew suspicious. He sensed she was pleading with someone.

'What trouble have you got into now?' he asked as soon as she hung up.

'Nothing.'

'If it's something that could harm Anandhi, I'll forget what Appa said and break your leg, got it?'

'Do you really think I'd hurt someone who's already been through so much pain and struggle?'

'Then who are you secretly talking to?'

'That was the production controller of my new movie. He's a good guy. Tomorrow is the release of Rajinikanth's *Petta*, right? I'm trying to get tickets for us.'

'And for that, you're pleading with him? If you give me some money, I can easily get tickets in black at any theatre.'

'I don't want just any theatre. I want tickets at Rohini Silver Screens in Koyambedu.'

'Rohini? You've got to be kidding,' Vetri scoffed.

Reshma's phone rang again. She answered immediately. Her face lit up with excitement as she listened. After thanking the person on the other line repeatedly, she spun Vetri around, holding his hands.

'Five tickets booked for the fans' show tomorrow at 4 a.m.! And they're VIP balcony tickets!'

Two

Anandhi remained awake after everyone had fallen asleep. She climbed up to the open terrace and sat on the concrete slab where the water tank was mounted, gazing at the twin stars in the sky. She heard footsteps approaching. It was Ram coming up the stairs. They exchanged a smile and looked up at the stars together.

'Your brother also turns to those twin stars every night like you, doesn't he?' Ram asked.

'Maybe not. He's in Australia now, and these stars aren't visible from there.'

'Oh.'

A brief silence settled between them.

'Even with different time zones and hemispheres, the moon is the same no matter where you are in the world, isn't it?' Ram asked suddenly.

Anandhi turned towards him, puzzled.

'We might not meet or talk anytime soon, Anandhi. Whenever I miss you, I'll look at the moon. I don't know if you'll ever miss me, but if you do, will you look at the moon, too?'

She didn't answer. Instead, she just glanced up at the moon.

Three

When the alarm went off at 3.15 a.m., Reshma woke everyone up.

Groggy but excited, they all got ready and set off to see *Petta* at Rohini Silver Screens in Koyambedu, all at Reshma's insistence.

When they arrived, the entire area was buzzing with energy, as Rajinikanth's fans had turned the place into a festive celebration. The parking lot was packed, so they had to park the car outside and navigate through the crowd. For Ram, it was his first time experiencing the fervour of Tamil moviegoers.

Reshma made a call. Soon, someone from the theatre's office came out and escorted them to the VIP balcony lounge on the first floor. Even before the movie began, the crowd below them was abuzz with excitement. Paatti and the rest of the group settled into seats in the back row, where a few well-mannered people were moving in and out of the VIP lounge.

At that moment, Reshma took Anandhi's hand and gave it a gentle squeeze. Anandhi was confused.

'Anandhi, before you leave us all behind, I should give you a special gift, don't you think?' Reshma said with a mischievous smile.

'Special gift? Don't be silly, Reshma,' Anandhi replied, playfully knocking her on the head.

'If my guess is right, something you've been yearning for is about to happen. Get ready to enjoy the moment.'

'Huh?'

'Yes, Anandhi. It's time for a big surprise.'

Just as Reshma finished speaking, a massive roar of excitement erupted from the ground floor and the VIP lounge.

They saw the door opening and Rajinikanth's wife, Latha, and his son-in-law, actor Dhanush, entered the lounge. The entire theatre exploded at the sight of Dhanush. He waved to everyone and took a seat in the front row, right in front of Paatti and her group.

Vetri and Ram could hardly believe their eyes.

But the real shock came when the next person walked through the door—actress Trisha, whom Anandhi adored. Anandhi felt her breath catch in her throat as exhilaration overwhelmed her. The roars of excitement from the ground floor and the lounge faded into the background.

Vetri, Ram and Paatti didn't notice the change in Anandhi's expression, but Reshma was watching closely, eager to capture the astonishment on her face.

'Now do you understand why I insisted we come here so early?' Reshma grinned. 'I found out just yesterday morning that Dhanush and Trisha would be here. I pulled a few strings to get these tickets.'

As Reshma spoke, Anandhi's eyes remained locked on Trisha, who was taking a seat in the front row. She watched every movement of her favourite actress with rapt attention, her cold hands tightly gripping Reshma's. Sensing her excitement, Reshma placed a reassuring hand on Anandhi's shoulder, feeling as if she had fulfilled one of her greatest responsibilities.

After the movie, Reshma didn't waste a moment. She gently pulled Anandhi over to where Trisha was, before she could leave the lounge. Anandhi got the chance to talk to her idol and even took a photo with her. After Trisha departed, Anandhi hugged Reshma tightly.

'Thank you, my sweetheart,' she said, her voice full of joy.

Reshma kissed her on the cheek with a smile.

It was nearly 7.30 a.m. when they finally made their way through the buzzing crowd to their car. They made their way back before the traffic kicked in.

Four

By the time they reached home, they were starving. Together, they cooked breakfast and sat down to enjoy it. Just as they began eating, Anandhi's phone rang. It was a call from the police station, as part of an inquiry into the call records of SI Farooq and Kathirvel, who had yet to reveal what happened that night.

Anandhi calmly explained that SI Farooq had called her regarding a missing person's case and that the missing individuals had since returned, prompting a follow-up call to inform her. The police officer on the line checked the files and confirmed her statement was true before ending the call.

Paatti and the others, who had been waiting anxiously, finally relaxed.

With that episode behind them, they realized they only had the rest of the day ahead.

Reshma and Anandhi went out to say goodbye to Principal Srinivas and to buy a bag and other essentials for Anandhi's journey. Meanwhile, Ram went to his apartment to pack for the next two days. He decided not to inform Bineesh and Kiran about the journey, planning to share details only after his return. Vetri also stepped out. With no one at home, Paatti lay down to rest.

They were all back at Paatti's house before noon.

Their plan was to start the journey at 4 p.m. Although the boat wouldn't depart until the twelfth, Amrith Das had instructed Anandhi to reach Cherai, near Munambam, by the morning of the previous day. He had even given her a phone number to call on once she arrived.

As Anandhi arranged her new yellow travel bag, Vetri entered the room. Paatti and Reshma were also there, sitting on the cot, watching her pack.

Vetri handed Anandhi a small wooden photo frame with a picture, a selfie of the two of them, taken at the beach the previous day.

'Oh! So you rushed out to get this, huh?' Paatti asked Vetri.

'Well, when she meets Raja, she'll definitely talk about me. What if he insists on seeing me? Unlike the rest of you, I have big responsibilities now. I'm the big brother of these two ladies, got it?' Vetri replied.

Anandhi hugged Vetri. 'Oh, my dear Vetri, please don't make me cry!'

Five

Vetri was the one who drove the Padmini out of the gate. As everyone walked towards the car, Anandhi turned back for one last look at the house. It felt like leaving her own home forever. Her eyes travelled from the water tank she used to clean to the door of the room she lived in to the outdoor bathroom she frequented. A flood of memories washed over her. When she saw the beehive, she remembered the incident with the senthatti powder and chuckled. She couldn't answer her own question: *would she ever get another chance to live in this house with Paatti and Vetri?*

Suddenly, she walked towards the car shed as if she had forgotten something. She lovingly looked at her Luna. She removed the two-day-old garland from it and kissed the seat.

'I'll definitely miss you,' she whispered, running her fingers over the seat.

As she walked away, leaving the Luna behind, she picked at the wilted marigolds from the garland and tossed them into Paatti's garden.

Ram stood by the gate, admiring the beautiful kolam. He knew that once he was back after leaving Anandhi, the first thing that would haunt him would be the absence of the kolam she drew.

'Shall we go?' Anandhi asked, looking at Ram, who was staring at the ground.

By then, Paatti and Reshma had already got into the backseat of the Padmini.

'Yes. Let's go.'

Ram tried to avoid looking at Anandhi's face as he turned to get into the car. Anandhi tugged on the edge of his shirt, pulling him towards her.

'Can you sit with me?'

Ram looked straight into her eyes, Just like Malli had said, he saw a secret love, long-hidden, reflected in them.

Ram asked Reshma if she could sit in the front. Paatti, who had her eye on that seat, promptly got out and moved to the front.

Ram and Anandhi got into the backseat and closed the door. Vetri prayed silently and moved the Padmini forward in first gear.

36

One

As soon as they crossed the city limits, Reshma opened Google Maps on her phone and set the destination as Cherai beach. Two routes appeared—one via Krishnagiri and the other via Salem. Anandhi suggested avoiding the Krishnagiri route since it would take them through Vaniyambadi. So, they went ahead on the Salem route.

'Vetri, if you get tired, let me know. I'll drive,' Ram said from the backseat.

'Then why on earth am I here? It's been a long time since I've had a good, long drive. Just forget about getting behind the wheel, dear,' Paatti teased, lightening the mood.

'Do you even have a licence, you oldie?' Reshma joined in the fun.

Paatti, with a smirk, reached into her purse and pulled out a renewed licence to show Reshma.

'Kolanchiyammal. Date of birth, 16 January 1951. Blood group, AB negative. Class of vehicle, motorcycle with gear, light motor vehicle, heavy motor vehicle … what!?!' Reshma couldn't believe her eyes. 'Hey oldie! Who gave you a heavy vehicle licence?' she asked, astonished.

Vetri and Ram were equally surprised.

'What do you think of me, huh?' Paatti asked, clearly amused by their stunned reactions.

'Well, if you promise not to make fun of me, I'll tell you something. When I renewed my licence recently, they mistakenly added heavy motor vehicle certification. It must be a printing error, but I didn't bother to get it changed.'

Anandhi burst into laughter, quickly followed by the others.

'You old trickster! As soon as we get back, I'll have the traffic police catch you. Just wait and see!' Reshma exclaimed.

'Give it back, you fool!' Paatti retorted, snatching her licence from Reshma and tucking it back safely into her purse.

Vetri placed his Bluetooth speaker on the dashboard and started playing the album titled 'Ilayaraja Hits' from his phone. On the way, they encountered a police checkpoint. When one officer called the Padmini an old rag, Paatti was furious and scolded him harshly. Vetri managed to smooth things over by slipping the officer a bribe.

As they continued, Anandhi, sitting on the right side, enjoyed the view while slightly leaning against Ram.

Throughout the journey, the Bluetooth speaker softly played Tamil songs.

Anandhi eventually fell asleep, her head resting on Ram's shoulder. He held her hand in his, watching her face in the glow of the streetlights. Despite Vetri's suggestion to get some sleep, Ram stayed awake.

When it was past midnight, Reshma woke up with a start and knocked on Vetri's head.

'Vetri, I need to use the restroom,' she said, as if jerked out of sleep by an alarm.

Vetri felt a twinge of irritation at the way she tapped his head to get his attention. He turned around, gave her a look and then pulled over near a cornfield.

Reshma glanced at the cornfield, then back at him.

'Save this spot for your mistress. Take me to a public restroom! Now!' she snapped, raising her voice.

They continued driving. After some distance, they spotted a Punjabi dhaba. Vetri pulled over.

Before Vetri could say anything, she darted out of the car and rushed towards the toilets. Concerned for her safety, Vetri followed after her. Paatti remained asleep in the front seat.

'Ram ...' Anandhi murmured.

Ram turned to face Anandhi, who was still resting her head on his shoulder, her eyes closed.

'Even after hearing all my stories and knowing that I'm leaving you forever, I don't understand why you keep me close like this.'

He smiled at her question.

'Anandhi, this might sound strange, but let me share a story. Once upon a time, we had a fish farm in the pond next to my house. We raised pearl spot fish, which is delicious and in high demand. I heard about their unique nature on a radio programme. It turns out they're monogamous for life, with deep bonds between each pair. If a male, especially, loses its partner, it won't find another one. When a pearl spot fish is caught, its mate will come to the surface and wait, as if hoping for its return. They wait until the fish dies. After hearing this story, I went to the pond and saw many fish on the surface, waiting for their lost partners. From that day on, I couldn't bring myself to eat pearl spot fish. I pressured my family so much that they eventually stopped fish farming. Chennai is like that pond, Anandhi. And I am one of those pearl spot fishes in it,' he said.

Anandhi looked at Ram, her eyes tearing up.

'I need to tell you something, Ram,' she said, gently pressing his palm.

But before she could continue, they heard Reshma and Vetri outside.

'The folks at the dhaba mentioned that there is another checkpoint near Pichanur. Since it's the Kerala–Tamil Nadu border, bribing the police with small amounts won't work. We'll need to hand over at least five hundred,' Vetri said, leaning through the back window.

Paatti, who had been asleep all this while, opened her eyes at the sound of his voice. 'What's going on? What happened?'

'Oh, nothing much. But do me a favour—sit at the back. Keeping you in the front is like inviting trouble. And stay quiet until we get through. Got it? Now, out you go,' Vetri said, opening the door for her.

Ram felt a twinge of disappointment as he left Anandhi's side, but he took his place in the driver's seat.

Two

Ram knew that once they crossed the border and reached Palghat, they wouldn't have to worry about the police. However, he was unfamiliar with the area beyond that, as he had only made a brief visit to Munambam, near the Ernakulam–Thrissur border, and Cherai as a child. Relying on Google Maps, he followed its directions.

It was early January. A thin layer of fog blanketed the road.

'*Kausalya supraja rama poorvaa santhyaa pravarthathe, uthishta narashaardoola karthavyam daivamaahnitham,*' Paatti recited softly, gazing out of the window.

As they reached Kodungallur, Anandhi received a call from Amrith Das, asking for her location. He gave her a new phone number, informing her that the contact person for Cherai had changed. He also reminded her to use the code '34' while dialing the new number.

Just then, Google Maps announced that Cherai beach was thirty minutes away. None of them had fully grasped the sad reality that Anandhi wouldn't be returning to Chennai with them. As they neared the beach, a wave of sadness washed over them all.

'Paatti, you'll make some sweets and send them to me, right?' Anandhi asked, leaning on Paatti's lap, noticing the happiness fading from her face.

'Do you really want to go, Paappaa?' Paatti asked gently. Anandhi covered her mouth, stopping her from saying anything more.

'I think Vetri was right. You should switch to silent mode,' Anandhi said, getting up from Paatti's lap with a forced laugh.

Ram continued driving the Padmini, following the directions of the female voice on Google Maps.

'Call me as soon as you get there, okay?' Reshma said, gripping Anandhi's hands firmly.

'You're being ridiculous! I'm not going to a foreign country for a job. How can I call you the moment I arrive?' Anandhi replied, gently pressing Reshma's cheek.

By this time, the Cherai beach was close. People were out to exercise and take their morning walks. Ram parked the car near the long walkway by the beach, paved with tiles, and turned to Anandhi.

'Are you sure you want to go, Anandhi?' Ram asked, his voice heavy with sadness.

'Why are all of you talking like this? I've explained everything. It's better if you all switch to silent mode until I leave,' Anandhi said with a strained smile. She then took out her phone and dialled the number Amrith Das had given her.

'Everyone, please be quiet. I'm about to make the call,' she said, almost like a warning. The four of them exchanged disappointed looks.

After five rings, a male voice answered.

'Hello, annaa. 34 here. I've reached the destination.'

'34? Wait a second! Oh, you're under Das's care, right?' the man replied, as if he looked up and found her details.

Anandhi assumed this was how they referred to Amrith Das.

'Yes, I'm under the care of Das.'

'You came by train, right?'

'Yes.'

'How did you get here from the station?'

'I took an autorickshaw.'

'Did you have any conversation with the autorickshaw driver?'

'No.'

'Okay, good. Can you see a two-storeyed ice cream parlour near the beach?'

Anandhi scanned the area through the front windshield. She spotted a small two-storeyed building near the beach. It had a sign that read 'Ice Cream Parlour'.

'Yes, I can see an ice cream parlour,' Anandhi said.

'Alright. Stand next to it, facing the sea, as if you're enjoying the sea view. In ten minutes, an autorickshaw named 'Aaron' will arrive. Get into it. And since you've reached the destination, it's best to switch off your mobile phone now. See you soon.'

Amrith Das had already warned Anandhi not to disclose any details to anyone, as this was an illegal journey. If anything went wrong, it would have serious consequences for everyone involved, including the passengers on the boat.

'They'll be here in ten minutes to pick me up. I told them I came alone. If they see me with you, it can cause trouble. So, let's skip the formal farewell. Bye.'

As she said this, their faces fell.

'Why such a hurry? We can have tea together before we part ways,' Paatti asked anxiously.

'Paatti, it would be really sad if I ended my story with a full stop right here, don't you think? We'll have that tea when we meet next,' Anandhi replied.

Paatti began to sob, words failing her. 'Are you really going?' she asked.

Anandhi gently held Paatti's head with both hands and kissed her firmly on the forehead. It was the hardest kiss Paatti had ever received. Anandhi then did the same for Reshma.

She ruffled Vetri's hair, who was sitting in the front seat. 'Let me take my leave, dear brother ...'

Vetri avoided her gaze and stared out at the sea, his eyes glistening with unshed tears. Ram sat in the driver's seat, his head bowed.

'Oye ... Ram ...'

He didn't hear her at first.

'Ram ... Ram ...'

'Huh?' he responded, still not turning back.

'Look at me.'

'Why?'

'Just look at me.'

When she insisted, he wiped his eyes quickly and turned around. Anandhi lifted her little finger and smiled, then carefully lifted both ends of his moustache with her finger. As she lifted the second end, tears from Ram's eyes soaked her fingertip. She quickly withdrew her hand, bowing her head, unable to look at him.

Anandhi felt overwhelmed by the immense love she had received from the moment she arrived in India. Yet, the love and longing for her only blood relation was even stronger. She held everyone's hand one last time, then opened the door and stepped out.

Ram opened the boot and retrieved her yellow travel bag. He looked into her eyes, surprised to see that her tears did not reflect the sadness of parting.

When Anandhi reached for the bag, Ram hesitated and held on.

'Ram, it's time. I need to go,' she said, tugging at the bag.

'Just answer one question before you leave, Anandhi. Did you like me? Just a "yes" or "no". I need to hear it from you.'

His eyes were filled with tears. Anandhi stood silent, unable to respond, overwhelmed at the thought that her answer could profoundly impact his future.

'Anandhi, an autorickshaw is coming. Could that be them?' Reshma asked, leaning out of the window.

Anandhi quickly and forcefully jerked the bag away from Ram and set it down. Then she retrieved her diary and its key from a hidden compartment and handed it to him.

'Read this only after you're back in Chennai. The answer to your question is in there.'

She lifted the bag on to her shoulder and walked away without saying goodbye.

'Ram, that autorickshaw is getting closer. Hurry up and get in. She shouldn't face any issues because of us,' Reshma said loudly from the car.

Ram got back into the car. All of them watched with heavy hearts as Anandhi walked away, her bag slung over her shoulder, not looking back once.

Three

Anandhi's eyes overflowed with tears as she travelled in the autorickshaw named 'Aaron', uncertain of her destination. At the same time, Ram's eyes overflowed with tears that fell on to Anandhi's diary, which he held tightly.

Four

Even though Anandhi had left, their hopes had not faded. They firmly believed that just before the boat departed early the next morning, Anandhi would call one of them and return with them to Chennai. So, they booked rooms in a hotel near the Cherai beach and waited anxiously for that call.

Five

12 JANUARY 2019 (THE NEXT DAY)
2.10 A.M.
MUNAMBAM BEACH

A groyne extended from the Munambam beach into the sea. To its right was an estuary where the River Periyar met the sea. Fishing boats navigated from the deep sea to the Munambam harbour and the Malyankara area via this route. Along the groyne, a high mast light illuminated the area. Workers on either side of the groyne were busy lifting Chinese nets. They looked suspicious as an old woman, two young men and a young woman passed by at that hour. It was an unusual time for visitors. The waves roared against the rocks, and the endless sea was dotted with the faint lights from distant fishing boats.

It was that time of the night when the fishing boats that had ventured into the deep sea the previous evening began to return through the waterway. Ram and Vetri had learned from the hotel's security guard that the boats from Munambam took this route to reach the deep sea. Paatti, Ram, Reshma and Vetri sat on the rocks at the edge of the groyne, their eyes scanning each boat that moved towards and away from the shore under the high mast light.

Finally, after 4 a.m., a boat named *Dayamatha* came into view. On one side of the boat, several travel bags were piled up, while the other side was covered with a large tarpaulin sheet. They could make out the shapes of the people beneath the sheet, their heads like faint spheres. Ram spotted the yellow travel bag among the pile and pressed Vetri's hand firmly. Without needing to speak, Paatti, Reshma and Vetri also recognized the bag. Anxiety gripped them as they all rose to their feet. *Dayamatha* passed right in front of them, carrying their last shred of hope of Anandhi's return.

Ram wanted to scream her name, desperate to see her face one last time. Instead, he remained silent, gripping Vetri's hand tightly as the boat drifted away. Paatti and Reshma's eyes overflowed with tears. They stood there, watching until the boat vanished from sight …

37

After returning to Chennai, the first thing Ram did was to read Anandhi's diary, with Reshma's help. On the first page, in bold letters, it was written: **ANANDHI, C/O RAM**.

The second page was filled with the name 'Ram', written over and over again. The following pages were filled with all the moments she had cherished with him. She had meticulously noted down every time Ram had looked at her, the colour of the jeans and shirts he had worn each day, and even whether he had shaved or had a haircut—Anandhi had noted every detail carefully.

As the pages went on, she described how Ram had been her companion on their trip to Alligramam, and how much she had enjoyed playfully lifting the edges of his moustache while he slept. In the later pages, she had penned detailed accounts of how their love life could have been if she were a regular Indian girl, and what their future together might have looked like. She had imagined every tiny detail of their life together. Anandhi had even written that they would have had two children after marriage, a boy and a girl. Ram could choose the boy's name, but she would insist that their daughter be named Trisha.

As Ram and Reshma continued reading, a loud scream rose from Ram's heart, burning and breaking it at once.

38

12 JANUARY 2020
SOMETIME DURING THE EVENING
MUNAMBAM BEACH

The pages of a diary resting on Ram's lap flapped in the wind. On the cover, in big and bold letters, it read: **RAM, C/O ANANDHI**. The first few pages were filled with the name 'Anandhi'. The wind continued to flip through many of the pages, but Ram caught the last page before it could slip away and read it once more.

Dear Anandhi,

It's been exactly one year since you left. After you were gone, for almost a week, the headlines of all the major newspapers in Kerala were about the boat you left on. At first, that terrified me, but knowing that they couldn't find any information about you brought me some relief. I was happy that you would get to meet Raja, just as you wished. Not a single day has passed without me thinking about you, Anandhi. Sometimes, I feel like crying. Do you remember the story I told you about the pearl spot fish? My situation is pretty much the same. I keep wandering through the places that hold your memories, imagining that you're still there.

The temple festival at Alligramam was a few days ago. We all went together, just like last year. Paatti stood at the door of her train coach, staring at the platform at the Egmore station until the train left, hoping to see you. And you know what? After we reached Thanjavur, I didn't go with the rest of the group to Alligramam. Instead, I stayed at our old Dhanashree Lodge that night.

Well, I've got some good news to share! Remember the old man at the hotel? He has ditched his all-black getup and is looking stylish these days. They've adopted a smart, young, orphan girl. His wife brought her to the lodge when she heard I was there. They both seemed really happy and, of course, asked about you. I couldn't resist, so I fibbed a little and told them you'd definitely come with me next year. Our names are still there on the wall, untouched. I even stayed in the same room as we did last time.

At night, I took a walk down the mayflower path, all by myself. That iron bench, the road—nothing has changed. I threw some flowers on the spot where you sat that day. You kept saying I was such a boring guy back then. And hey, remember our deal about the moon? Whenever I miss you, I just sit and stare at it for a while. When I'm at Paatti's place, I go up to the water tank and gaze at Sirius and the moon. I know you're out there somewhere, doing the same when you miss me.

I've been using your Luna these days, Anandhi. I wash it every day and even put a garland on it. Sometimes I take it to places like that closed shop where we stood on that rainy night. I miss Malli, too, just like I miss you. When I do, I take her ghungroos and sit on the bench at Guindy railway station, where we used to hang out. They repainted that bench, so our names are gone, but I've got a photo of it on my phone.

Remember the bike that Malli's younger brother damaged? The guy from the showroom, Mani, fixed it up and sold it. He came to Chennai with the money, and that's when he found out Malli had passed away. He gave the money to her friends. Since then, they've been trying to find a safe place to stay, but no one's willing to rent them a house, no matter how much they offer.

Balaji Annan had suggested another girl for your room. I told Paatti about Malli's friends. When she heard what they were going through, she insisted on bringing them all home. Some of them are sleeping in your room now, while the others are in Paatti's room. Paatti's very clever though. She told them not to worry about rent, but managed to convince them to stop begging on trains and help her make sweets at home. Now, almost every bakery in Chennai has their sweets, and they're in demand. Guess what Paatti named their company? It's 'Anandhi Sweets'.

Even though my course is over, I still go to our college's reception and just stand there, staring at the area where I used to see you every day. The new receptionist thinks I'm crazy and keeps scolding me. She has no idea that you ruled that place like a queen.

Amma Unavagam is still the same, and the akka who served food is still there, too. Whenever I'm in Nungambakkam, I buy the same curd rice you used to love and sit at the same cement bench where you would eat. After that, I wander alone through the streets of Nungambakkam, where we used to walk during breaks. Your memories are etched everywhere, Anandhi. The only thing missing is Reshma, Vetri and you, chattering away while walking with me.

Guess what? Reshma's first movie came out, and it was a hit! She's done three movies in the past year and is super busy, so she doesn't get to wander around with us much. But whenever she can, she still shows up with some crazy stories. The main problem now is if we take her to Marina beach or Besant Nagar, people recognize her and start crowding. Still, I'm really happy for her. Even though she's made a lot of money, she's still living with Vetri in his room. With her support, Vetri also worked on three movies. Now he's gearing up to make his own.

Oh, a funny thing happened. Reshma's mom, who never even bothered to call her before, showed up as soon as Reshma got famous and made some money. She came to take her home, but you know what Reshma did? When the lady was standing outside, Reshma threw something at the beehive, dashed inside and locked herself in her room. Paatti came out and saw the lady running for her life. She hasn't bothered to come back since.

I just realized I've told you all about everyone else but nothing about myself. So, here it goes. I finished writing my novel this past year. I named it *Ram, C/O Anandhi*. I sent it to five publishing houses. Guess what? Yesterday, I got an email from one of them—they're going to publish it! That's my news. I'm done sharing everything about us. Now, I need to know about you. It's been a year since you left. Where are you, Anandhi?

There was an article in the paper today about the boat you left on. It said that even after a year, there was no trace or lead in the Munambam human trafficking case. The police made inquiries in several countries, including Australia, but it was all in vain. No one can confirm that your group arrived anywhere. The navy also confirmed that there were no boat accidents at that time. The newspaper mentioned that the police are still investigating. I've been searching for you in every way I can. I'm sure that wherever you are, you'll contact Amrith Das. I found his number and practically begged him for any news about you, but he keeps saying he doesn't know anything. He's blocked my number now because I kept calling. I'm planning to save up some money, go to Australia and fall at his feet if that's what it takes to find out something about you.

Oh, and I forgot to tell you. I went to Akka Thankachi Madom in Rameswaram, where you used to live. I sat by the pond for a while, where you used to spend so much time. The tall grass and the blue flowers are still there. I also met Dr Ramachandran, the one who treated you. He's such a kind man.

I still have so much more to tell you, Anandhi. I came home for two days from Chennai. Before heading back, I just felt like sitting here for a while, writing to you. I've booked my return train from Thrissur at 6.55 p.m. I don't want to be like you, catching the train at the last minute with some heroic stunt, so I'm leaving now. I'll write more after I reach Chennai.

Yours always,
Ram

Ram closed the diary and placed it inside his bag, which also contained the one marked **ANANDHI, C/O RAM**. As the sun began to set, he walked towards the main road.

39

17 JULY 2019
A NEWS SNIPPET FROM *KERALA KAUMUDI*
NEWSPAPER READ LIKE THIS:

> **Munambam Human Trafficking Case: Missing Persons Remain Untraced**
>
> Police struggling with investigation; progress stalled
>
> KOCHI: Despite the arrest of six individuals, including the main suspect, and the seizure of crucial documents, the Munambam human trafficking case continues to stall. The Kerala Police, the Tamil Nadu Police's Q Branch, the Intelligence Bureau, the Directorate of Military Intelligence, the navy, the Coast Guard and international agencies, have all been involved in the investigation. However, progress remains slow as they struggle to locate the eighty-seven people, including children, who escaped to Australia. The ongoing uncertainty has delayed the submission of the charge sheet.
>
> The police have received information that the individuals who escaped from Munambam have reached various countries, including Australia, New Zealand, Indonesia, Malaysia and Algeria. Despite launching an investigation with the help of Interpol, no significant results have been obtained. Some relatives of the missing individuals received missed calls from overseas numbers, but these couldn't be traced or verified. The calls were found to originate from the Annaba police station in Algeria. These numbers were handed over to the consulate, but the police were informed that they had no connection to the human trafficking case.
>
> Meanwhile, the foreign ministry has no updates either.

It was discovered that the boat had traversed the Pacific Ocean, prompting notifications to be issued to countries along this route.

The human trafficking occurred on a fishing boat named *Dayamatha*, which departed from the Munambam harbour in the early hours of 12 January. The trafficking ring had been operating out of Ambedkar Colony in Delhi, a densely populated area where Sri Lankan refugees and Tamilians live. The first clue about human trafficking emerged from the bags abandoned at Maliyankara Boat Jetty, where the police discovered birth certificates written in Sinhala. Critical information came to light when the police arrested an individual in New Delhi, who had failed to board the boat with the others.

Acknowledgements

Tamil Nadu has been a fantasy world for me ever since I was a child. Except for a couple of visits to Palani Temple and a visit to the college in Coimbatore where my brother studied, I didn't have many chances to explore the state. Later in 2016, I visited Chennai with my friend Vishnu Ram to participate in a film audition. When he went in for the audition, I strolled through the streets of Chennai. You know that particular vibe people talk about? I felt that same vibe right then and there. It was at that moment I decided I would write my next novel based in Chennai, after my novel *Ouija Board*. I even named it 'Chennai Diaries'. But how could I write authentically about a city after a single visit? For that, I needed to gain experiences and mingle closely with the natives. The novel wouldn't progress without these. That's how I landed up in Chennai in search of experiences.

Accommodation was arranged in the flat of Aneesh, the elder brother of my close friend Nidheesh. Aneesh loved and cared for me like his own brother.

Though I went to Chennai to write a story, the days that followed saw me running from pillar to post in search of a job to make ends meet. There were times when the purpose of my visit completely slipped my mind. I walked in and out of many call centres looking for a job. During those days, a person who fed me lovingly was Latha, despite the fact that we met through Facebook.

I made many Tamil friends in Chennai. And my dear Paatti entered my life quite unexpectedly. The ones who stood strong like pillars with me during the transformation from 'Chennai Diaries' to 'Ram C/O Anandhi' were my friends: Nidheesh Karthikeyan, Vishnu K Udayan, Harin Kairali, Akhil K T, Jerry, Vishnu Shaji, and Lachu.

Of course, Mark Zuckerberg, the owner of Facebook, also deserves a share of my gratitude. The platform he created was the breeding ground for the writer in me.

Dear Mr Ravi Deecee, Mr Ramdas who edited the Malayalam version, every staff member of DC Books who worked hard to make sure the book found its audience rightly; people who sell books in trains and buses; all the Malayalees who wholeheartedly accepted and celebrated *Ram C/O Anandhi*, HarperCollins who came forward to get a wider audience for this book, and Haritha who translated this book wonderfully—my heartfelt thanks and tight hugs to each one of you.

Lastly, but never least, my wholehearted thanks to my family members, who silently supported me when I was working on the final touches of this novel.

My sincere gratitude to each of these persons from the bottom of my heart: Director Jude Antony Joseph, Vipin Panappuzha, Anoop Shanmughan, Anooj Meera Niharika, Abhijith Joshi, Monichan Paili, Ajitha John, Sumitha Sanal, Saumya Chandrashekhar, writers Lajo Jose, Anoop Sasikumar, Nimya Narayanan who read the proof, writer Sreeparvathy, dear friends Akhil Anand Sagar, Fanto Varghese, Sajin Satheeshan, and Sreejith bro who stood by me through everything while I was in Chennai. Selvakumar, Viji Annan, Krishna Annan, Mani, Tamizh Deva, Abhayan who shared my flat, and the akka who serves food at the Amma Unavagam in Nungambakkam.

Glossary

1. Amma—Tamil/Malayalam word for 'mother'
2. Antakshari—a spoken parlour game played in India, using movie songs
3. Appa—Tamil word for 'father'
4. Aruvani—Tamil word for 'eunuch'. It's often used as an expletive.
5. Chechi/Akka—Malayalam/Tamil words used to address elderly sister-like women
6. Enke—Tamil word for 'where'
7. Ettan/Etta/Chetta/Chettan/Annaa/Annan—respectful words for addressing elderly brother-like men
8. Ghungroos—the anklets worn for dance
9. Idli—the soft, fluffy, savoury rice cake that originated in southern India and is often eaten for breakfast
10. Jhumka—a style of earring worn by women of the Indian subcontinent, characterized by their bell shape, which is often embellished with intricate filigree work, beads, and gemstones
11. Kaiyadi—Malayalam word for 'applause' and Tamil word for 'masturbation'

12. Karingali—bark of the Cutch tree. It's boiled in drinking water, and known for its vast medicinal properties.
13. Karuppamma—literally means 'a dark person'
14. *Kausalya Supraja Rama Poorvaa Santhyaa Pravarthathe, Uthishta Narashaardoola Karthavyam Daivamaahnitham*—the opening lines of Venkatesa Suprabhatam, which is considered a very significant and much sought after prayer, because it is in the form of singing the Hymn of Morning Salutation to Lord Venkateswara
15. Kolam—decorative designs drawn on the floor, traditionally with rice flour, etc. in southern India
16. Machaa—Tamil word for 'buddy', denoting friendly affection
17. Mone/Mole—affectionate way of addressing a male/female in Malayalam
18. Moodevi—refers to the Hindu goddess of misfortune and adversity, Jyestha. She is the sister of Lakshmi, the goddess of prosperity, and is often considered her opposite.
19. Paappaa—Tamil word for 'daughter'
20. Paatti—Tamil word for 'grandma'
21. Pallu—the decorated end portion of a saree that hangs loose from the shoulder
22. Payasam—also known as 'kheer'. It is a pudding or porridge popular in the Indian subcontinent, usually made by boiling milk, sugar or jaggery and a grain or fruit of our choice.
23. Podi/Poda—casual way of addressing a female/male while dismissing something
24. Pongal—a harvest season; also a food item in southern India
25. Roti—chappati/flatbread

26. Sambar—a staple food in southern India, which is a lentil-based vegetable stew, cooked with pigeon pea and tamarind broth

27. Semmozhi Poonga—a botanical garden in Chennai set up jointly by the Horticulture and Agricultural Engineering department of the Government of Tamil Nadu

28. Senthamil—a term to refer to refined standard and pure Tamil

29. Senthatti—the nettle plant defined with Tragia involucrata in various botanical sources

30. Sundakanji—A local variety of alcohol made from fermenting rice in earthen or mud pots covered with cloth and buried under the beach sands of the coastal areas

31. Thaathaa—Tamil word for 'grandpa'

32. Thevidiyaa—a Tamil derogatory term used to insult someone, particularly a woman, in a vulgar manner

33. Thirunangai—a Tamil word that means 'respected woman' and is used to refer to the eunuchs and transgender community in Tamil Nadu. The word was coined in 2006 by former Tamil Nadu Chief Minister M. Karunanidhi.

34. Unavagam—Tamil word meaning 'eatery'

35. Uruli—big round brass vessels used in home for cooking and in Ayurvedha to make medicines

36. Vanakkam—Tamil word meaning 'Greetings' or 'Hello'

About the Author

Akhil P. Dharmajan is a bestselling novelist and scriptwriter. He holds a degree in Mechanical ITI along with diplomas in mechanical engineering and filmmaking. He made his mark in the Malayalam film industry as the screenplay writer for the movie *2018*, India's official entry at the 96th Academy Awards. A prolific contributor to digital discourse, Akhil is very popular on various online media platforms and passionately engages with digital communities. His previous books are *Mercury Island* and *Ouija Board*.

About the Translator

Haritha C.K., a translator based out of Kerala, excels in bridging linguistic and cultural divides. A post-graduate in social work, she has translated acclaimed works of fiction and non-fiction from English to Malayalam, such as *The Girl on the Train, Warren Buffett's Management Secrets, The Hidden Hindu* and *The Midnight Library*. She is also an expert at English subtitling Malayalam short films. Known for her meticulous attention to details, cultural sensitivity and passion for storytelling, Haritha is a valuable asset in the literary and translation community. She is currently translating several popular Malayalam novels into English.

HarperCollins *Publishers* India

At HarperCollins India, we believe in telling the best stories and finding the widest readership for our books in every format possible. We started publishing in 1992; a great deal has changed since then, but what has remained constant is the passion with which our authors write their books, the love with which readers receive them, and the sheer joy and excitement that we as publishers feel in being a part of the publishing process.

Over the years, we've had the pleasure of publishing some of the finest writing from the subcontinent and around the world, including several award-winning titles and some of the biggest bestsellers in India's publishing history. But nothing has meant more to us than the fact that millions of people have read the books we published, and that somewhere, a book of ours might have made a difference.

As we look to the future, we go back to that one word—a word which has been a driving force for us all these years.

Read.

Harper Collins | 4th | HARPER FICTION | HARPER NON-FICTION | HARPER BUSINESS | HCCB HARPERCOLLINS CHILDREN'S BOOKS

HARPER DESIGN | Harper Sport | HARPER PERENNIAL | HARPER VANTAGE | हार्पर हिन्दी